The Wrong Side of Twenty-Five

Kate Armitage

CROOKED
CAT

Copyright © 2018 by Kate Armitage
Design: Tom Armitage
Editor: Maureen Vincent-Northam
All rights reserved.

No part of this book may be used or reproduced in any manner whatsoever without written permission of the author or Crooked Cat Books except for brief quotations used for promotion or in reviews. This is a work of fiction. Names, characters, and incidents are used fictitiously.

First Crooked Love Cats Edition, Crooked Cat Books. 2018

Discover us online:
www.crookedcatbooks.com

Join us on facebook:
www.facebook.com/crookedcat

Tweet a photo of yourself holding
this book to **@crookedcatbooks**
and something nice will happen.

To myself.

*Refer to this on days when you
don't think that you are good enough
or capable of achieving things.*

About the Author

Kate Armitage is a writer from England who has three cats, two children and one husband. She lives an alarmingly conventional life which surprises everyone who speaks to her for more than five minutes. She spends her days knee-deep in play-doh and spends her nights elbow deep in manuscripts. Sometimes she lets the children also use the play-doh but only if they promise not to mix the colours.

You can find Kate on social media under @itskatearmitage or through her website www.katearmitageauthor.com.

Acknowledgements

I'd like to thank my former boss who called me by the wrong name before unceremoniously firing me during the middle of a twelve-hour shift, with the reason that I wasn't a good fit. That night I went home humiliated and mentally drained. I was twenty-five, unemployed and apparently 'not a good fit' in the only thing I was qualified to do and to be honest, didn't really want to do. I had no direction and things felt bleak. The only thing I had ever wanted to be was an author, but had considered it a pipe-dream. With nothing to lose, I decided to give it a try. I sat down at my ancient computer and began to type. Less than two years later, here I am, a published author. I didn't think I would make it, but someone who always knew that I would was my husband, Tom. Thank you for reading scores of early drafts in a genre you don't even like and encouraging me to keep going.

But I fully believe that my manuscript would have lived and died in my hard-drive if it weren't for the help of my editor, Stephanie Roundsmith. Steph painstakingly guided me on how to get my manuscript to its full potential. She was incredibly supportive, not just with my book but in general, and I am truly grateful.

I would like to thank Crooked Cat Books for taking a chance on me. Laurence, you have no idea what this means to me, thank you. Thanks also to Maureen Vincent-Northam for giving my book a final edit and polish. I can't wrap this up without acknowledging my fellow Crooked Cat authors for being so welcoming and supportive. My former boss was right: I wasn't a good fit. This is where I fit.

Lastly, thank you to everyone who has offered kind words and support during my journey to publication.

The Wrong Side of Twenty-Five

Kylie

The sink is blocked again. The plug isn't in and yet there sits a murky pool of water. I don't have time for this. I only dashed home to change before I go to Mum's, but upon arrival I was greeted with a large note on the fridge from Lucie saying *I cleaned the kitchen but I'm not cleaning the mess you made in the sink – sort it out!* The sensible thing to do would be to leave it until later but it doesn't bear thinking about if she comes home before I do and finds the sink as she left it. Lucie might be petite, but she's strong from years of gymnastics and running. Instead, I poke at viscous water with a wooden spoon. But it does nothing except make me look like a modern-day witch hovering over a cauldron. It's a shame I'm not, I could do with a spell. The sink belches and bubbles and for a moment I think I've done it, but nothing else happens and the water remains. I look at the clock on the kitchen wall. Shit. If I don't get ready now, I'll miss my train.

Does anyone else have an area in their room dedicated to clothes that aren't dirty enough to justify washing but don't want to wear two days in a row? I like to think we all do but some are more vocal about it than others. If you genuinely don't and you're thinking I'm disgusting well, I'd like to let you know that washing perfectly wearable clothes is a waste of water and electric. I'm just doing my bit for the environment. That's my excuse and I'm sticking to it.

My clean-enough clothes live on the chair that I bought so I could sit at my desk and be productive. I stand before it, wondering what to wear. So many clothes lay before me; some even spilling off the chair and onto the desk, which itself is buried under half-finished notebooks, important paperwork, bus tickets, receipts, the contents of a make-up bag, an empty make-up bag and books that I have been meaning to give to charity for the past year. They're mostly vampire books, back when vampires were crammed in to every new piece of literature. I fell for the vampire craze hook, line and sinker… but I'm over them now. Right, on with the hunt for something to wear. I take off my leggings, because I don't plan on wearing a dress and wearing them as trousers just won't do. 'Leggings are not trousers' Mum will say. I find some black skinny jeans from the floor and a respectable top from the pile on the chair. It looks good, if a little creased. I would iron it but I don't think I own an iron. Instead, I reach over for my hair straighteners and switch them on. As they heat up, I start applying the least amount of make-up that I can get away with. I rub at my eyelids with eye shadow, because despite how often I watch tutorials on how to apply make-up, it's still a mystery to me. I won't be hashtag-declaring myself as a make-up artist any time soon. Besides, it looks so exhausting. When did everyone start filling in their eyebrows?

The straighteners are ready so I press them around the collar and hem of my top, taking care not to burn my body or worse, face. I'd rather not do that again; last time I ended up with a nasty blister on my chin. With my top looking almost respectable, I turn my attention to my hair. The thing about my hair is that it's neither straight nor curly but just cavemanesque. In my nearly twenty-five years of life I haven't figured out what to do with it except take the outer layer of hair that has frizzed from a night of being smushed against my pillow and create waves with straighteners. I don't own a curling tong. Necessity is the mother of invention, right?

Speaking of mother, I better catch a train and see mine. I slip into some shoes and pick up my phone when I notice a message from Alexa. *Don't miss your train!*

Sometimes I'm sure she has a camera installed in my house. I look around, paranoid. *Don't worry, I'm absolutely on top of things.*

I doubt it. Are you ready for Saturday night? Have you

decided what to wear?

I roll my eyes at Alexa's incessant need to be prepared for everything and reply *Of course I'm prepared. I was born prepared. Don't worry about it.*

But I do worry, Kylie. And you weren't born prepared, you were three weeks late and needed medical assistance. So once again, have you decided what you're going to wear?

Yes, yes, a thousand times yes. Anyway, must dash.

I knew it, you're running late. Have fun!

Have fun, she says, after all she knows about my mum. She's so sarcastic when there's no one but me to witness it. I put the phone in my bag, head downstairs and take one last look at the kitchen clock. Shit. I might have to run after all.

I ring the bell and Mum opens the door. Is it just my imagination or is she disappointed to see me?

'Come in,' she says as she heads to the kitchen, without so much as a 'hello', let alone a 'nice to see you'. Instead she stands with her back to me, preparing the kettle to make a round of drinks. I don't care, my attention is on the array of finger food before me: egg and mayonnaise sandwiches cut into triangles, party rings, hot dog sausages, and cheese and pineapple on sticks are displayed nicely on the dining table as well as a chocolate caterpillar cake sitting proudly in the middle. It's not a birthday without a chocolate caterpillar cake.

'This looks amazing,' I say as my mouth salivates.

'Yes, well, I did offer to take you out but you insisted on a finger food buffet.'

I almost laugh at the exasperation and pain in her voice. 'I love finger food, Mum. It's the best bit about my birthday.'

'Yes, your appetite has never truly matured. We could have gone somewhere nice.'

I roll my eyes and help myself to a sausage roll. 'This is fine, Mum. Honestly.'

'We could have gone to that posh gastropub that's opened up around the corner.'

'Putting the word gastro in front of the word pub doesn't

make it posh, Mum.' In fact, the name alone puts me off seeing as gastro as a prefix is generally reserved for stomach problems.

'Oh sorry, Kylie, we aren't all as cosmopolitan as you.'

There's annoyance in her voice now as she puts a cup of coffee in front of me and taps my hand, which is shovelling food into my mouth.

'Wait until everyone gets here, please.'

'Who's coming?'

'Oh, just Nan and Grandad, and Auntie Julia.'

'Oh, that'll be nice,' I lie. We sit and sip our hot drinks together. I can't help but notice she's looking at me, with a frown on her face that tells me she's mentally scrutinising my appearance. 'How's Robbie?' I ask, as a distraction. Robbie's my brother. He's much younger and we have little in common. What we do have in common is that we were named after pop stars. He was named after Robbie Williams and I was named after Kylie Minogue, if you hadn't guessed already. The whole naming-your-kid-after-fleeting-celebrities is a bloody awful idea, thanks Mum. I could have had a normal name with potential for nicknames but no I had to be Kylie. A name that sticks out for all the wrong reasons. It can't be shortened unless I want to be Ky, which I don't, or Lee which I can't because that's my surname. Yep. My name's Kylie Lee. Mum must have hated me from the moment I was conceived.

'We've just found out he's got in to the college of his choice for September.'

I nearly choke on my tea. 'College?' Surely not. Am I missing something?

'Yes, college. Why?' She looks at me like I'm mad.

'But… he's like thirteen!'

'He's sixteen next month, Kylie. You do exaggerate.'

I do the maths in my head and she's right, he's sixteen next month. 'Unbelievable.'

Nan, Grandad and Auntie Julia arrive and I stand accepting hugs and greetings from each of them while Mum calls down Dad and Robbie.

'Kylie!' Grandad hugs me and stuffs fifty pounds in my fist at the same time, like he always does when he sees me. 'I can't believe you're nearly twenty-five, how does it feel?'

'I can't say I feel much different, Grandad.' After all, age is but a number.

'So, Kylie. How are you getting on in the city on your own?' asks Auntie Julia.

'Good, thanks. I've been living there years, it feels like home now.'

'Oh, of course, but I mean how are you getting on in terms of finding your feet? Any promotions recently? Any big plans?'

'Not exactly.' By not exactly, I mean, not at all.

'No? Too busy running around the city chasing boys and drinking cocktails?'

'Er, well…' I don't know what to say. The truth is far from chasing boys and drinking cocktails. More like stalking boys on social media and drinking whatever is on buy-one-get-one-free.

Thankfully Dad pokes his head through the door, cutting my conversation with Auntie Julia short. What a shame.

'Hey, love. Happy Birthday for Saturday.'

I smile at him. 'Thanks, Dad.'

Just then, Robbie plods in, clearly coerced by Mum who stands unnaturally close behind him. 'Right, now that everyone's here, Kylie can open her presents. Oh, hang on, I need to take a photo.' Mum spends the next few minutes setting the scene, making sure everything is perfect. 'Come on you lot, stand closer together.' She gestures us to move closer.

As Mum sorts the lighting, I see Dad roll his eyes to himself. It makes me happy knowing Dad feels somewhat like I do in regard to Mum and her business of making a fuss.

'Okay everyone, say Happy Birthday!'

'But it's not her birthday,' says Robbie.

'I know but she's too busy to see her parents on her actual birthday so this will have to do.' There's resentment in her voice, and a sense of 'woe is me'. Everyone clearly senses it too, and plays along.

'Happy Birthday!'

'Lovely, let me just check it looks nice and no one was blinking—'

'It'll be fine, Marie; can the poor girl open her presents now?' Only Dad could get away with undermining Mum like this.

I open my gifts and look pleased when I'm supposed to and thank everyone for the usual loot of chocolate and toiletries. I always need toiletries and if I manage it well I can make my Christmas toiletries last until my birthday ones and make those last until Christmas. When I open a card from Mum and Dad, £300 falls out. Kerching! 'Thanks, you guys!' Oh, the things I could buy. What do I need? More importantly, what do I want? I'm already mentally spending the entire amount.

'That's enough for a provisional license, theory test and a handful of lessons,' Mum says.

'What?' I'm not even listening. I've pulled my phone out for a spot of online shopping. It's enough for something nice from Michael Kors. Who needs a man to buy me nice jewellery when I can buy my own? I'm an independent woman. Although I wouldn't mind a man buying me nice jewellery…

'Well, you're twenty-five on Saturday. Don't you think it's about time you learned to drive?'

'Oh, Mum, no one drives in the city. There's never anywhere to park on the street anyway.'

'Even if you don't get a car straight away, you don't want to wait too long to learn to drive. My biggest regret was waiting too long. You don't want to be like me and take your test with a massive bump behind the wheel.'

'I certainly don't want to do anything with a massive bump.'

'Which is why you should do it now, before you have kids.'

'I'm not having kids,' I say. Certainly not any time soon anyway. No thanks.

Dad clears his throat for attention. 'Right, I've got an important call to make. Bye, love. Enjoy spending your money.' With a final nod and a typical Dad smile, he slinks away.

Mum looks horrified and follows Dad. 'Pete! You do not walk out when I've planned a nice event. How do you think that makes me feel?'

Mum can't help but make everything about her, even my birthday. I would be annoyed but I'm just glad the attention has been taken away from me and all the kids she's planned for me to have.

Mum sits back down, her face thunderous. 'Where were we? Before we were rudely interrupted.'

'We were about to—'

Auntie Julia cuts in, 'Kylie was saying she's not having kids.'

'Ah, yes. Well you can't know that for sure, darling. I didn't think I was but then I married your dad and eight months later, there you were. Some things just happen.'

I shrug, 'and some things just don't happen, at least not for a long time.'

'You never know. Maybe soon you'll finally be serious with someone. Do you have a boyfriend?'

Happy birthday to me! I can't think of anything better than declaring my long-term singleness to my immediate family. 'No...'

'Marie, maybe she's one of those lesbians. It's very trendy now,' says Nan, to my horror.

Mum shakes her head, 'she's definitely not a lesbian.'

'But what about that girl who comes as her plus one to everything?' asks Nan, as if I'm not in the room, 'Alexandra?'

'Oh goodness, she's not dating Alexa. I'll admit, they're unnaturally close but it's purely platonic. No, Kylie's definitely straight. And single.' The last word echoes around the room, bouncing off everybody and coming back to bite me.

'I am here you know!' I tell Mum in a huff.

'I know you are, darling.'

'Well, can you not talk about my love life, or lack-thereof as if I'm not?'

'Sorry. I'm just worried, Kylie. Maybe if you put yourself out there a bit more... And looked a bit more presentable. You could start by styling your hair before you leave the house.'

'What's wrong with my hair?'

'It's just like your father's was in the 80s before he started balding and I finally got him to shave it.'

'Leave her alone, Marie. I think all the young women have hair like that nowadays.'

'Thanks, Auntie Julia.' You're wrong but I appreciate the support.

'You're right, Julia.' Mum takes a deep breath, 'I'm sorry, Kylie.'

Good God, I wonder if I can get her to say it again and this time record it.

'Now don't worry,' she soothes, as if she wasn't the one who started this, 'it'll work itself out. Do you go to the pub often? I found your dad at the local pub quiz a cold winter's evening. We had a joint mortgage by summer on this house.'

'Marie, I'm sure she gets out plenty living in a city. I bet she goes on loads of dates when she's not chasing her career. Young women nowadays are all about their careers.'

'Is that true, Kylie? Are you all about your career?' Mum looks at me, wanting reassurance and hoping that my life isn't as shit as she fears.

'Yes, I am,' I lie. I've lied in this kitchen a lot, but it's been a while. The last time I lied here I was seventeen and swearing to Mum that I wasn't hungover, but genuinely just sick. I laid it on thick and she eventually bought it and tucked me up in bed. Later that day, Dad brought me up a bacon sandwich with a knowing smile. Somehow, he knew and he was happy to keep it a secret.

'Well,' says Mum, collecting herself now, aware of herself, 'then I guess you have nothing to worry about. I'm sure you'll make good choices on how to spend your money, although I do suggest driving lessons.'

I smile with appreciation and reach for another sausage roll. 'And maybe a gym pass,' she says as I stuff it into my mouth.

I sit, no longer eating, and wait while Mum buzzes around the kitchen fussing over everything until she decides it's time to light the cake. No one smokes anymore and Mum flaps about looking for a lighter. 'Oh, this is ridiculous, Pete,' she huffs, addressing my Dad who isn't even in the room. 'You might not smoke now but what if we had a power cut and needed to light some candles? Do we even have candles? If there's an apocalypse how will we survive?' she looks through the drawer of miscellaneous crap. You know the drawer, the one crammed with take-away leaflets, spare keys, plasters, and hopefully a lighter or Mum will definitely have some sort of nervous breakdown.

'Are you looking forward to college?' I ask my brother, who has his head in his phone.

'Yeah,' he grunts in response.

'Good,' I say. Well, what a riveting conversation that was. Why do I bother?

Suddenly I'm plunged into darkness. The room is filled with everyone singing Happy Birthday slightly out of sync with each other as the cake, and now fully lit candles, is placed on the table.

'Make a wish, Kylie!'

What do I want in my twenty-sixth year of life? I thought I wanted something nice by Michael Kors and for my favourite black dress to fit me again, but now I can't help wonder if my priorities are wrong. Maybe I should wish for a solid career. Perhaps a boyfriend. After all, I'm twenty-five tomorrow and have neither. As I sit having an existential crisis with all of my family waiting expectantly, melted wax drips onto my cake. Shit. I close my eyes and think. *I wish to have all the things I should, and also to fit in my favourite black dress.* Then I blow out the candles and everyone cheers. The lights come back on and I pick the face off the chocolate caterpillar cake.

Alexa

I get through the front door with a sigh of relief and switch the kettle on. Kylie's at her mum's for the evening, so I can't call her until later, which means until Priya gets in from work, it's just me and a cup of tea.

I make my way to the living room, holding my favourite cup in both hands, receiving its warmth and comfort. I sit down, sip my tea and wonder what I will have for dinner. I think I'll find out what Priya's having first. Priya's my house mate, and a great cook. She should be home any minute. That's why I like living with Priya; she sticks mainly to a routine and I always know where I stand with her. It's exactly why I couldn't live with Kylie; she has no idea what she's doing or where she'll be from one minute to the next, and she's a terrible cook.

Kylie's my best friend, there's no doubt about that, but we're an unlikely pairing. We met on the first day of university, outside our first class, both late. However, we were late for very different reasons. Kylie had slept in, where as I had been overcome by anxiety and needed to take a moment in a toilet cubicle to calm down. University was important to me, as it should be, but I took it so very seriously that as a result it all became too much before it had even started. When I arrived, the class was already inside and the doors were shut. I was mortified but then my attention quickly turned to this girl bulldozing her way towards me. She had dyed-black hair that had been meticulously straightened and accompanied by a side fringe that impeded her view. She wore skinny jeans with rips at the knees, not one but two belts, some band shirt of which I have forgotten, and two different shoes. I stood there, rooted to the spot in my most 'flattering' boot-cut jeans and 'respectable' jumper ensemble (we'll pretend I didn't have blonde streaks through my hair), as this girl came to a stop before me, flashed me a smile, asked if I was late too and guided me in to class. We had to sit together at the front, side by side. She's been by my side ever since.

I hear the front door unlocking. 'Hey, I'm in the living room,' I shout. I hear Priya take her shoes off, put them in the cupboard and switch the kettle on.

'Hey,' she says, 'have you eaten?'

I smile to myself. 'No, do you have anything in mind?'

Priya sets to making a stir fry and I can't wait. I haven't eaten anything since lunch when I nibbled on an over-priced sandwich that tasted of cardboard from a shop two doors down from work. What a waste of three hundred calories! By the time I've set up the trays, dishes, cutlery and drinks, Priya's ready to dish up. We take our meals to the living room and settle in front of the television.

'You're out this weekend, aren't you?' Priya asks.

'Yes, I'm off out with Kylie on Saturday. It's her birthday. Do you want to come?'

'Actually, I can't. I've got a date.'

'Oh? Do tell.'

Priya fills me in on the details. She met him last week at a work event. He's taking her to Zizzi's. 'He actually remembered my name and what department I'm in, tracked me down and rang me at work,' she says.

I pause from eating to process this. 'So... he's a stalker?'

'He's not a stalker, Alexa, thank you very much.'

'I dunno. I think there's a fine line between romantic and creepy.'

'Well I can assure you, this was very romantic.'

'I'm sure.' Although I'm not sure and Priya can tell.

'Don't you ever believe that maybe true love just finds a way?'

There's no point in lying to her, she can always tell, 'No, not really.'

'You will. Maybe not now, but one day. Maybe when you

finally fall in love.'

'I've fallen in love before…'

'Really?'

I think about it. My last relationship was a year ago with a guy called Scott who I met at a coffee house. We both wanted the last shot of hazelnut syrup in our cappuccinos. He let me have it, in exchange for a date. It was a fine relationship but it fizzled out quite naturally and amicably. It wasn't love. All of my past relationships have been mediocre to be honest. I've never had my heart broken but I've also never broken anyone's heart. But so what? Are either of those things achievements? 'I'm far too busy, anyway.'

'Too busy for love?' Priya shoots me a doubtful look, with an added eyebrow raise.

'Well, no, it's just, I'm not interested in seeking it out or hoping it "finds its way" to me.'

'If you say so…'

'I just mean I don't need to be validated by a man.'

'What if you just want to be dated by a man?'

'Very funny.'

'Are you seriously saying if love found its way to you, you'd be too busy?'

I look at Priya and her judgemental eyebrow. She's lucky she's such a good cook, or I'd be wishing I was still alone tonight. 'Fine,' I concede before my dinner gets cold, 'if love literally finds its way to me, I'll let it in.'

Kylie

'Did you read the note at all?!' says Lucie as I walk through the front door.

'Yes! You asked me to sort the sink.'

'So, why haven't you?'

'I tried! Honestly! But nothing worked and then I had to get ready to go to see my mum.'

'You tried everything? Did you try the drain cleaner in the cupboard?'

'Oh... which cupboard is it in again?'

'The one with all of the cleaning products in.'

'Right, that one.' I wrack my brain for memory of this mythical cleaning cupboard, all the while trying to look casual.

'It's under the sink,' says Lucie through gritted teeth.

'I know it is, obviously,' I lie as I reach down for the drain cleaner.

'See to it while I'm out.' She nudges past me to fill up her water bottle.

'I will, I promise. Are you still joining us tomorrow night?'

'That depends on if I have killed you by then.'

She's going for a run. Voluntarily. For fun. And she's already thin. I don't know what possesses her. I pour drain cleaner down the sink until she leaves and then head upstairs.

As I rest my legs and tuck into a chocolate bar, I wonder if I should take up running. I've always been reluctant to run anywhere, unless I'm running late. And I've always said chocolate is worth the wobble. But maybe it's just something else I can't do. Maybe having never taken part in a so-called 'fun' run or a colour run is just another milestone I haven't achieved.

Great, that's put me right off my Mars Bar. I fold the wrapper around the chocolate and put it on the coffee table. It takes a lot to put me off food, but if anyone can do it it's Mum. Her comments today are swirling around my head, filling me with doubt. Everything was fine until she used my birthday as an opportunity to remind me how much of a disappointment I am. And worse, as an opportunity to control me by withholding money and reserving it for driving lessons. I don't want driving lessons; I want to spend frivolously and buy all the things I've been eyeing up recently but can't afford on my pittance of a salary.

Then again, maybe it is time I learned how to drive. I know a lot of my friends can drive from all the dashboard selfies littering my social media. Not being able to drive is just another milestone I have yet to achieve. Like being in a long-term stable relationship or working my way up a career ladder. I guess I got complacent, and thought I had more time. But now the question burning into my stomach and ruining my appetite is: is twenty-five the turning point in which you should have your shit together? I should ask Alexa.

As if by telepathy, Alexa messages me *How did it go?*

Should we be at a point in our lives where we're on track with careers and life partners?

I take it your mum got in your head, again.

She gave me money for driving lessons and asked if I'm dating or chasing a career.

Tell me all about it tomorrow at the café. Usual time.

I get up and make my way to the wardrobe, opening it up and peering inside. It's jam packed full of clothes but I already know there's nothing in there that is twenty-fifth-birthday worthy.

Actually, I think we might need to meet earlier and go shopping.

Alexa

Sacrificing the majority of my lunch break is unfortunate, but necessary if I'm going to finish my work on time today, which I must. It's okay, I often eat 'al desko', because I can't say no to people and end up taking on more than I can manage. Take today for example; on Fridays I usually meet Kylie at our favourite café at 5pm. But instead, I've agreed to meet her at our bench at 4pm so we can walk back into the city together in time for her to shop before everything shuts for the day. She told me many times she had an outfit for her birthday, and then at the final hour she told me she didn't. Since then I've had exactly twenty messages begging me to meet her as early as possible to go shopping. I'm hardly going to say no, but it does annoy me how unprepared she is despite the fact that tomorrow night's plans have been the main topic of every conversation for a month.

Sip, type, sip, type. Lunch today is a black coffee and a few nibbles. I can't resist carbs, which is a pity. When you sit at a desk all day like I do, not to mention look like I do, you don't need carbs in the form of crisps. Crisps are unhealthy and delicious in equal measure. They're irresistible, which is why I'm not.

I sneak a crisp in and keep on typing. There's several infuriating emails I must respond to in a professional manner. They must sound sympathetic but assertive. I can do that. I can send assertive emails to clients.

'Alexandra,' someone says, causing me to jump. I look around. It's the big boss, John.

'Hello. Can I help you with anything?' I ask, whilst discreetly trying to hide my crisps.

'When you've finished your lunch I have something I

would like you to help me with, if you're not too busy?'

Actually, I am too busy, and I think he should ask someone else. 'Oh, sure. That'd be fine.'

'Great,' he says, 'I'll email it over to you now. Can you leave it on my desk before the end of the day?'

'Absolutely.'

'Brilliant, thanks for this.'

Yeah, brilliant, for him. I pop the crisps back in my bag, now having no time to eat if I'm to fit another task in. I sip coffee and type furiously, although ensuring my words aren't furious ones. You wouldn't believe the emails I get. Sometimes they're snide beyond belief and full of contempt. The worst bit is none of their upset has anything to do with me. I'm just an administrative assistant. What's the phrase? Don't shoot the messenger? But they do, and I can't help but take every bullet personally.

By some miracle, I've squeezed everything in by 3:50pm. There's just enough time to pop up to John's office and hand in the extra paperwork. I grab my bag and head upstairs. It's nicer up here and not just because it's spacious with white walls as opposed to the cramped office that I work in, with motivational posters on every wall and junk in every nook and cranny, but it's also quiet. What I would do for some peace and quiet while I work. I leave the paperwork on John's desk and I'm about to leave when I'm stopped by a woman.

'What did you just put on John's desk?' she asks.

'Oh, erm, just some paperwork for him.'

'I'm John's personal assistant,' she says in a superior tone.

'Oh right,' I say. So what? I think.

'I'll let him know it's there,' she says.

'Okay, thank you,' I give her a nod in acknowledgment and then hurry to leave. As I do, I can't help but hear people talk about me.

'Who's that?' someone says.

'I don't know. She had something for John,' says John's personal assistant.

'Why?' asks a new voice.

'No idea,' says someone.

'Does she work here?' asks John's personal assistant.

'I think so. I think she's called Alexandra,' says another.

'Must be a new girl.'

Nice to see I've made an impression in my five years of service. Good job I have friends outside of work, like Kylie, who I'll be seeing any minute when I reach our bench.

It's 3:59pm and I'm rushing up the hill to the bench. My calves burn but I carry on, huffing and puffing until I reach the bench with seconds to spare... and she isn't even there. Disappointed and annoyed in equal measures, I slow my pace and make my way to sit down. I can't believe I rushed; I should have known she'd be late. Five minutes go by without any sight of her so I message *Where the hell are you? Have you even set off?*

I sneak a crisp from my bag and receive a message back *Yes of course I've set off, what do you take me for?* I roll my eyes and decide to check my social media. Zoe had croissants and summer berries for breakfast. Everything she does looks like a work of art. My muesli wouldn't have got any likes at all.

As I stare down at my phone, a pair of feet appear in my peripheral vision. I recognise the feet, or rather the odd socks on said feet give me a clue as to who the owner could be. All through university she wore odd converse shoes, one black and one white. She lets people think it's a quirk, a style choice, but I know she's just forgetful and loses things.

'You're late.'

'Sorry.'

Any annoyance I had melts away when I look up and see her sheepish smile. 'You're only hurting yourself you know. You're the one who apparently needs to go shopping.'

'I do need to go shopping! Desperately. Come on, let's go.' She stands up and I follow her back into town.

'So, where are we going first then?'

'I dunno. Whatever we come to first along the way.'

And so we enter the first clothes shop that we come to,

because that's how Kylie lives her life - just on a wing and a prayer with no real plan. The shop isn't my type of place with its revealing clothes and ungenerous sizing. I won't even entertain the idea of trying anything on because I know nothing here would complement my body shape. Who needs the soul-crushing horror that is not fitting into clothes and ugly crying at their reflection in the dressing room, in several mirrors at once? Kylie, however, is slimmer than me. She'll have no problem fitting in the many clothes she's oohing and ahhing. I leave her looking at dresses as my attention is taken by what looks like adult-sized jelly sandals. 'Kylie! Look at these. I can remember running about on the beach in a pair of jelly sandals as a kid and they weren't fashionable even then.'

Wait, where did she go? 'Kylie?' I call out, just as I see her enter the changing rooms. Damn. I make my way over, but a sales assistant with supermodel looks stops me in my tracks. She glares down at me from her 5'9" height with a look that says, 'you don't belong here…'

I look up at her and clear my throat, 'Oh… can I just, get in… my friend, she's in one of the cubicles…'

'Alexa?' shouts Kylie from behind a changing cubicle curtain.

'That's me, I'm Alexa…' I add. The sales assistant purses her lips and lets me pass.

'Alexa? Are you there?' asks Kylie.

'I'm here,' I say as I reach the other side of her curtain.

After a while, she pulls back the curtain and looks at me. 'Right, what do you think?'

She stands before me and smiles a crooked smile that reaches her hazel eyes, which sometimes look greener, sometimes browner, and therefore suit her completely because Kylie is anything but decisive. The dress, although garish, fits her enviable figure like a glove. I feel self-conscious in such a nice shop, in front of Kylie as I stand in a frumpy dress. She looks like a goddess and I am the physical embodiment of porridge: pale and lumpy.

'I think you look great, but I'm not sure about the dress,' I admit. After all, if your best friend can't be honest, who can?

'Too much?' she asks, frowning and studying herself in the mirror.

'Well, what are you trying to convey with this dress?'

'That I'm fun and youthful.'

'Can you be fun and youthful in something a little more sophisticated?'

'Sure. How about a turtle-neck jumper and overalls? What about a nun's habit? Would that please you?' she rolls her eyes at me but I know she's joking.

'Actually, that would be perfect.'

I head to the counter with Kylie, standing close to her and fixing my stare at the floor to avoid eye-contact with the myriad of mirrors.

'Look at this bracelet!' says Kylie who has been taken in by the display of jewellery next to us. She picks up the bracelet and inspects it.

'It's nice,' I say, glancing at it.

'I think I'm going to get it. Although I'm totally broke.'

'What about the driving lesson money?'

Kylie sighs, 'Mum kept the driving lesson money as she didn't want me going home on my own with that much cash on me aka she doesn't want me to blow it on my birthday weekend. She's transferring it into my account on Monday, but that's no use to me now. So, shall I buy it?'

'I think if you're totally broke until Monday, don't buy it until Monday.'

'Well that's not a fun answer.'

'But it's the right one.'

'I think I'm going to get it now.'

'Okay, whatever you want.'

'Oh, but are you able to buy my sandwich today? I'll pay you back.'

'No,' I should say. 'Yeah, that's fine,' I tell her.

'Thanks, Alexa! You're the best.'

She buys the green dress and the damn bracelet and we leave to grab a bite to eat. I order my usual, which is a salad sandwich and cup of tea, as well as a chicken and bacon baguette, and a brownie and latte for Kylie. We sit down at our usual table and I watch Kylie pour copious amounts of sugar into her latte. It looks divine and I feel envious.

'Stop staring at my latte and get one yourself,' she says, reading my mind.

'I can't. I'm on a diet.'

'You seriously don't need to be on a diet. You look amazing.'

'These hips don't lie.'

'Men like hips. Men like all body shapes. They're really not that fussy. It's us women who are fussy. And not about each other, but ourselves.'

This is one of those moments where Kylie shows how smart she really is. I should point it out, but I don't want to respond and acknowledge that I am critical of myself, and maybe I shouldn't be. 'Are you ready to be twenty-five?'

'Not now I've realised how little I've achieved in a quarter of a century. No career, no boyfriend and definitely no husband or mortgage. My life is depressing.'

'Your life is fine, don't listen to your mum.'

'But she has a point. I'm in the same job, same house and doing the same things as I was when I was twenty-one. I should have moved on somewhat. I should have a better job, my own place, a boyfriend. And what about learning how to drive or travelling?'

'You've got plenty of time to do all those things.'

'Have I? I've been thinking about it and once you hit twenty-five, you're no longer in your early-twenties. You're mid-twenties. It's a slippery slope to thirty. Are you ready to be thirty?'

'No,' I say as I prepare my sandwich to be just how I like it, 'because I'm not thirty for five more years.'

'You'll be thirty before you know it, as will I. Face it, Lex, as of tomorrow, I'll be joining you on the wrong side of twenty-five.

Kylie exaggerates often and lets her imagination run away with her. I'm used to it. 'Speaking of tomorrow, what's the plan?'

'I don't know... come to mine in the morning, we'll have breakfast and lounge around until it's time to get ready.'

I pick at a sad slice of tomato that hangs from my sandwich. 'What time in the morning?'

'Oh, whenever I get up.'

'So... 11am?'

'Yeah something like that.'

I eat the slice of tomato as Kylie breaks her brownie in half and puts one half on my plate.

Kylie

I'm roused by pings and buzzes coming from my phone beside me. I open my reluctant eyes that have sealed shut with last night's mascara and grab the phone. Various messages wish me happy birthday. Oh that's right, it's my birthday.

Not one to let a birthday pass without childish excitement, I jump out of bed in just my faded old My Chemical Romance top and knickers and run downstairs to make breakfast. Seeing as it's my birthday, it's only right that I live a little this morning and have a mixture of cereals; all chocolate.

With breakfast out of the way, all that's left to do is to wait for Alexa to arrive. I'd like to relax some more, seeing as it's my birthday, but I really, really, need to clean. She'll be horrified if she sees it in this state. But what to tidy away first? How do people know what to prioritise? I'll start with the food wrappers and moulding cups of unfinished tea on the coffee table.

As I'm loading the washing machine with a backlog of laundry from the floor of my bedroom, I hear knocking at the door. 'Let yourself in!' I shout.

The door creaks open, 'I hate letting myself in,' says Alexa as she walks into the room.

'Why?'

'It doesn't feel right.'

'Oh Jesus, Alexa. We're a little past formal greetings don't you think?'

'Probably. Which is lucky for you, because I'm staring at a pile of your underwear.'

'Nah, I show everyone my underwear.'

'I know... anyway, happy birthday!'

'I'm too sad to celebrate my birthday,' I joke. 'I'm old. I'm past it.'

'Come on, let's open your presents.' She gestures to the gift bag she's holding and leads me to the kitchen table. I open her gifts excitedly, and eagerly. Then I see what she has given me. I'm confused.

It's a framed picture. Except it's not a picture, it's a quote. 'It's a...'

'It's an inspirational quote.'

'What's it for?'

'You can put it on your wall and feel inspired from the moment you get up,'

'It says "Behind every successful woman is herself"...'

'It's so inspirational, isn't it? There's never been a better time to be a woman. We can be successful in our own right, without men.'

'I suppose that's true.'

'I thought you were a feminist?'

'Of course I am.' But feminism doesn't require cheesy quotes in metallic print. 'I love it,' I lie.

'Open the rest of them!'

I'm nervous now. What else has she got me? As I peer into the bag I see a large box inside, which I take out with both hands. I shake the box, trying to guess what it is and Alexa is grinning like a Cheshire cat. What would be in such a big box? Probably something sensible. Like a year's supply of tampons. Although that wouldn't be so bad. I peel back the wrapping paper and find a shoe box. 'Shoes?' I say, thinking out loud.

'Have a look!' she looks confident in her gift choice. Excited, even. It's unnerving.

I open the lid. To my surprise, inside are two converse shoes. But they're not a pair; one is black, one is white. 'Oh my God!'

'You can wear them and re-live being on the right side of twenty-five.'

'I love them!' I say, 'but wait, how did you manage to buy

an odd pair of shoes?'

'I didn't, obviously. I bought a black pair and a white pair.'

'What will you do with them?'

'I don't know. Do you want them?'

'Oh, well, maybe. But I only like them in this order. The left white, the right black.'

'You're so weird. Anyway, there's one more present for you.'

I look in the bag one last time and gasp as I pull out a bottle of Lambrini, with a bow wrapped around the neck. 'You're an angel.' The nectar of my youth, the taste of university. It's cheap and easy on the palate.

'Only the best for my best friend. I knew you'd like it.'

'So what shall we do now?'

'What time are Sam and Laura getting here?'

'About 5pm.'

'How can we kill a few hours until then?'

We do what we always do when we have time to kill; watch telly. Or rather, half watch telly and half sit on our phones looking for interesting stuff. It's considered rude to sit with your head in your phone when you have company, but Alexa isn't company, she's like an extension of myself. We amuse ourselves until I notice it's 5pm.

'Right, come on, time to get ready.' I get up and go to leave the room.

'Are you not turning the television off?'

'Nah.'

Sighing, Alexa turns it off before following me. Once upstairs, we sit on the floor crossed legged in front of two mirrors propped up against the wall. I pour out the contents of my make-up bag, ignoring Alexa's sighing. Where's my eyeliner?

Alexa expertly applies her make-up while I watch on in wonder and aimlessly smother my own face in the only foundation I own. She's brought a huge bag and is starting with something called primer. No idea what that is. I can't keep up with brands.

I rub concealer on my many blemishes and turn to Alexa, 'How am I old, and yet still suffering from bloody spots?'

'Because you don't wash your face before bed.'

'I do!' I protest, 'mostly...'

'Just get into the habit of doing it. It's not hard.'

'I remember a time I didn't have spots.'

When I was young, I couldn't wait to be an adult and eat ice cream for breakfast and go to bed without washing my face. Now I'm an adult I can't do either without worrying about my thighs and acne.

Don't grow up, it's all a lie.

Alexa

'I'm excited to go out tonight,' I tell Kylie. 'I haven't let my hair down in a while.'

'Literally. You wear it up for work.'

'Oh, that's hysterical, Kylie. Have you thought about a career in comedy?'

'Anything would be better than a career in pandering to Janine.'

'Is she still giving you grief?'

'Oh yeah. Big time.'

'What's her problem?'

'That I'm distractingly beautiful and intimidatingly clever?'

'Or,' I offer, 'that you never quite turn up on time or do what's asked of you.'

'Unfair! I turn up practically on time every day.'

I roll my eyes at this obvious lie, now unable to speak as I apply lip-liner.

'Oh, that's a gorgeous colour!' says Kylie, 'can I borrow it? Pretty please, it's my birthday!'

I continue applying slowly as a means to stall giving Kylie my precious lip-liner. When finished, I slowly put the lid back on and try to ignore Kylie staring at me hopefully. Inevitably, I cave and hand her the precious liquid. It *is* her birthday after all. 'So, forgetting all the stuff your mum said, are you having a happy birthday?'

She raises her eyebrows at me in exasperation and finishes lining her own lips before replying, 'Yeah it's great. Although I can't help but feel down about some things. Even without my mum getting in my head, being twenty-five isn't how I thought it would be.'

'Why?'

'I figured I would be in some fabulous job, with money to burn, and running off to Europe for long weekends with hot men. Instead I have a shit job, no money, and no men.'

'You don't have the work ethic for a great job.'

'I know, but I have a degree in psychology, as do you. Four years ago we stood and threw our caps in the air and thought the world was our oyster. Ha! One time, that was enough.'

'One time, five-hundred quid a month was enough to rent an entire house. Things change, times change.'

'I guess so. How do you feel about being twenty-five?'

'I feel okay about it.'

'Really?' says Kylie with doubt in her voice.

'Oh, thanks very much!'

'No but, are you really satisfied?'

'I have a nice job… I like where I live…'

'But what about your career goals? Aren't you worried you'll be stuck in office work forever?'

'I've got time…' Haven't I?

'If you say so…'

The conversation comes to a close as Kylie experiments with eye-shadow. I carry on getting ready, pushing down the seeds of worry that Kylie's planted into my mind. And yet, questions keep sprouting up. Am I doing okay at twenty-five? Where should I be? Should I have an established career? A great man? Great, now Kylie's mum is getting in my head, too.

'Any chance I can borrow some eyeliner?'

Seriously? I look through my make-up bag and sacrifice my least favourite eyeliner, because there's no way I want it back. 'You know, it's not hygienic to share make-up'.

'But we're best friends!'

'Hygiene doesn't care.'

'Hygiene's such a savage,' says Kylie, applying flicks on the edges of her eyelids. 'Oh damn, I never get my flicks even. I'll end up looking like Amy Winehouse by the time I've finished.'

After a shameful amount of time we're ready. Kylie's paired her new green dress with leopard print heels that would look disgusting on anyone else. I'm in black skinny jeans (which aren't just for skinny people), bright pink heels and a black glittery top. I like all the versions of us as friends, but dressed to the nines side by side is my favourite.

'Right,' she says, 'let's go open that Lambrini.'

Downstairs, Kylie opens the plonk as I look for glasses, to no avail, 'Where are your glasses?'

'Oh, I dunno. Just get anything.'

'But there's nothing here suitable.'

'What about them two mugs?'

'Mugs? Are you serious?'

'Why not?'

'Well, it's not very classy.'

'We're drinking Lambrini, Lex. The classy ship has sailed.'

The door opens and Lucie comes in. 'Hello, girls!' she says, 'Happy birthday, Kylie!'

'Thank you!' Kylie pours Lucie a mug of Lambrini and hands it to her, 'Have a drink!'

Lucie sniffs the drink cautiously, 'What the hell is this?'

'Lambrini,' I tell her.

'Good God. It's no Pinot Grigio.'

Kylie frowns, 'It's the nectar of my youth.'

I'm guessing it wasn't the nectar of Lucie's youth. She's a bit too far on the posh side for Lambrini, what with her sports degree, her job as a personal trainer and not to mention the fact she has bags of money and only rents because she doesn't want to be tied to a mortgage yet. After all, she's only twenty-two.

'Oh that reminds me, I bought you a birthday present.' Lucie goes to her personal cupboard in the kitchen and produces a bottle.

I read the label, 'Gin?'

'And tonic.' Lucie grabs another bottle.

Kylie frowns. 'I've never had gin and tonic before.'

'It's as good as calorie free,' says Lucie.

'Sold!' Kylie laughs and Lucie makes us both a gin and tonic, in glasses.

'So why are you drinking the "nectar of your youth"?' Lucie asks.

'Alexa, why exactly did you buy the Lambrini?'

I swallow a mouthful of gin and tonic, which is disgusting by the way, 'Erm, well, it's what me and Kylie used to live on in our student days.'

'It made up at least a third of our diet,' says Kylie.

'Along with cereal and ice cream,' I add. 'Oh, and pizza!'

'Yes, so it made up a quarter of our diet.'

'Some great memories were made with the help of this drink.'

Sam and Laura, our old university friends, arrive. We drink G&Ts and what's left of the Lambrini and then hit the town, arm in arm, wobbling down the hilly street towards our favourite bar in the city centre. It plays the best music and by best, I mean music from when we were young and carefree. At twenty-five, and apparently going nowhere fast, it'll be nice to feel carefree for a night.

Kylie

All of my senses are alert. Disco lights flash and they illuminate people all around me, blending and blurring them together. My shoulders rub with other shoulders and my body tingles with adrenaline. Sweat and musky odours permeate the room. Alcohol lingers on my lips and leaves a burning sensation in my throat. Laughter and music fills the air.

When the current song finishes, I look around and find Alexa dancing up a storm. I've managed to dance myself a bit away from her while I was caught up in the moment. At the same time, almost instinctively, we reach out and grab hands and shuffle to meet each other through the crowd. I sing along to the next song that comes on although my imperfect pitch thankfully goes unheard what with all the other noise in the room.

Alexa pulls me towards the bar, 'Come on, let's get another drink.'

We stand and wait to order and I'm glad for the break. I'm not as fit as I used to be. I never did start exercising like I said I would at the start of the year. My good intentions fell flat before the end of January. My sports bra became a lounge bra, running trousers became lounge pyjamas. Is lounging an exercise? I hope I look better than I feel. As I catch my breath, I look around. Where have the other girls got to?

Alexa stands next to me, getting out her purse. 'Laura and Lucie hit it off and are in the corner swapping diet tips, and Sam has hit it off with this gorgeous girl. They're in the corner swapping saliva.'

I look around and see Sam indeed sucking someone's face in the corner. 'Lucky cow.'

'What can I get you two ladies?' says the man behind the

bar.

Alexa looks at me and I know what she's thinking. We nod to each other in unison before she turns to order. 'Two Cheeky Vimtos, please.'

'Literally anything but gin,' I add.

'It was bad, wasn't it?'

'It tasted like detergent.'

'Cheeky Vimtos are worth the calories anyway.'

We drink at the bar; I try to keep up with Alexa. She looks unassuming but she can drink me under the table and has, many times. As I sit, I look around the darkened room. There are some very nice-looking men but of course they're already dancing with women. Groups of men, or should I say boys who have clearly only just turned eighteen, or maybe they're seventeen, are huddled together in the corners. Every now and then one strays to try and snare a girl on the dance floor. Boys like that are the reason this place stinks of spilled lager. No, I don't want a boy.

Alexa nudges me. 'Who're you looking at?'

I gesture to the other side of the room, 'Them boys.'

'Why?'

'Could you ever date someone so young?'

'I don't think so. Not that young.'

'I've just done the maths and if they're eighteen they were born in 1998.'

'Really? That's horrifying.'

'It's enough to drive anyone to drink.'

'Indeed. So, drink up. I love this song.'

Just as I'm finishing up, Alexa grabs my arm and pulls me into the crowded dance floor.

'What about him?' I shout at Alexa over the music whilst furiously gesturing to a guy in the corner with my eyes.

Alexa sneaks a peek and frowns, 'No way!'

'But he's so your type!'

'I can tell he's only after one thing.'

'So? Clubs are modern day mating grounds. Dancing is literally a mating call.'

Alexa pulls a face that's a mixture of doubt with a touch of disgust.

'Honestly, you should go over. They won't just come to you and offer you everything on a plate.'

'I don't come here to find men, I come here to have a good time,' she says. I roll my eyes at her. Why can't she do both? And then our song comes on so we dance and don't stop.

At two in the morning, I find myself being dragged out of the club by Alexa.

'Just one more song! I've not finished my drink!' I say.

'No, we're going now. You're way too drunk, you need some supper.'

'I don't need supper! I don't need anything except music and a dance floor!'

'You need a hot meal and some sleep. Move it.'

I give in to Alexa and we set off walking, minus Sam, the only one who got lucky tonight. The cool air sobers me up some, but not completely because I still feel weightless and giddy.

We approach my favourite takeaway, its aromas inciting me inside. 'Ladies! Let's stop for some food!'

'Like what?' asks Lucie.

'Something hot, greasy and alcohol-absorbing.'

'Oh, not me, thanks. I'm working on my summer body,' says Laura.

'What does your winter body look like?' I ask.

'All the better for being under layers.'

I disagree, 'you look like a hot piece of arse any season.'

After getting food, Laura and Lucie take the lead in front, each nibbling on a chicken wrap. Fools. It won't be grease and alcohol absorbing. They'll be regretting that tomorrow morning. Meanwhile, Alexa and I stumble behind them, sensibly sharing a serving of cheesy chips and garlic mayonnaise.

'Kylie! You're hogging all of the cheesiest chips!' moans Alexa, a little louder than she would ever talk sober. Her northern accent, which she tries to disguise day to day, comes out when she's drunk.

'I'm sorry. I'm cheese deficient though so I'm only doing

it for my health.'

'You're bloody something deficient! How do you stay slimmer than me when you eat more?'

'My misery burns calories.'

'What are you miserable about?'

'I'm not really but... I wore my new cleavage enhancing green dress to showcase how *volumptuous* I am and how fun and quirky I am and yet as always, I'm going home alone.'

Alexa sighs, 'Firstly, that's not a word.'

'What?'

'Volumptuous. It's voluptuous, no "m".'

'Oh, sorry, grammar Queen. I'm having a quarter life crisis here.'

'Secondly, you're not going home alone; you've got me.'

'I know but I can't shag you. Although, I wouldn't kick you out of bed if you're offering.'

'I've been single for so long that I'm tempted.'

'Do you think it's easier to hook up when you're gay? Sam never goes home alone.'

'I don't know. Sam is a knock-out though so it's not fair to make assumptions on an entire sexual orientation based on her pulling power.'

'Very wise, Alexandra Jane Chapman.'

'Why thank you, Kylie Louise Lee.'

'At least we have each other.'

'Yep. For better or worse.'

We get back to mine. Laura heads to her own home and Lucie goes straight to bed. I bring a duvet downstairs while Alexa washes her face. I put the telly on and find a re-run of Sex and the City. Together, we make up a bed for the night.

'They should make a new version where Carrie is an online clickbait article journalist and after spending the majority of her income on rent, barely has enough for a pair of high street retail flip flops.' Alexa smooths a blanket over the sofa as I fight a pillow into its case.

'Or a vlogger,' I add, 'I always hoped that Sex and the City was realistic and this is what my life would be like. Fabulous cities and designer shoes. Alas, no.'

'Do you know what made me realise it was a true work of fiction? The fact that Carrie can run in heels.'

'In the real world, Carrie would have bunions and resort to wearing espadrilles.'

I realise the pillow case is inside out, but whatever. I throw two pillows on one side for Alexa and two on the other side for myself. 'No. She'd just suffer and wear heels anyway. You're a Miranda by the way.'

For a moment, Alexa looks offended, 'Why do you think that?'

I shrug and spread the duvet out, 'You wear sensible shoes. You're very sensible like Miranda.'

Alexa lends a hand and I can't help but notice she's made her side much neater than mine, 'she's also smart and independent.'

'Oh, you're both of those things too,' I say as we get under the covers.

'Who are you?'

'Duh, I'm a Carrie. A fatter, less successful Carrie.'

'Oh yeah, you're such a Carrie.'

We lie together, eating biscuits by the light of the telly. When I next look, Alexa's asleep. So this is how I end my twenty-fifth birthday; sleeping next to Alexa instead of a guy. Still, I could do worse. And I love Alexa. Life would be easier if we were a romantic couple. Soothed by her rhythmic breathing, I close my eyes and give in to sleep.

Alexa

Kylie's snoring wakes me and I find that it's the morning after the night before. I don't remember falling asleep but I must have done, and in a terrible position. Kylie's curled up like a cat next to me, with eighty percent of the duvet, which is so typical of her. She sleeps like she's dead, too. Speaking of dead, I feel like the walking dead as I stand up and plod to the kitchen for a glass of water. Now, the question is, will Kylie have any food in for breakfast? She definitely won't have porridge, my usual, but maybe cornflakes. As I open her food cupboard and look, three different types of chocolate cereal, all opened and left open, look back at me. They stand with salt, chilli powder, a sad bulb of garlic and half a packet of custard creams.

'You won't find anything good in there,' Lucie says as she comes into the kitchen.

'I didn't think I would.'

'I'll make you some of my toast, it's gluten-free if that's okay with you?'

'That's fine, thanks.' I sit at the table as Lucie puts two pieces of gluten-free bread into the toaster. It's become very de rigueur to be gluten-free. There have been stranger trends but this one is dubious none-the-less. What did gluten ever do to anyone?

'Any plans today?' Lucie asks brightly. She's seemingly unaffected by last night.

'Erm, not really,' I answer. By that I mean, of course I have plans, just not interesting ones. I change my bed linen on Sundays and prepare my outfit for the next day. It's necessary but not exactly thrilling.

'I'm going to hit the gym soon.'

'Sounds good...' I'm too tired and hungry for small talk so instead turn my attention to looking in my overnight bag as she slides a slice of buttered toast in my direction.

Why can't I be someone who finds exercise easy and enjoyable? I've gone on a run before, waiting for some sort of epiphany, but instead getting a sick feeling and buckling legs. I can't help but think about the slice of toast that's about to sit in my gut, and turn into an extra pound in weight. More than the toast weighs itself. That's how my body works somehow.

'I think I'm going to pop for a shower, if that's okay?' I ask.

'Sure.'

I should have brought a towel. The only one I can find is damp and hangs curiously on the door of Kylie's wardrobe. Trying not to think about where it's been, I grab it and head to the bathroom. Oh, for God's sake. The door still hasn't got a lock. I told Kylie last time she needed to get one.

Through suds and shower spray, I hear the door creak open and the laundry hamper drag across the floor.

'I'M IN HERE!' I shout, desperately trying to cover myself with my arms and feeling helpless.

'It's just me, morning babe!'

'Kylie! I'm in the shower!' I can't believe it. Only a misty shower door separates Kylie's eyes from my naked body.

'I know you are. Oh, are you using coconut shampoo? It smells gorgeous. Can I borrow some afterwards?'

'No, do you realise how much it cost?' I say in my head. 'Maybe,' I say out loud with a sigh, 'if you shut the damn door and leave me to shower in peace!'

I see the cloudy silhouette that is Kylie leave, and feel relieved. That was a close one. Being caught naked is my worst nightmare, even by Kylie! With a body like mine I generally keep public viewings to a minimum. I quickly rinse my hair, grab the towel and wrap it around my body before stepping out and standing against the door while I get dressed. As I pack my things to leave, I place my shampoo on the side with a sigh. Never mind, it was half empty anyway.

Kylie

I switch on the hot tap of the bath and pour in as much of Lucie's bubble bath as I can get away with. She can't know that I used it, not again, she'll kill me. It's not that she's selfish, but admittedly I use her stuff a lot. Well not a lot, but often. She's very set in her ways. I think it's only-child-syndrome. Although come to think of it, she has a brother, so that theory doesn't fit. Anyway, she uses my stuff all the time but I never complain, and I wouldn't use her bubble bath if I didn't have to, but I've ran out and I feel too rough from last night's events to pop to the shop. All I need is enough to make a few bubbles to cover my modesty in case anyone walks in.

The bathroom door lock doesn't work, in fact I should make a mental note to buy one. Lucie and I know to knock if the door is shut, but recently she had some friends over and they didn't know of this little rule. There I was, enjoying a relaxing bath, singing along to my bath playlist (guilty-pleasure songs) and the door burst open, revealing a horrified guy. Whether he was horrified by my rendition of Toxic, or my body, I don't know, but he left quickly. Lucie tried to reassure me that he swore he didn't see anything, but he so did. After the initial shock wore off, I was fine with it anyway. I have good boobs. They're not the perfectly-spherical kind with gravity-defying nipples that you see on the telly, but they're fine. That said, I could do without a bathroom encounter today. I can't handle a hangover like I once could, and feel terrible.

But I don't just feel terrible physically; I also feel mentally drained. I'm not going to lie, it's disheartening that even though I sent myself to the bottom of my overdraft buying a dress that resulted in the most likes I've ever got for a selfie, I still failed to attract male attention. What's wrong with me? And if I can't find a man on a night out, then how? There's no eligible bachelors at work, in fact no eye-candy at all. I need to broaden my horizons, but how?

I spot the shampoo Alexa left me and smile. I knew she'd leave it; she knows I love it but it's well out of my price-range. It smells like a thousand coconuts and has an instant affect on my mood and it's like the clouds have shifted and I can see the light. The truth is, we had a great time last night. No, we didn't meet men, but we didn't need them. We never do. The truth is, as long as I have Alexa by my side it's all going to be okay. I have good boobs and good friends. The rest will come. I rinse my hair and lie back to enjoy the rest of my bath before the bubbles fizzle away.

Alexa

I wish I could be one of those women who fall out of bed and look beautiful, effortlessly. Do those women exist? Or have I fallen victim to magazine propaganda again?

This morning, I fell out of bed looking bedraggled. It takes me longer to recover from a night out than it ever has. Whereas once I could fall asleep drunk, get up and feel as fresh as a daisy, today it took an extra hot shower to feel human again and two coats of under-eye concealer to look respectable enough for work. Now I'm drinking extra-strong coffee at my desk before the madness starts. No one who works in an office likes Mondays and I'm no exception.

The big boss, John, is mooching around and it's making me nervous. Last time he was hovering over me, he asked me to do him a favour. Perhaps he thinks he can get me into the habit of doing him favours. I'm way too tired for this. I try to look busy but in my peripheral vision I can see him looking at me and – oh God, he's coming over.

'Alexandra, can I see you in my office in ten minutes?'

'Sure, no problem,' I say, hoping to come across as breezy, but inside I'm in a state of panic.

After ten enduring minutes, I make my way to his office and tentatively knock on the door.

'Alexandra? Come in.'

I enter his office, sick with dread. What could I have done? Is it about the paperwork I did for him last week? Am I in trouble? Am I liable for something huge? He gestures me to sit and I do, and then he looks at me. He might as well have positioned an overhead spotlight on me. I feel exposed, vulnerable and anxious. It feels like he's been sat looking at me forever, but it must only be a few seconds. Then he says,

'How do you think you're getting on in your role?'

'Well, good I think. I hope.' I wonder if he's ever had a response like: 'Oh I'm terrible at my job and I just hate it here.'.

'But it's not what you want to do? Someone as ambitious as you surely wants something better.'

How do I answer that? No, it's not what I want to do, but I can't afford to be fired. I look at him, trying to figure him out. What's the right thing to say?

'Okay, Alexandra, I won't beat about the bush. I'm looking for a personal assistant and I think you'd make an excellent choice. It would require a little more responsibility but you'd only be answering to me and you'd get your own office and a small pay rise.'

I'm stunned. Why me? 'I can't believe it. I don't know what to say.'

'Do you want the job, Ms Chapman?'

'Yes!' I say, although inside all I can think is *of course* I want the job! What kind of question is that? Of course I want a promotion, a raise, my own office, a change of scenery. I want to gush about what an incredible opportunity he's giving me, but I won't. That will surely ruin the sophisticated persona I have given myself to get the offer in the first place. I collect my thoughts and clear my throat, which has somehow been affected by all the internal screaming I've just done. 'Yes, please. It would be an honour.'

'Brilliant. Well, you'll have to stay where you are for the rest of the week until we replace you downstairs and then you can move up here and start your new role. That will be all.'

I nod and leave the office calmly and then hop and skip all the way back to my desk where I sit back down in a state of shock. I can't believe it. I've been promoted. I've been noticed. Me! My relentless organisation and attention to detail has paid off. Being me has paid off. It's not my dream role but it's definitely a step up. I can't wait to tell Kylie my good news!

Kylie

'I hate Mondays,' I tell Alexa as she answers my daily phone call.

'I know you do. Listen, I have news. I've been dying to call you all day but I've been too busy!'

'Me too. I could have done with a year-long rant this morning, but Janine was hovering over me.'

'Why was she hovering over you?'

'I don't know. Probably because I've been lagging behind. I can't help it. I had half of Thursday off and then after Mum's encounter I suffered through Friday with a mild case of PTSD.'

'You need to just push through. It'll all turn out okay.'

'I suppose. I just wish Janine would back off. She's on my case, Mum's on my case…'

'You're taking it too personally. Your mum just cares about you, and Janine's not on your case she's just watching over you. It's her job.'

'There's watching over me, and there's stalking me. Every day she finds new ways to catch me out. I think it's because I'm still on probation from the incident last month, which was ridiculous but you know about it already. Anyway, today she asked if she could have a "word" by which she meant she wanted to berate me for ten minutes, finishing by telling me I need to "up my standards". I asked her what that meant because I do my job just fine. Honestly, she just has it in for me.'

'I guess it does seem a bit excessive…'

'I know, right? She's asking for me to move the Earth and what for? A shit job that pays sod all. I went to university; it wasn't supposed to be like this. I'm on the wrong side of twenty-five *and* the wrong side of success. Great. How depressing. Now I'm going to sulk and stalk people online who are doing better in life than I am.'

'Sounds like a plan. Avoid looking up Jessica Burke unless you're feeling particularly masochistic.'

'What are you having for dinner?'

'Priya said she's making us Cajun chicken with a side salad. You?'

'I'm heating up a shepherd's pie as we speak.'

'It's summer…'

'It's the first thing I pulled out of the freezer.'

'Fair enough.'

For a while, neither of us speak. I sit and watch my sad shepherd's pie go around and around in the microwave. This is what has become of my life. A bubbling microwave meal of unidentifiable slop after a day of being unappreciated. No, something has got to give. If I can't change my career just yet, I must change other aspects of my life.

'Kylie? Are you still there? I have something to te—'

'I've got it! I'm going to sign up to one of those dating apps.'

'Seriously?'

'Yes. Everyone's doing it. It's like blind dating except not blind at all. You get their picture and an entire profile. Like a boyfriend resume.'

'But what if they put up a pretend picture and you get catfished?'

'Oh God! Don't say that. Look, I have to try. I have no other way of meeting men. I don't go anywhere except work and I have no hobbies in which to join a club. I have to.'

'Okay then… Listen, I—'

The microwave dings. 'Got to go, I'll call you tomorrow after work and let you know how the dating app sign up goes.'

I hang up, take my dinner out of the microwave, burning my fingers in the process and head upstairs. I'll sign up to a dating app whilst I eat my dinner, I can't wait another second.

One shepherd's pie and far too many biscuits later and I'm in. It took a while. Dating is exhausting and I haven't even started. Before I do start, I'm going to get comfortable and snuggle under the covers with a hot cup of tea by my side. Now that I have all the characteristics of a grandma, I'm finally ready to judge men by their appearances. Fun!

James, twenty-seven, likes guitar. He's cute, except the hair. Bry, twenty-eight, ugly jumper. Ellis, weird name. I've quickly fallen down the rabbit hole. Too many cats, sleazy, needs a shower. I could never be a match with someone whose profile picture is of themselves hiking. Same goes for a man who has a picture of a sports car as his profile picture. What's he compensating for? Andy, thirty, looks like a serial killer. Dante, too pretty. I judge and scroll to the next person and then the next. Wait, this guy might be okay. He has a mop of black hair and a cheeky smile. He looks a little grunge. He's called Jason. Worst possible name, given my own moniker, but I'm in no position to be so picky. It says he works in media. How cool!

I begin to message him and pause. What to say? 'Hi, I like your face?' No, it's creepy. I have no reason to message him. Dating services take the mystery away from the whole thing. We will never see each other's faces for the first time across a crowded room; merely I see his face in my darkened bedroom. It sounds sinister now that I've thought about it.

Okay, I'm going in.

What does a guy like you get up to on a Monday night? Cringe. Is this my best attempt at flirting? What is wrong with me?

Quicker than expected, I receive a reply. *Just having a go on my guitar. Do you play any instruments?* he asks. A guitar player!

No. I like watching people play though.

I'll be playing at Fox and Duck on Thursday if you'd like to see me play? We could have a drink together?

Wow this dating app is effective. *That sounds good. What time?*

7pm. Wear that dress in your profile picture, you look hot

as Hell.
A guitar player thinks I look 'hot as Hell'. I've still got it.

Alexa

It's hot today. I mean, it's June so it's somewhat to be expected but it's not your average summer's day kind of hot. Heatwaves in England occur at most once or twice a year and cause the country to go into melt down. Trains inexplicably refuse to run and the supermarkets run out of bagged ice and disposable barbecues. We lose our minds when it's exceptionally hot. The heat goes to people's heads. For example, every other person I've passed in the street today is in a state of undress. Maybe it's because England is so consistently mild that people crave extreme weather. I, however, am not one of those people. I like consistency and I won't be rushing to put on a bikini or have my dinner in the garden any time soon. The only acknowledgement I've made that it's hot is buying a frappuccino to drink as I walk home.

I live a bit out of the city centre, away from the loudness and the chaos. My street is long and rather quaint. Zebra-striped birch trees line the pavements and flower boxes full of pansies decorate most yards. It all adds up to making it a very nice place to live. The neighbours keep to themselves and cats roam freely, accepting treats when I have them. Nothing exciting happens on this street, which is just how I like it. What I don't like, however, is my front door opening when it shouldn't. I guess Priya is home from work early. But when the door fully opens I see it's a man. Although he doesn't see me, in fact he bumps into me.

'Ah!' he cries as we collide, 'I'm so sorry I didn't see you there.'

'That's okay…' I comfort the strange man leaving my house and can't help but think how ridiculous this is. I should ask who he is but I can't. Maybe he's a burglar, although he doesn't look or sound like a burglar. Not that I'm sure if a burglar looks or sounds a particular way, but he doesn't look like he's up to trouble. He looks kind, and rather handsome. Maybe he's Priya's new boyfriend. The stalker. Sorry, romancer.

He takes a lingering look at me and I feel self conscious. 'I'm Shaun,' he says.

'I'm Alexa.'

'Alexa...' he repeats my name slowly, as if trying it out on his own lips. It's weird.

'Well, nice to meet you. Can I just... I just need to get past...' I try to sneak past him, but he keeps getting in the way. It becomes a kind of awkward dance until finally I'm free on the other side of him. 'Thank you,' I tell him as I finally open the door and quickly shut it behind me.

Priya greets me as she enters the kitchen, 'Hey, how was work?'

'Good. I've just seen your new boyfriend out there. Very nice.'

'What?' Priya gets herself a drink, 'Oh, no that's just a guy who came to fix my laptop.'

'Ah, I see.'

'You think he looks nice?'

'What?'

'You said he was "very nice" when you thought he was my boyfriend. I have his number if you want to give him a call?'

'No definitely not, you've got the wrong idea.' I feel my cheeks colouring. 'Anyway, I think I'll head upstairs for a bit.' I like to be alone after work, to gather my thoughts and unwind. I need to escape from encounters with strange men and talkative house mates.

I retreat to my room and shut the world out, taking my shoes off and taking refuge on the bed. All I need is an hour to myself, to relax and do nothing. There's something very underrated about doing nothing.

My phone begins to ring and it pierces the silences with shrill tones. Who's that now? Great. It's Kylie. Maybe I'll just let it ring this time… damn it!

'Make it quick, I've only just got in and I need to unwind by avoiding everybody's existence.'

'Okay, okay, I'll be quick. Four words: I've got a date tomorrow!'

I want to tell her that she used five words, not four, but I'm too intrigued by the information to bother. 'Really? Through that dating app?'

'Yep. A guy called Jason. He works in media. He plays the guitar. And he's fit!'

'No. You know that the person in the picture is fit. You don't know that picture is really Jason. He could be a murderer. He could be seventy. He could be a seventy-year-old murderer.'

'Well, as long as he plays the guitar.'

I sigh, 'Are you at least meeting in a public place?'

'Yes!' Kylie says with triumph, as if that is enough to put an end to my concerns.

'Well that's something. Just be careful. Ring me before and after, please.'

'I will. Aww, you're so cute worrying about me.'

'I do worry. I worry one day you'll run out of lives and actually die.'

'I always land on my feet.'

She does. I'm grateful for that. 'Well that's great news then. It could be the start of some great love story…'

'Steady on, I just want to be wined and dined.'

'Do you believe in love at first sight?'

'No, what a load of rubbish.'

'I don't believe in love at first sight either. I believe in lust at first sight, sure, but not love. Love takes time.'

'Totally. You need to be able to see someone at their worst before you'll know if you love them. I believe in the toilet test.'

'The toilet test?'

'Yeah. If you accidentally see your other half on the toilet and you don't mind, it's love.'

'That's disgusting.'

'That's real love, baby. Warts and all.'

I hear a commotion in the background, it sounds like Lucie and she doesn't sound happy.

'Ah shit, Lucie's off on one because I used all her almond milk. It wasn't worth the impending argument either, it was disgusting. Got to go, see ya.'

Suddenly I remember my promotion, 'Oh Kylie, wait! I have some—' but she hangs up, having not heard a word. I guess I'll just tell her on Friday.

Kylie

No time for a phone call – It's D-Day!
 No, it's not? That was in June Alexa replies.
 What? It's D-Day. Date day. With the guitar player!
 Ahhh, I see. How long have you got to prepare?

The answer: one hour. So needless to say, I'm in a rush. I rushed through work, rushed home and now I'm trying to piece an outfit together. I'm going to a pub to hear live music so I need to look sexy but not too sexy because it's a Thursday and also, I need to look a little edgy, a little grunge. He asked me to wear the dress in my profile picture on that dating app, but it's my green birthday dress and it's not appropriate. Besides, it's still in the laundry basket.

I'm standing with my head in my wardrobe looking for a miracle, hoping it will take me to fashion Narnia. It's a small IKEA wardrobe and contains everything from a hideous Christmas jumper to my old university hoodie to several dresses that will never fit again without some radical diet change or the removal of several organs.

I decide to go with some high-waisted black skinny jeans that have rips in the knees and a crop top. Don't worry, the high-waistedness hides my wobbly bits. I can just about pull it off… But it's a good reminder I need to start doing some sit-ups now and then.

My hair is a mess. A wild mop. I spray at it and scrunch it up, trying to make it work. Messy chic, is that a thing? It is now. I scramble for my eyeliner, fail at the first try of getting a good flick and have to make it twice as thick. Damn it.

Right I'm ready. This is it. After grabbing my bag and having one last look at my appearance, I head out in the direction of the Fox and Duck. I haven't been there before but I know where it is and I know it will be like every other pub: sticky carpets and weird smells, but that's fine. I just hope we hit it off and the conversation flows as I'm not great at enforced small talk.

The pub looms before me and I tentatively head inside. People glance at me as I enter, which is pretty normal in pubs, but they quickly return to their pints. I look for Jason, and see a band setting up. He'll surely be one of them. A guy is sorting out some amp leads and looks like Jason but I don't want to go up in case it isn't or in case he's horrified by me and shows it. Instead, I'm just going to sit in a corner and text that I'm here. When it sends, I'll be able to figure out which one's Jason because he'll check his phone. I see a guy get his phone out, read a message and reply. *Where are you?*

In the corner near the door. I watch him read my reply and look until he spots me and smiles. I smile back. He looks friendly and decidedly young. Take that, Alexa! Then he beckons me over. This is it. I approach the band area where the band is busy setting up. There's a small disagreement between two of them and I feel like I'm intruding. Jason hasn't stood up to greet me, he's still squatted down sorting out cables. I feel like a spare part.

'Kylie, right?' he says, looking up at me. He looks shabbier up close.

'Yeah…'

'You want a drink?'

'Oh, totally.'

'Good. Could you grab me a pint while you're there? I'll come see you in five minutes.' He continues sorting out his cables. He looks almost like a chimp trying to figure out a puzzle.

Help.

'Okay. No problem.'

No problem. Is it? I know it's the twenty-first century, but really? I buy a pint and a glass of white wine from the bar and go back to where I was sitting and take a gulp of my drink; a little dose of courage. I promised Alexa I would text her to let her know I'm safe, *I'm at the Fox and Duck. He's real and not old or murderous-looking.*

Good! Have a great time and tell me all about it when you're home and safe!

So far, my night isn't worth talking about, but I should be patient. He did say he was playing tonight. I didn't expect his undivided attention. Oh no, he's coming towards me.

'Thanks, babe.' He sits close to me and takes the pint, drinking it almost in one go. 'For five minutes, I'm all yours. Then I've got to go and do my thing. So, your name's really Kylie huh?'

'Yeah.'

'That's so weird; I don't know anyone called Kylie.'

I get this a lot. 'Well you know, except the famous Kylie.'

Jason looks confused for a second. 'Oh, of course, Kylie Jenner.'

'Who?'

He begins to answer but is called by his band who look ready. 'Got to go, babe.' He finishes the last of his pint and leaves.

A long haired, greasy guy takes the microphone and settles the crowd. Jason picks up his guitar and positions himself, taking it all so very seriously. I'm ready.

'Hello, hey guys, hey. We're Codeine Dreams and this is Get Out of Here.'

The music starts with a bang, but not a good one. Spotlights hit the stage, illuminating Jason, and the light isn't kind to him. The music builds up in vain to a crowd who just aren't feeling it and then awful 'singing' starts, which is thoroughly anticlimactic and not just because I can't make out any of the words. I don't know how to describe it more succinctly than it's just… not good. The crowd seem to agree with me and I suddenly feel awful for Jason and his band.

I feel sorry for me now. This is never ending. I've died and gone to hell. Oh, hang on. Is it? Yes, it's over. Thank God. Jason puts down his guitar and high fives people. Who is this guy? Calm down, Bono. Oh God, he's coming over.

'So, what did you think?' he asks.

I force a smile; it hurts my jaw. 'Amazing,' I gush as well

as I can. 'Really good. Have you finished now?' Fingers crossed.

'Yeah, that's it for now. That's all the material we have really.' He sits back next to me and I can see he's sweaty. It's to be expected, I guess. But the fact remains.

'Why are you called Codeine Dreams?'

'I broke my leg last year and was given Codeine. They gave me these intense dreams that inspired a lot of my songs.'

Cringe-worthy. 'Makes sense.'

'So, tell me about yourself then. Where do you work?'

'I work in the city for a distribution company; it's really boring. I'm just a receptionist.'

'That sounds cool, working in an office. I like a girl in office clothes. Very sexy.'

'Mm.' There was nothing sexy about my outfit this morning. 'What about you?'

'Oh, I work in a video games store.'

'On your dating profile, it says you work in media.' I try to hide my shock.

'Yeah, babe, video games are a type of media.' He says it like it's obvious.

Oh wow. 'Oh, I get it now,' I say, wondering when I can leave.

'Play your cards right and I'll get you 10% off any game,' he says, as if this is going to get my knickers off. He sits closer to me.

'Mmhmm.' I take a sip of my drink. Then another. I finish the glass.

'Steady now, it's only a Thursday night. I don't want a drunk girl on my hands.' He looks like he does. I've had some pretty bad chat up lines and attempts at flirtation, but this tops it. I'm suddenly wishing this was my own codeine dream… my own drug induced nightmare. 'You're right. I need to get going soon anyway, early rise tomorrow for this office worker.'

'Oh God, I never considered that. Where do you live?'

'Only about ten minutes' walk away. What about you?'

'Me and the band live in a house share nearby. I'll take you to see it sometime.'

He smells strongly of fresh ale and body odour, and I can't imagine his house smells much better. 'I'd love to,' I say, 'another day, but now I have to go.' I get up.

'I'll walk you home,' he says, getting up also.

'No, please, you stay. I'll be fine, I've lived around here for years.'

'All right. Well, see ya babe.' He leaves and walks to the bar, to buy his own drink.

I walk out and the first thing I notice is fresh air. Despite the smoking ban many years ago, the pub reeked of cigarettes as well as stale beer, which I anticipated. It also had a faint odour of sweat and disappointment. Beginning to shiver, I set off for home whilst messaging Alexa, *I'm going home now.*

Dud or stud? she asks.

Dud. Capital D.

Shame. Better luck next time.

Let's hope so!

Once home, I plod up the stairs and once in my room, peel off my clothes, put on a t-shirt and get into bed. I'm exhausted despite the very brief and uneventful date. I think mentally exhausted is more like it. So, my first date as a twenty-five-year-old was a failure. But at least he wasn't a seventy-year-old murderer. He did seem nice, and I'm not a music or a work snob but he was just so… not the guy for me. Not the guy I see myself with. It's times like these that I'm glad I keep a stash of snacks in my bedside cabinet. I text Alexa goodnight and open up the dating app to check for any new messages.

'I wonder what you look like in the morning… in my bed.'

'I want you to wear a killer pair of heels for me and nothing else…'

I open one more message. 'I love a woman with a nice sized pair of tits.' Okay, that's enough. I'm going to sleep.

Alexa

Although Kylie invited me out tonight, I've feigned a headache because what I'm craving is a quiet weekend in after the last one and a busy work week on top. We've just been to the café for a drink and catch up but no, I didn't manage to tell her about the promotion. I was going to, honestly, but the moment she arrived and started telling me about her date last night, I was so captivated that it wasn't until two hours later on the way home that I realised. I find Kylie's adventures with this dating app fascinating and I'm living vicariously through her. She's daring and as much as I frown and disapprove of almost everything she does, I have to say I respect her for it. She's just so effortlessly cool and never shies away from going out and getting what she wants. As it turns out, Jason isn't what Kylie wants. Priya and I are going to watch a film and share some dinner right after I slip into something a little more comfortable.

I choose some leggings and a slouchy top before heading to pre-heat the oven. We're having pizza tonight, but to make it seem better than it is I'm going to serve it with salad and calorific dressing. I can't wait. What can I say? I like food, more so than I like the idea of being super thin.

'Something smells good!' Priya comes downstairs also in leggings and a comfy top.

'I've made a salad. Do you think we need anything else?'

'I have some posh crisps. They cost me three pounds.'

'For one bag? That's outrageous!'

'Yes, but they're from Waitrose.'

'Ah, well that explains it.'

We spread our dinner out on the coffee table. Pizza, salad, crisps and some coleslaw that I found in the fridge. We fill our plates and discuss what we should watch.

'Something romantic,' says Priya, sighing and curling up on the sofa with a plate of food.

'Oh God, do we have to?' I fill two glasses with wine with a sense of dread. We don't clash on a lot of things, but movies are always a source of dispute in this house.

'What do you have against romance?'

'Nothing. I have nothing against romance.'

'Then why can't we watch something romantic?'

'Because rom-coms never depict real romance.'

'Of course they do!'

'I bet you can't name one rom-com that does.'

'I can and I will: *The Notebook, Never Been Kissed, She's All That.*'

'How about: no, no and no. Come on, Pri, let's be the sophisticated, degree-educated women we are and watch something more intellectual.'

Somehow, we end up watching *10 Things I Hate About You*. Priya is remarkably good at getting what she wants. Although I like the film, I can't let Priya think she's won.

'See now, this is a bad romance.'

She gasps, in genuine horror. 'You take that back.'

'But he's not pursuing her with honest intentions.'

'Only initially, but then he falls for her. Love finds a way.'

I roll my eyes. 'I think you have a warped idea of what love is.'

'You just haven't been romanced in such a long time that you're becoming cynical. You just need a cat or two and you're all set for your spinster life.'

I take a big gulp of wine, finishing the glass. 'Maybe that's true. Kylie has resorted to using a dating app on her phone. I might join her.' I get up, taking the empty plates through to the kitchen.

'It might be a good idea. Oh, grab another bottle of wine while you're there.'

The plates are put to soak when I hear a knock at the door. How odd, we're not expecting any visitors. I open it to find the guy who I bumped into the other day – the computer repair guy.

'Oh, hey.' I say. Priya hasn't mentioned her laptop is broken again. Even so, why would she go to the guy who failed to repair it properly? Why on a Friday evening? 'Are you here for Priya?'

'No, actually.' His attention seems to turn to a small card in his hands that he's fiddling with, before he finally looks back at me. 'Alexa, right? We met the other day…'

'That's me…' Is this a sales pitch? I don't need my laptop fixing. 'How can I help you?'

'I was erm, just wondering, if you'd like to hang out sometime. Maybe grab a drink?'

'Me? Erm, well, I guess I don't know—'

'Think about it,' he says, interrupting me and holding out a card. 'Get in touch if you do.'

'Okay,' I say, 'thank you, Shaun.'

He smiles with closed rosebud lips and looks at me. I smile back, feeling my face warm with embarrassment. 'Well, nice seeing you again.' He says 'bye' and turns to leave. I watch him exit the yard before closing the door.

'I told you,' says Priya, causing me to jump out of my skin. I had been caught up in the moment and forgot she was only in the other room. Had she seen the whole encounter?

'You told me what?' I ask, trying to sound casual. But Priya looks amused and victorious.

'Love finds a way.'

Kylie

Tonight was going to be lost to binge-watching Grey's Anatomy in bed. It's a perfectly respectable way to spend a Friday night, but with my dating app messages on a decline, and the disastrous date with Jason still fresh in my mind, I'm itching for something good to happen. And it's not going to happen in bed clutching the remote.

So, I've decided I'm going out. And it'll have to be alone, because Alexa has a headache. I don't like going out without her, but since my birthday tea at Mum's I've had this inner voice nag at me to get out and do more. I've chosen to listen to the inner voice because I need the push and maybe it'll be good for me. What's that inspirational quote on the print Alexa got me? 'Behind every successful woman is herself'? Maybe it's true. I'm an independent, twenty-five-year-old woman and I'm going to get myself out there and see what happens. What do I have to lose? I'll just binge-watch Grey's Anatomy tomorrow.

I walk into the first bar I see; a place I've never been before. It's a rather quiet and dark space that doesn't smell of stale beer but instead an intoxicating mix of perfume and spirits. The men are in nice shirts, the women totter about in heels and tight dresses. I don't belong here but I'm going to pretend I do. I'm going to fake it until I make it and act like I come here every day of the week. I stroll up to the bar and sit on a high stool, which I do with less grace than I would have liked.

The barman comes over to me, 'What can I get you?'
'A cocktail please.'
'Which one?'
'A Cosmopolitan,' I say, the only cocktail name I know.

The barman hands me a small cocktail glass of something red. It costs the best part of ten quid and I try not to look shocked. It tastes okay though, very fruity. I try to conjure up an out-of-body experience and imagine what I look like perched on a stool drinking a cocktail. I imagine my posture to be terrible and sit up better whist trying to keep my legs together. Yes, I bet I look perfectly sophisticated. A fine twenty-five-year-old. Until I miss my mouth and slosh what is, let's face it, overpriced cranberry vodka down my front. Damn it.

'Whiskey on the rocks and whatever this lovely lady is having.'

I turn my head and there's a guy looking at me, smiling. 'Hey, I'm Harry.'

I stare at him, open mouthed for a second, and then give him what I hope is a demure look, 'Kylie.'

'Kylie? That's a beautiful name. You don't hear it very often.'

The barman gives us our drinks and Harry pays. 'Are you here with friends?' he asks, looking around.

'No. Just me.'

'Really? That's bold. Do you want some company?'

'I'd love some.'

He leads me to a table in the corner and we get talking. He's wearing a smart shirt, tucked into dark, tight-fitted Levi's. His fragrance, probably designer, is more intoxicating than the Cosmopolitan. I feel like a complete slob in comparison but he doesn't seem bothered by my appearance, quite the opposite.

'So, what's a girl like you doing in a bar like this alone on a Friday night?'

'A girl like me? Do I not fit in here or something?' My insecurities slip out.

'Of course you do. But alone? You're too fun to not have people flocking around you.'

'I chose to come on my own,' I purr, putting emphasis on the last word. 'I wanted to discover something new.' Or rather, someone new.

'Well, I hope I'm satisfactory for you,' he growls back, putting his hand on my leg.

'What's a guy like you doing in a bar alone on a Friday night?'

'I had a free night, but no friends to join me, so I thought I'd make new ones.'

'So, what do you do for work?'

'Ah, I'm an accountant. It's very boring stuff. What about you?'

I was dreading this question, 'I'm an administrator, but I have a degree in Psychology.'

'I could see you as a psychologist.' He looks bemused, but in a good-natured way, 'Are you going to lay me down and start asking me about my childhood?'

'I might lay you down but there won't be any talking.' Wow did I really say that? These cocktails are potent. So is Harry. He looks me in the eye and keeps his gaze, as if he's deciding something. I return the gaze, into his rich brown eyes that are framed by impossibly long eyelashes. He has a smouldering look with sun kissed skin. I've never met such an attractive man. I feel hot and tingly. A result of Cosmopolitans and the urge to rip his probably very expensive shirt right off his body.

He knocks back his whiskey and squeezes my thigh, 'Shall we have another drink before we go?'

Alexa

I wash my face, brush my teeth and get straight into pyjamas, short cotton ones, and put on moisturising cream. All the while holding the business card that Shaun gave me. Priya teased me about it for the rest of the night; she's convinced this is the start of something big. 'Love finds a way,' she kept saying. She's unbearable when she's smug.

This guy, Shaun, doesn't even know me. He saw me once, fleetingly, and then came back to hand me a business card under the guise of wanting to grab a drink. I don't believe it. He's probably trying to drum up new customers, not ask me out. But try telling that to Priya who has spent the whole night gushing about it being a romantic gesture. It's ridiculous.

So why am I still holding his card? Granted, it's a nice card with a minimal but professional look to it. It says his name is Shaun Abbott, 'For all your computer repair needs and more'.

His number is on the card.

When I first met him I told Priya, when I thought he was her boyfriend, that he was cute. I wasn't just saying it to be complimentary to Priya. He has a crop of blonde hair and kind brown eyes. He's unassuming but handsome, kind of like Justin Timberlake circa 2004 and well dressed with it. I could do worse. What if he was genuine about wanting to grab a drink?

I type his number into my phone and send him a text message.

Hey, it's Alexa. Is this a bad time to text?

Is it too soon to message him? What if he's in bed? After all, I am.

But I get a text message back almost immediately, *Hey Alexa, it's not a bad time at all. I'm glad you text.*

You are?

Yes. I'm just in bed but I can't sleep.

I try not to think how he looks in bed and reply, *I'm in bed too.*

Did you have a good evening?

Yeah I guess. I just watched a movie with my house mate.

Priya, is it?

Yeah.

She seems nice. She doesn't clear her laptop out often enough though.

I knew it. Apparently Priya is a hoarder in real life and virtually. I message him back, *I tell her all the time. She never clears anything out.*

Are you more organised?

Erm, yes. Obsessively. It's quite sad.

Not at all. I'm the same.

Already it feels easy and natural to talk to him. I can't help but worry what if I'm getting my hopes up and he's just buttering me up as a potential new customer? I'm not one to initiate things, but all I can think about is the chat I had with Kylie when we were doing our make-up on the night of her birthday. As someone who has been single since before I even joined the wrong side of twenty-five, what do I have to lose in asking him out for a drink? And more importantly, what could I gain?

So, about that drink...

Kylie

I wake up in a very big bed, on a crisp white sheet, my head pounding despite it resting on a very soft pillow. I sit up but the world still feels topsy-turvy. This isn't my bedroom, that much is certain. I soon realise I'm naked and pull at the duvet for modesty before leaning over to grab my clothes, which I see are strewn on the floor beside me. Harry isn't here. Now what? For starters, I should get dressed.

I've never had a one-night stand before, believe it or not. I'm not against them, but this is new territory for me. I've only seen one-night stands on the telly. Is he going to bring me in a stack of pancakes on a tray with a rose in a small vase or is he going to tell me to leave and never come back? Do I sneak out or find him?

'Morning.' He enters the room just as I'm wiping sleep out of my eyes. Oh God. He stands near me, holding out a mug of coffee.

'Morning.' I try to avert my mouth and breath from him. This is terrible. He reaches over and gently lifts my head up with his finger so I'm forced to look at him. He smiles and looks just as hot as last night. 'You okay, gorgeous?'

'Yeah,' I say whilst keeping my mouth as closed as possible. 'Just, feeling a little rough.'

'Too many cocktails last night.'

'Definitely.'

He walks to the mirror, checking his hair, 'What are your plans for today then?'

'Oh...' Shit. I don't have any plans. No reason to leave and no reason to say no if he invites me anywhere. I sip my coffee. It's soothing and helps clear the brain-fog. 'No plans, I guess.'

He finishes looking at himself and turns to look at me, 'You want to go for dinner tonight?'

A date with my one-night stand? Is that the done thing? I'm not sure about this. Besides, I'm broke. Although, he's probably not short of cash. 'Oh, well...'

He smiles, 'I'll pay.'

'How can I say no to that?' I ask, smiling. No, seriously, how? He walks back over and takes my coffee mug.

'Jot down your address, go home, freshen up, drink lots of water and I'll pick you up at 7pm.' He kisses me on the mouth. It feels slightly forward; I barely know him. Then I remember we had sex last night. I don't remember much but I do remember that it was the tearing-at-clothes, passionate kind of sex. If anything, a kiss is a step back. I accept the kiss and try to smile graciously, 'I look forward to it.'

I set off home, in the same clothes as last night so I feel a tad self conscious and very over-dressed. This is what people refer to as the walk of shame, right? Except I'm not ashamed. Why is it called that? Because everyone can tell you've slept over somewhere and probably had sex? Harry is nothing to be ashamed about. He's a successful, older, handsome guy who is taking me to dinner tonight. This is what it's like to date as an adult. I should be skipping home, delighted. Only, my head is rocked and I feel groggy despite the coffee and fresh air. What did Harry say? Drink water?

When I finally make it home I kick my shoes off and wander into the kitchen, drink two glasses of water. It doesn't do much for my hangover but it soothes my throat, dry from shouting over music to converse with Harry. Adrenaline floods over me as I think about the events of last night and the early hours of this morning. As tired as I am, I feel exhilarated. It gives me the energy to rush upstairs where I dive onto my bed. It's much smaller than Harry's bed, but it's mine and it's my safe place. I lie back, stretch out, and flick the telly on. Everything's how it usually is, except I have a date tonight.

My instinct after any significant event is to call Alexa and tell her all about it, but I wonder if she will disapprove of going to a bar alone and going home with a stranger. Alexa isn't a one-night stand kind of girl. She's better than that. She's classy. What will she think of me? I don't need her lecturing me over the phone while I nurse a hangover. I don't want her to put me off going out tonight for what will almost definitely be a very fancy meal with a handsome man who has seen my wobbly bits and doesn't mind. For now, I'll keep it to myself.

Alexa

Cake or cookies? he asks.

Hmm. That's a tough one. *Cake. Tea or coffee?*

Tea

Me too!

We've been doing this all evening, and it turns out we mostly agree on everything. We haven't been for a drink, but it's on the cards. Instead I've been in my bedroom messaging him back and forth. We get on so well. I lie back on my bed, feeling relaxed and yet at the same time excited. My phone buzzes and I rush to look at the message.

Chocolate or flowers?

You're supposed to pick two different things that fall under the same category.

I have. The category is 'things to receive as a gift'.

Oh, I feel silly now. Well the truth is, I've never received either. But if I had to choose... *Flowers. I buy myself chocolate but I never buy myself flowers.*

Interesting.

He's clearly asking in case the occasion comes up to buy me anything, right? Or am I getting carried away? Maybe I'll meet him at a bar and he'll be sitting there with a single white rose. No, that's cheesy. What's wrong with me? A day of male attention and my brain has turned to mush.

I get up, and head out of my room. I'll make some tea and think of what question to ask Shaun next. I don't want to know if he prefers Quavers to Wotsits. I want to know something real, something gritty. What's beneath his handsome and well-polished exterior? What does he suppress before delivering kind and well-spoken words? I need to find out before I get too attached.

'Hello,' says Priya when I enter the kitchen. 'I don't believe we've met. I knew there was someone upstairs glued to their phone, but it's been so long since I saw their face I've forgotten.'

'Har-har.' I walk across to her and peer over her shoulder at the simmering pan of food. 'Something smells nice.'

'It's curry. Do you want some?'

'Yes please! Is it your mum's famous curry?'

She turns to me, looking annoyed. 'No, it's Patak's Tikka Masala. Honestly, Alexa, that's so racist.'

I'm hit with a pang of guilt, 'Oh God, I'm so sorry.'

But then her face turns and she beams a huge grim at me. 'I'm totally kidding. It is my mum's famous curry. She gave me a vat of it when I was there yesterday.'

'I thought it was! The smell brings me back to the last time I visited.' I get two bowls out of the cupboard in anticipation as I realise I haven't eaten all day.

'So did you get a chance to talk to Shaun?' Priya asks. 'Or have you been texting someone else for the last twenty-four hours?'

'What? Oh, Shaun.' I try to sound nonchalant. 'We exchanged a message or two.' Or fifty.

'Well? What's he like?'

'He's…' I think about it, and then say, for lack of a better word, 'nice.'

Priya frowns, 'What's that supposed to mean?'

I shrug, 'That he's nice? I don't know. He's nice. He says the right things. I've yet to find a flaw or a quirk. It's kind of unnerving don't you think?'

Priya rolls her eyes, 'What's wrong with being nice?'

'He's almost too nice. He looks nice, he says the right things.'

Priya stares at me, eyes wide open, looking incredulous '…and?'

'He seems perfect. But no one's perfect.'

'Well, I guess you'll have to keep talking to him until you find something not-so-perfect about him.'

'Maybe later, if I'm not busy.' I start to eat a little quicker.

Kylie

It's 6:58pm. Time to make a move. I doubt I'll need any money but I do want to take a bag as I feel naked without one. I fill it with essentials: phone, lipstick, deodorant, perfume, condoms and a chocolate bar.

As I fasten my bag, there's a knock at the door. Shit. I was going to meet him outside my house so he didn't have to come in. Maybe I can open the door and sneak out before he has time to look at anything.

I crack open the door and there he is; every bit as handsome as he was last night. He stands, looking pristine from impeccably quaffed hair to shiny shoes.

'Hey,' he says with a smile, 'are you ready?'

'Yeah,' I say, and then realise that I'm not, damn it. 'Actually, I've left my bag upstairs. Give me one moment.' I bolt upstairs as quick as these heels will carry me, hoping he doesn't come in and look around. When I come back down, he's still standing at the doorway, but with the door open. That over-flowing laundry basket displayed before him is sure to shit all over the version of me he met sat at a cocktail bar in a little black dress.

'Are you ready now?' he asks.

'Ready.'

We sit close together in the back of the taxi and the hot air mixed with his expensive fragrance and the desire to get even closer to him makes me feel hot and dizzy.

'You'll love where I'm taking you,' he says with complete confidence.

'Is it fancy?' I sound intrigued, and hopefully not as anxious as I feel. What if it's too fancy? I'm suddenly reminded that Harry's loaded. And while that's nice, I hope I won't feel too out of my depth.

Harry shrugs, 'It's charming, although not half as much as you are.' He snakes an arm around my shoulder and rests his other hand on my waist, pulling me in and suddenly I couldn't give a toss what the restaurant is like. I almost tell him to forget it and take me to his, when the car stops.

He gets out and opens the door for me. 'Come on.' He offers me his arm and we walk in together. A waiter leads us down to our table, past rows of smart-looking men and sophisticated-looking women.

'Allow me.' He pulls a chair out and waits for me to sit down. I sit down and shuffle my own chair in but he insists on helping.

'Have I told you how lovely you look this evening?'

'No.' Although I wouldn't blame him for not telling me. As I smooth a napkin over my lap, following his lead, I realise just how green this dress is. It's fine on the dance floor, but here amongst a sea of suits and little black dresses I stick out like a Christmas tree in July.

'Well, you do.'

'I can't help but think I should have worn a different dress.'

'Nonsense,' he says, although I'm not sure he means it.

'It's nice here.' I try to change the subject.

'Yeah, I like it. So, have you recovered from last night?' he asks, opening the menu.

I take a menu for myself and open it. Christ! Look at those prices. 'Just about', I say, distracted. Who has this kind of money? 'What about you? Have you recovered?'

'From the alcohol? Yes. From you? I'm not sure. You certainly gave me a run for my money.'

With as much money as he clearly has, I should have charged him.

A waiter appears, 'Hey Harry, what can I get you tonight?'

Harry closes his menu and hands it to the waiter, 'Whiskey on the rocks, medium rare sirloin and the stuffed mushrooms for me. Kylie?'

The problem is, I don't know what anything on the menu

is. Where are the chips? The burgers? I can't see lasagne printed anywhere. I've heard Lucie say she likes risotto so I know to avoid that. Chicken seems like a safe choice but will it seem too common and uninspired? Harry and the waiter are looking at me, waiting for me to order. Just choose something, Kylie, anything. Say the next item you see.

'The grilled halloumi, please,' I say, closing the menu and handing it to the waiter. I didn't read what it came with, but surely it'll come with mashed potato or something that isn't completely alien to me.

'And a Cosmopolitan for her, Steve,' adds Harry. The waiter, Steve, nods and leaves with the menus. I regret my choice already, but try to focus my attention on Harry.

'So,' he says, 'I didn't know you were vegetarian.'

'Sorry?'

'The halloumi…'

'Oh, right. Well, I'm not exactly… I just like to be healthy.'

Harry smirks for a moment and then changes it into a smile, 'I getchya. Smart. Then again, I should have known you're smart, being a graduate.'

'I'm not known for my smarts…'

'Nonsense. Renting that tiny terraced house made me realise how smart you are. Saving money is a dying art. I should know, you should see the clients I have on my books. They're terrible with money.'

I really don't know what to say to this. Should I go along with it? Or admit I'm terrible with money? No, better not. Then I see the waiter coming back with our drinks.

'Here you are, Harry.' He places the drinks down, 'here you are, Madame.'

It's just occurred to me that the waiter knows Harry by name. Why is that? The waiter leaves and I can't help myself but ask, 'How often do you come here?'

'Oh, now and then. When I have good company.'

'How do you manage to have such a great life?'

Harry laughs, 'I don't want to talk about my life. I want to talk about you. What do you do for fun? Do you like skiing?'

I nearly choke on my Cosmo. The closest I've ever come to skiing was going out in heels when the paths were iced over. 'Erm,' I say, 'not really, I'm not that brave.'

'Yes, after I said it I realised my mistake. No, extreme sports don't seem your thing. I can imagine you in the resort instead. Sipping on a hot chocolate, watching everyone else ski.'

'That does sound more like me.'

'I go skiing every January. It really is incredible, there's nothing like it.'

'I'd love to go sometime.' I always imagined a mini-break with a boyfriend would be in Italy or France in the summer. But a skiing trip is definitely romantic. Plus, I won't have to worry about looking good in a bikini.

The waiter arrives and puts a plate in front of me. Is that all of it? A few slivers of halloumi sit on a bed of leaves. Other vegetable pieces punctuate the plate and everything's drizzled in some kind of sauce but as dressed up as it is, the meal still looks as tiny as it is.

'So, I was talking to a friend at lunch time,' says Harry, 'she works at a clinic and she mentioned she was looking to hire a few more psychologists. I thought of you.'

'Really?'

'Yeah. Shall I send her your details? I know you said you want out of the job you're in.'

'Oh,' I carry on chewing so I can think of how to get out of it. The truth is, I don't really like psychology. I know, I know! I have a degree in it. But I didn't know what to take at university and Mum pushed for psychology because it sounds impressive. Sadly, not only did it bore me to tears but I had to rely on Alexa to scrape a 2.2, 'Sure. That'd be nice. Although I have some other options.'

'It's nice to keep your options open, though.'

'It is,' I say, and carry on eating. You know, this halloumi isn't so bad. In fact, it's pretty good. I could definitely get used to it.

Alexa

It's Monday and Shaun's still perfect, despite us speaking all Sunday. As a result, I've started to come around to accepting that maybe he just is perfect. I guess time will tell, we have a date on Friday.

Either way, it's time to put him to the back of my mind as today's the big day: today's the day I start my promotion. I know it's not my dream career, but it's a step up and I've earned it. I feel proud of myself, which doesn't happen often.

I enter the building I've entered every weekday for years without much fuss. Everything's the same, but something feels different. The elevator takes me past my old floor and it's all getting very real.

The elevator doors open and there it is, my new work floor. It's very white, like a blank canvas. I tentatively step out of the elevator. Now what?

But before I have time to decide, my boss strides towards me. 'Morning, Alexandra, shall we?'

I should speak but I can't, instead I nod and a few sounds come out and I follow him to a room. Is all of this mine? It can't be. We walk over to what I presume is my desk. It's beautiful. I try not to swoon at an IKEA product and act like a professional.

'This is your office; I trust you like it?'

It's all mine. It's bigger than my bedroom. My mind is racing with themes and ideas of how I could decorate this space, but first I should probably answer my boss. 'I love it, thank you.'

'Good. Because this is where you'll be more often than not. It's a lot of work but I'll try to make you as comfortable as possible. Coffee?'

I'm not sure if he's offering me coffee or if he wants me to get him coffee. 'Do you mean you want me to make you coffee?'

'It's like you read my mind. One sugar, please.' He smiles and leaves, shutting the door behind him.

I put my bag down on my chair in my office. I can't stop thinking how all of this is mine. And it's so quiet! I'll no longer be subjected to loud, gossiping colleagues within elbows distance of me. I won't be constantly interrupted.

Suddenly the door opens and a huge bouquet of flowers walks in, 'Delivery for Alexa.'

Could they really be for me? I ask the talking flowers to clarify. 'Alexa Chapman?'

The bouquet lies on my desk and a man appears, 'That's right. Sign here please.'

I sign the man's clipboard, thank him and watch him leave before I pounce on the bouquet, looking for a clue.

A card reveals the mystery gifter, 'To Alexa, good luck for today, Shaun.' I put the flowers on the side, making a mental note to buy a vase on my lunch break. My face turns as pink as the flowers, overwhelmed with the events of today. It's not even 9am and I've got a new job and a man who sends me flowers. I need to tell Kylie. But how do I tell her all of this? It sounds ludicrous to have gained so much in a weekend. It *is* ludicrous. And yet it's true, so I have to tell her, and I want to tell her. But first, coffee.

Kylie

I scour the floor for my underwear, 'Do you know the number for a taxi company around here?'

'No. There are no taxis. There's only a bed.' He grins and puts his hand on my waist. I feel him gently pull me closer.

I don't want to resist, but I must. 'I have to go to work.'

'Forget work, you hate it there. You don't hate it here, though, do you? So stay.'

I lean in and kiss him, 'I do hate work but I like money. I need money.'

'Your work pays you peanuts. They don't appreciate you. I told you, I know a friend who can get you a job. The pay is great.'

I stop him kissing my neck, pull away a little, and look him in the eyes. 'But can you really get me a job?'

He looks back at me so seriously that I can't imagine why I would doubt him. 'Of course,' he says, 'call in sick, stay in bed with me and when I go to work later I'll make some calls.'

'Fine. You've twisted my arm.'

He puts his arms around my waist once more and pulls me to him, skin on skin. 'I would never twist your arm. I'd never hurt you.'

It's so cheesy but I believe it. He's invited me into his home, he wants to get me the job I deserve and he wants to help me have a better life. I glance at the clock. I'm meant to be at work in ten minutes, I should call Janine. But he pulls the sheets over us and my mind turns to mush. Janine can wait. The world can stop turning for all I care.

Some hours later, the world resumes turning and Harry has

to go to work. I lie in his bed as he jumps in the shower. My phone is showing seven messages, six missed calls and four voicemails. No prizes for guessing who the voicemails are from. Who even leaves voicemails anyway under the age of forty?

Harry comes in, buttoning up his shirt. 'What are your plans for the afternoon?'

'I guess seeing as I'm not at work, I'm free. Do you need me to leave when you do?'

'No. You can see yourself out when you're ready and post the key when you do. Is that okay?'

'It's perfect.'

He comes over and kisses me, See you, babe'.

'Have a good time at work.'

'Knowing you're naked in my bed? How can I possibly have a good time?' He flashes me a pearly white grin and sets off out the door. When it shuts, I ache for him.

I'm torn between having a good snoop around and having a nap. But first I should listen to my voicemails.

Hello, Kylie, this is Janine. I can't help but notice it's 9am and you haven't arrived. When you do, could you come and see me as soon as possible, please?

Shit. She sounds pissed. I need to call her back, but while I work up the courage to do so, I'll check in on Alexa and tell her about Harry before my head explodes with all this information that I'm keeping to myself. It's vital. I call but there's no answer. Shit. She's at work. I'll message her instead, then she can read it when she gets the chance. *Lex, huge news! So, I didn't tell you but I went out that night you had a headache and I met this guy. I think it's getting serious!*

I sit back, feeling better at having told Alexa. It felt wrong keeping it to myself. Sooner than expected, I get a message back. *You met a guy? You kept that quiet. But that's brilliant news! And you say it's serious already? Tell me more.*

We only met recently. It was so random, but we really hit it off. I know it sounds crazy, but it feels serious already.

Just take it steady, Kylie. You barely know him. Don't do anything drastic.

Typical Alexa, ruining things with her sensible nature. She makes me feel impulsive and naive. And although she's right in some ways, she doesn't know Harry like I do. But I think I'll leave it now, I probably shouldn't tell her much more yet. *I know, don't worry about me. But it's all going well so far. Is that so wrong?*

Of course not. I'm happy for you!

I lie back and stretch out in Harry's bed. I'm happy for me, too.

Alexa

Today, the office is a circus and I'm doing a juggling act. My boss has given me a huge list of tasks to complete and I'm drowning in emails and files to the siren of the phone ringing. I feel like answering and screaming for help. But no, I must keep calm and collected.

But how can I when the printer inexplicably won't work? Damn it! Don't flake on me, printer, when I need you the most. I clench my fists but resist punching the display screen that's telling me there's an 'error' and storm out of my office to find Adam, the IT guy.

I race across the hall, powered by the steam coming out of my ears, but appear to run out of steam as I near him. 'Hi, er, oh… excuse me?' I say from a distance.

'Can I help you?' He looks at me like I'm a stranger.

'I hope so, it's my printer, there's something wrong with it.'

'What's wrong with it?'

'It's not working.'

I can see him almost roll his eyes and stop himself. He sighs, 'Could you elaborate?'

'It says "error"…'

'Which office are you in?'

'The one over there,' I say as I point to it, 'the one with my name on the door.'

'Right… and what's your name again?'

If my face wasn't red from anger, it is now but from embarrassment. 'Alexandra,' I tell Adam Johnson, 33, the IT guy, whom I've known as a colleague for five years.

'Okay. I'll be over in ten minutes, Alexandra.'

'Thank you.'

Brilliant. I can't move on with my workload until the printer's fixed. I head back to my office, shut the door, and sit at my desk, which is in complete disarray. What now?

But my fate is decided for me, as Kylie messages.

I'm thinking of going on the pill.

Really? Things must be pretty serious between you and this new guy.

I like to think it's getting serious. But also, I'd like to not have to use condoms. We had sex five times last night. After a while it starts to chafe.

Oh Jesus.

You should still use condoms. What about sexually transmitted diseases?

He says he's clear!

They always do. I roll my eyes. *Oh well, by all means risk it then.*

Really?

NO! Obviously not. Ask him to get tested.

I can't ask that.

If it's serious, there's no reason why not.

You suck the fun out of everything.

I lean back on my chair and relax, *I know. Want to come to mine tonight? We need to catch up. I have stuff to tell you.*

Can't. Harry's booked us a table already at some restaurant.

Aww. So his name's Harry. Well, have a good time. Let me know how it goes asking if he's diseased.

There's a knock at the door and I shove my phone out of sight just in time for Adam to come in.

'Hey,' he says, 'is it this printer?'

'That's the one.'

I perch on the edge of my seat, feeling awkward, as Adam goes about fixing the printer. I wonder if he has an STD. No! God, why would I even think that? I wonder if Shaun has, although it's not really my business. It's been a long while since I've had to worry about contraception. That's the great thing about Kylie though, she's not afraid to just seize the moment. She's not afraid to ask me if she should get the pill.

She's fearless. That's why I invited her over tonight, so I could tell her about everything. The next time I see her, I'm telling her, without fear. What am I afraid of anyway?

Kylie

I'm running for work in last night's heels, still hungover and now intoxicated from all the dry-shampoo I applied this morning to look somewhat respectable. The automatic doors open and I skid through the lobby and into the lift.

What a shame the lift walls are mirrored. I really don't need to see how awful I look. Still it gives me a chance to rub yesterday's eyeliner back into place. I catch my breath and stand, composed, as the doors open. If I'm lucky, I can make it to my desk without anyone noticing I'm late.

I load my computer up and shuffle files, pretending to be in the middle of working hard. My phone sounds off in my pocket. Shit. Rachel looks over her computer monitor at the commotion. I smile, shake my head and tut, 'bloody thing I thought I had put it on silent.' I wait for her to stop gawping so I can read my message.

I just had to pop back to mine. You left these on my bedroom floor, a photo of said pants accompanies the message.

My face turns red and I laugh out loud but stifle it with a cough and shove my phone under paperwork as Janine walks by.

'Morning, Kylie,' she says in the way she always does, pained and resentful as if I've just given her a bikini wax against her will.

'Good morning, Janine. I've been working on these papers all morning but I'll have them for you by lunch.'

'Very good, Kylie.' She walks back to her office and shuts the door. She probably wants privacy while she snacks on live baby chicks or whatever it is she does behind closed doors. That's what I imagine, anyway. I check the coast is clear and message Harry.

Oops! Now I have to spend the day at work commando!
I'm okay with that. It makes for good fantasising.

Talking to Harry by any means always makes me feel giddy. He's charming and always knows the right thing to say. *Pop to mine after work and I'll make that fantasy a reality.*

I will. I'm going now, I have a meeting with Charlotte.

Charlotte is the women who has a job opening that Harry thinks I'll be perfect for. *Put in a good word for me?*

Of course, babe.

Harry is my knight in shining armour. Everything's coming together. Maybe this isn't the wrong side of twenty-five after all. I put my phone away and get on with work. It's tedious beyond belief but tolerable now that I know I won't be doing this forever, or even for the rest of the year.

'Kylie, can I see you in my office, please?'

I look up from my monitor to see Janine towering over my desk. Despite having completed the majority of what I'm working on and promising Janine I'd have it ready by lunch, it's only 11am. 'Oh, I'm not quite finished yet. I did say lunch time, but I can get it to you quicker, perhaps in half an hour—'

'That's fine, Kylie, but I'd still like to see you in my office.'

She looks happier than usual. Her lips are pursed but her eyes are smiling. It's unnerving.

'Okay, sure.' I get up and follow Janine to her office.

Janine's office always throws me off as it contrasts with her personality. Instead of being a darkened lair full of discarded baby chick bones and jars of stolen hopes and dreams, it's floral and smells of talc. I walk past a 'best nan' bear and feel nauseated.

'Have a seat, Kylie.' She beckons me to a seat on the other side of her desk. I sit.

'Is everything okay?'

She makes a song and dance of carefully sitting in her chair, smoothing her skirt and straightening a folder with my name on it. Then she leans back and looks at me, 'Kylie, how long have you been an employee here?'

'About five years?'

'Yes. *About* five years, as you say. How do you feel you have progressed in this time?'

'Pretty good, I'd say. I know where everything is and I do my work.'

'Mmhmm.' She opens the folder and appears to look through it, 'but it doesn't take very long to learn where everything is and what one is expected to do in one's job. Or at least, it shouldn't. It certainly shouldn't take, *about* five years.'

I don't like where this is going, 'well, I do everything that's asked of me...'

'It isn't enough to simply do what is "asked of you". You don't go above and beyond, and if we're being honest, you don't always do what is asked of you. You often arrive late, for example.'

A breeze travels around the room, or is that her sucking the life out of me? I muster a smile through gritted teeth, 'come on, Janine, a few minutes late now and then isn't a big deal.'

'But it's not a few minutes. From my observation, it's more like ten minutes or even twenty, or several hours.'

Shit. So, she did notice that I came in late today. I need to think of something to say that will appease her, before it's too late. 'Janine, if I could just—'

'I'm afraid, Kylie, we've come to the end of the road. I just don't see what else working here could do for you, or for us. We're going to have to let you go.'

Shit. I sit, soulless, defeated. Janine offers an apologetic face, but I know it's just a mask to hide her true form. She's talking and I hear the words, 'two weeks' notice' and 'P45' in the distance, but everything seems fuzzy. I need to get out of here.

'Okay, thank you,' I say inexplicably before my legs carry me out of the office. In a daze, I walk to my desk, grab my bag and leave the office for the last time. Fuck the two weeks' notice, I can ask Harry to sort me that job sooner. Maybe this is a blessing in disguise.

As I walk home I call Harry but he doesn't answer. He's probably still in that meeting so I'll message him.

Harry, huge news! Work fired me, bastards. Do you think you could ask Charlotte to sort that job opening sooner than planned?

I keep on walking, waiting for a message back. As I walk it hits me that I no longer work for Janine and no longer have a job. I'm unemployed. I want to freak out, cry, drink, eat, and call Alexa. But I'll wait to see what Harry's plan is. He'll sort it all out for me. There's no need to worry.

You actually got fired? Shit. I'm still in talks with Charlotte, I don't know much yet...

It's fine, it's early days yet. *That's okay. I can wait for a bit, don't worry.*

Maybe you should look for other jobs anyway, just in case.

I'll never find a job as good as the one Charlotte's opening up.

I get home and feel a sense of relief. I head upstairs and find my room to be the mess I left it in before I stayed over at Harry's last night. He said he would come over after work, so I better clean up. As I tidy my floordrobe I realise he never messaged me back.

Come over whenever you finish work; I'm home now and waiting, minus pants.

As I'm making my bed and imagining him in it, my phone buzzes, *hmm we might have to schedule for another day, babe. Something's come up.*

Disappointment crushes down on me and I fall back onto the bed in a heap, really? *Can't you come over for a little bit? I've had a really shit day and I need you.*

He doesn't reply. I kick off my heels and curl up in bed. Maybe I'm jumping to conclusions and being sensitive, but I'm worried now. If Harry doesn't pull through for me, I don't know what I'm going to do.

Alexa

Kylie's late, which comes as no surprise but is annoying none-the-less. I've been at the café where we said we'd meet for half an hour. I sip my black coffee alone, with only a lukewarm latte and an empty chair for company. Where the hell is she?

Today is the one day that I really needed her to be on time because tonight I have a date with Shaun. I'm going to tell Kylie about it too, if she ever bloody gets here. I want to know more about this Harry guy seeing as we missed our chat yesterday. She messaged me saying she didn't feel good. Maybe that's why she isn't here.

No reply.

Hmm. She wouldn't still be at work, no way. Kylie has never stayed at work late. I find Kylie's number in my contacts and press call. It rings and rings for what feels like eternity. Come on, Kylie. Just then I hear the phone connecting. 'Kylie?'

'You have reached the O2 messaging service for...'

Knowing she doesn't listen to voicemails, and not prepared to sit here on the edge of my seat any longer, I end the call, stand up, pass Kylie's sad cold latte and set off to hers.

It's only a five-minute walk to Kylie's place, but I rush anyway, breaking into as much of a run as I can stand with my general fitness and these work heels. I start to feel sick, which might be my body reacting to actually doing some cardio, or might be because my mind is racing with all the possibilities of why Kylie hasn't been in touch. It feels like a part of myself is missing and I won't be whole until I find it.

I reach Kylie's and knock furiously. No one answers.

Should I go in anyway? There's a spare key under a porcelain tortoise by the front door, for emergencies just like this, but I don't like letting myself in. I knock some more, but nothing comes of it. Sod it, I'm going in.

It's quiet in the house, and rather messy. 'Kylie?' I shout. I head upstairs to her room and when I open her door, there she is. 'Kylie? Kylie!' I gasp, good God, is she dead? I know she isn't asleep because she isn't snoring. 'Kylie? What's wrong? Are you ill?'

'I'm not ill,' Kylie says quietly. She doesn't look at me.

'Then what's the matter? Why are you in bed? I don't understand.'

Kylie mumbles through tears, 'It's all gone wrong, everything's ruined... I don't know what I'm going to do.'

'What do you mean? Is this about Harry? Did he dump you?'

'Yes.'

'Oh, Kylie! Oh, but don't let him get to you, don't hide in bed on a Friday evening. It could be so much worse.'

'It is worse. I got fired.'

'Seriously? What happened? Was it Janine? That bitch!'

Kylie looks at me now. She looks drained and so sad that my heart breaks for her.

'I messed up, Lex.'

'What does that even mean?'

'It means I'm out of a job.'

'Well, fuck her. You hated that job anyway.'

'I did hate that job. But I need that job to live. What am I going to do?'

'I don't know, but we'll figure it out.' I put my hand around hers and give it a squeeze. 'What happened with Harry?'

'I was an idiot.' She sits up, blinking away tears, 'I should have listened to you.'

'But what happened?'

'He was so nice... or at least he acted so nice... and he built me up and made me feel good about myself, you know? He told me he would get me a job, a good one. He told me he would never hurt me. I believed him. Then yesterday I got fired and he turned distant. He cancelled coming over, and stopped replying to my texts. I thought he was busy and he'd call me later, but he didn't call me all night. And then finally, this morning, he messaged me saying we're just too different as people and he couldn't give me what I wanted and maybe we'd had our wires crossed.'

'Why would he do this to you?'

'I don't know.'

'Well, fuck him. Fuck them both.'

Kylie frowns at me with a look of bemusement, 'It's not like you to f-bomb.'

'Well, I guess that's just how strongly I feel about two certain people.'

Kylie looks at me, a bit happier. She grips my hand, 'What would I do without you?'

'That's not something you have to worry about.'

She scoots over and I kick off my shoes and get into bed with her. We sit side by side under the covers and for a while we just lie there and say nothing. I was going to tell her about my new job and Shaun today. It doesn't seem right now. It would be insensitive.

'I miss when times were simpler,' Kylie says suddenly.

'Oh God, me too.'

'Do you remember when we used to set up camp in my dorm? With good music, bad alcohol and snacks. Our biggest worry was completing assignments.'

'You mean my biggest worry was completing assignments. Your biggest worry was if you could change my assignment enough to look like it was your own.'

'I needn't have worried. I always successfully plagiarised your work.'

'That's true.'

Kylie leans onto me for support. 'Look at us now though; both on the wrong side of twenty-five, neither of us with great jobs or great guys.'

Wow, this is awkward. I smile at Kylie and hope it doesn't show. 'But at least we have each other.'

She nods. 'We have each other.' She sounds much better than she did when I found her. Which is good, because I need to leave.

'I better be going,' I begin to shuffle out of bed.

Kylie stops me, 'Oh Lex, please stay with me tonight. I need you. We can order a take-away and watch terrible movies. Please say you'll stay.'

How can I say anything else? I so desperately want to go on my date tonight with Shaun, but…

'Of course I will. Of course I'll stay.'

Kylie smiles and I see the relief in her eyes.

'I'll pop and get us a cup of tea.' I slink out of the room whilst Kylie snuggles back under the covers. I guess my date with Shaun will have to wait.

Kylie

I woke up to Alexa calling my name. I told her everything, well almost everything. I told her I was fired and how Harry broke my heart. Bastard. I wish I had just stayed in that night I met him. If I had wanted a broken heart, I would have just watched Grey's Anatomy after all.

Alexa sat by my side, as my shoulder to cry on, all night. She's my guardian angel. We reminisced about the good times and watched telly whilst squashed up in my sad single bed together with a pizza to share, cheap wine and chocolate. Cadbury chocolate is a healer.

On Saturday, we spent the day decluttering my room. Or rather, Alexa did. She said a calm environment would calm my mind. I think she just wanted an excuse to clean my room. Still, I'm glad she did and I actually do feel much calmer. She left yesterday to prepare for work.

Now it's Monday and life continues, except mine doesn't. I don't have anywhere to be. Whenever I've had week days off before, I've woken up late in the morning feeling elated, but today I woke up at 10am feeling deflated, tired of sleeping in. Over-sleeping makes me feel groggy. I listened to an unlikely playlist consisting of Beyonce's Lemonade and everything by My Chemical Romance before I got hungry and thudded downstairs to have cereal in front of the telly. I'm still here now, cradling an empty bowl while Lucie runs around getting ready for work. She looks at me sympathetically, 'So they fired you with immediate effect? That's terrible.'

'Actually, I had the option of continuing work for an extra two weeks but I can't face going in and working for Janine. Having to see her smug pigs-arse-esque face for another second will send me over the edge.'

Lucie sighs as she packs her bag, 'You really should have worked the two weeks. What will you do for money?'

'Don't worry, I have it all figured out.' A lie, and I think we both know it. I have nothing at all figured out. Now uncertainty lies ahead and I feel uneasy.

'Well, you better do. I can't afford to pay rent for us both.'

'You probably can actually,' I point out. Lucie is always loaded. I should become a personal trainer. No, forget it; that sounds like far too much effort.

'Nice try. Come on, you can turn this around. I'll help you look for something when I get back.'

'So, you're off then?'

'Some of us can't lounge around on the sofa.' She grins and heads for the front door.

'See ya.'

Some of us don't want to lounge around on the sofa, but have nothing better to do. I curl up, ready for the next show. It's about people finding property to buy, something I'll probably never do. These days you're either rich or stuck waiting for one of your relatives to pop their clogs so you can inherit property. My parents own their house but they're also a long time from being dead. Damn it.

I hear Lucie leave the house. It's raining outside and people are rushing by under umbrellas while I curl up, comfortable and dry. Okay, so right now it isn't so bad. I get paid a month in arrears so I can afford to relax for a week or so before I have to start job hunting. It could be like a holiday. I can explore the city and enjoy the sun when it decides to show its face. Yes, that's exactly what I'll do. Lucie's right, I can turn this around. What was I fretting about?

Alexa

My phone vibrates. It's a text message from Shaun: *How's work? Are you too busy to talk?*

I'm never too busy to talk to you.

You were too busy for most of the weekend.

Sorry. Kylie held me hostage. She's going through some stuff.

You're a good friend.

That's debatable.

I still haven't told Kylie about my new job or Shaun and I feel so guilty about it. I mean, I was going to on Friday but obviously I couldn't when she was in such a state over her work situation and love life. I can't believe what's happened to her. If I ever meet this Harry, I'll kill him. And as for Janine, I honestly think she was too harsh. Sure, Kylie is a bit unorganised, okay very unorganised, but she did her job just fine. She's not a brain surgeon, what does it even matter if she's sometimes late or not the most enthusiastic?

I'm worried about Kylie. She isn't one to be defeated and when I found her in bed upset it shocked me. I still feel a little shaken. In fact, I'll ring her now.

'Hello?' I hear background noise, and then crying, 'Kylie? Oh my God are you okay? Has something else happened?'

She sniffles, 'I just watched this thing about a couple who were together seventy-five years and died holding hands. Seventy-five years! Even if I found someone this year, I'd have to be one hundred years old before I could say I had been with someone for seventy-five years.'

She has lost the plot. 'Well… it could still happen. Or you could—'

'It won't happen. I won't live that long, I have awful genes.

Every single person on my dad's side of the family have bad hearts. Mum's always on at Dad about his cholesterol. He's not allowed to eat cheese. Can you imagine?'

I cannot sit and listen to Kylie crying about such nonsense in the middle of the day. Although, a life without cheese sounds awful. 'Kylie, turn off the daytime television.'

'But what else is there to do, at 11am on a weekday?'

'You could go out?'

'I'd need a shower first. And then find an outfit and do my hair. And go where? No, it's too much effort.'

'Well then stay in but do something productive. Go online and job hunt.'

'I just need time, to get my head around it all. I'm hurt... I'm grieving.'

Kylie always dwells and dithers when upset. It's not my style. But I'll let her have a week to get back on her feet and then I'll help her get sorted. 'Take some time and clear your head. I better go, I don't want to get caught on my personal phone.'

'Oh shit, sorry. Call me tonight?'

'Will do.'

I hang up and put my phone down but it lights up as it lands on the desk, buzzing and displaying another message from Shaun, *Don't have a big lunch because I'm taking you out for dinner tonight.*

What? He can't be serious! *Tonight? I thought we had rescheduled for Friday.*

I can't wait until then. How's 7pm for you?

In all honesty, it's a little short notice. I feel unprepared and also, a little rushed. But Kylie had an entire relationship and break up in a week. What am I waiting for? *Sounds great. I can't wait.*

Kylie

'Please tell me you haven't sat on the sofa watching telly since I left for work this morning.'

'Of course not! I turned it off, it was too upsetting. But now it's evening and evening telly is never as upsetting so I came back.'

Lucie drops her bag down and sits next to me, 'So what have you been doing in between daytime and evening telly?'

'I did some laundry, cleaned out my food cupboard, ate some pretzels that I found in the back of said food cupboard...'

'...You managed to do all of that while I was out? Wow Kylie, don't overdo it.'

'Did you know that there are endless channels dedicated to kids' shows now?'

'Yes. Everyone knows.'

'I didn't. In my day you could only watch kids' shows right before school, or after, unless you were lucky enough to have cable. Which I wasn't until I was eight.'

'Wow, grandma. Tell me more about life in the nineties.'

Lucie was born in 1993 but I get what she's trying to say, and decide to ignore it anyway. 'In case you're wondering, all of the classics have either been ditched or redone with CGI.'

'Fascinating. Did any mail come for me today?'

'No.' I carry on, 'Speaking of mail, Postman Pat now has the option of helicopter as a mode of transport. And he looks younger than ever. Is anything safe from Photoshop and retouching? Also, I'm unsure whether Jess the cat is the same cat or another sneakily replaced so that the kids didn't cry. Cats don't live that long.'

'Oh, Kylie, one day of unemployment and you've lost the plot. Shall I put the kettle on?' She gets up and goes to the kitchen.

'I think we should get a cat... I've always wanted one. Mum never let me. She always said that they're messy and disruptive but she's wrong. It would just lounge around the house being fluffy and cute. I would make a great cat-owner.'

Lucie comes back into the room looking exasperated. 'You can barely look after yourself.'

'You're such a spoil sport! We could record it doing cute things and put videos up online.'

'No.'

'At least have a think about it, please?' I pull a silly pout.

'I'll think about it if you go and get off this sofa.' She turns the telly off and holds the remote captive.

I pout again, only this time it's genuine. 'And do what?'

'Perhaps go for a jog.' But then she sees my smirk, 'or maybe borrow one of my Yoga DVDs?'

'Oh God I can't think of anything worse!'

'I can. It's called sitting in front of the telly all day, turning to mush. At least get on your laptop and do something productive.'

'But—' I whine.

'Go. I'll bring you coffee.'

Reluctantly, I get up from my comfy spot. 'You're like my second mum. Only marginally less annoying.'

I go to my room, switch on my laptop reluctantly, and curl up on my bed. Having the internet at one's fingertips is beneficial beyond compare. There's just so much to do, read and learn on there. The possibilities are endless. The problem is, I'm a serial procrastinator.

The door opens as Lucie comes in with coffee in my favourite mug. 'How's it going?'

'Brilliant.' I take the mug of coffee. 'Nikki's in Spain on holiday. She's been bragging about it for weeks and now she's finally there and it's raining.'

Lucie peers over at my screen, 'I hate it when that happens.'

'Me too, but I'm amused because she's always so smug about everything. Not today.'

'Anyone else having a shit day that you can poke fun at?'

'So far, no. But there's always Ellie.'

'Naturally.'

'Right? Another day, another pathetic humble-brag. But I see through them.'

'Not to mention, her recent hair style is tragic.'

'Exactly. Whenever I'm feeling down, I like to have a quick nosey at her social media. Cheers me right up.'

'Well seeing as you're feeling better, do you want to come to Pilates with me? I could get you in without a membership.'

I look her up and down and try to conjure up an expression that looks thoughtful, like I'm deciding if I fancy going when I absolutely don't. 'No thanks, I think I'm just going to have a night in and snoop on people through the powers of the internet.'

'Okay. Maybe you could look for a job too?' She stops to wrinkle her nose at the pile of chocolate bars littering my bedside table. 'See ya.'

'Thanks for the coffee!'

I sip and sigh. Coffee is usually enough to fix anything, but it's just not doing it for me tonight. Being on social media is depressing me. Sure, there's an Ellie here and there to make you feel better about yourself, but it doesn't make up for the endless newsfeed of 'friends' who are on their third, fourth, fifth gap year to a foreign country. Or who are riding elephants while I'm riding the bus, or having pizza in Italy while I'm having toast in my living room. Even off social media, Lucie is out doing Pilates while I'm engaging in some sort of bed yoga. Sitting crossed legged is yoga, right? I know, I know, I could have gone out with her. I just have no motivation to do anything but carry on scrolling, in spite of myself.

My phone rings. 'What?' I answer, without looking at who's calling. How the hell did Lucas become a published author? Maybe I should write, now that I have nothing better to do...

'Kylie? Is that really how one answers a telephone call?'
Shit. It's Mum.
'No, sorry, Mum. I'm a little distracted.'
'Well could you not be? I've taken the time to call you, the least you can do is give me your undivided attention.'
Yes, Mother dearest. I roll my eyes, 'Okay, fine. What is it?'
'Well as you know, it's Robbie's birthday in a fortnight so I was wondering if you wanted to come.'
No, I don't. 'Of course, where and what time?'
'Friday, we're going for a posh meal so dress up nicely. With matching shoes, please.'
'Okay.' Not that it will matter what shoes I wear, because Pizza Express or the nearest rural pub doesn't call for dressing up nicely.
'Right, good. Okay, darling, well I better go, I won't keep you. You're probably busy preparing for work tomorrow or something.'
'Bye, Mum.'
No, I haven't told Mum I've been fired and I don't plan on telling her either. I need to find a new job so I can pretend I quit. I feel shit enough just on my own without her making me feel worse.

Alexa

I thought I had until Friday to see Shaun, but now instead I have ten minutes. I dashed out of work as soon as possible, jumped in the nearest taxi and dived into my most flattering dress, suitable for most occasions. Although I assume we'll be going to some bar or restaurant. I pack money, lipstick, my purse and phone into a small clutch bag before having a quick look at myself in the mirror. God, my make-up needs redoing. Quickly grabbing my make-up bag, I start touching up my mascara when I hear a car sound its horn.

Seconds later, my phone buzzes in my bag, and when I look it's a message from Shaun: he's outside. Flustered, I make my way downstairs and get to the door. With shaky hands, I open the door and there he is, standing before me. The last time I saw him he stood in this exact spot looking at me like he is now. Except the last time, he was a stranger. It's surreal.

'You're early,' I can't help but say.

'You're beautiful.'

He leads me to his car, opens the door and gestures me inside. I try to slide in with elegance and grace but my knees feel weak. I put the seatbelt on, hoping it won't crease my dress. Wow, this is a nice car. It looks modest from the outside, but inside it has a sleek interior and leather upholstery. A part of me feared it would be grubby with takeaway wrappers in the footwells and I'd feel uncomfortable but it doesn't and it smells of vanilla not grease. I look around until he gets in and we're sitting side by side. He starts the car and it gives out a low purr. Houses and trees pass in a blur as he drives off.

'Where are we going?' I ask.

'You'll see.'

He doesn't drive towards the city centre and parks up on a little side street. Where on earth are we?

'See that little place there?' He gestures towards a small restaurant. 'It's the best Italian restaurant around. Come on, you'll love it.'

It's dark inside, illuminated by candle light and lamps that are dotted on surfaces. Glasses clink together and people laugh as Shaun leads us to the front desk. We're taken to a small table in the corner and once again Shaun helps me into my seat.

'Did I tell you how lovely you look?'

'You did, but thank you again.'

'You didn't have to dress up; you could have come in your work clothes.'

'Oh no, absolutely not. I looked hideous.'

'You didn't look hideous when I first saw you. You were in work clothes then, weren't you?'

I smile, 'I was. I can't believe you remembered.'

'More like, haven't forgotten. You've been on my mind a lot.'

I'm living some sort of cliché movie moment. Our eyes are locked across a small table in a nice restaurant. It feels so intimate, like in this moment we're the only two people in the world.

'Are you ready to make your order?' says a waiter, reminding us that we're actually in a busy restaurant.

We make our orders and Shaun orders a bottle of House Red. When the waiter comes back with our wine, Shaun pours me a glass and I take a sip.

'How's the wine?' he asks.

'Oh, very good. But I have to admit, I don't know much about wine. I only know "good" and "not so good".'

'I think the truth is no one knows one wine from the next, only if it tastes good to them or not.'

'Why do people pretend otherwise though?'

'I don't know, to feel smart and cultured?'

'I think you're right.'

'I didn't get a taste for alcohol until a few years ago. Which is embarrassing.'

'Neither did I. I started at eighteen drinking Lambrini with Kylie and even that was quite strong for me.'

'Kylie?'

'My friend... my best friend.' My best friend who doesn't know I'm on this date.

'Tell me more about her.'

Where do I begin? 'She's... a tornado. She shakes up your life and you're not quite the same afterwards...' I could talk about her for days. She's almost as much a part of me as myself. I really need to tell her about all of this. I will when I get home, I'll tell her everything.

'I'd like to meet her one day. Maybe we could all hang out sometime.'

'I'd love that.'

Our meals arrive. Suddenly I feel very self-conscious. I don't want to spill anything. Why is everything Italian red? Red sauce, red wine.

'How's your pasta?'

'Oh, delicious. This place is amazing; how did you find it?'

'This place has been open for a long time. My dad took my mum when they first started dating.'

I'm thankful I'm seated because I suddenly feel light-headed. This is where his mum and dad fell in love? He wouldn't just take anybody here. It's either the sweetest thing I've ever heard or the best line I've ever fallen for.

'How are you so perfect?' I can't take it anymore; I need to know.

He smiles graciously, 'I'm not perfect. I'm just doing what I was taught to do when you meet a beautiful woman and want to get to know her.'

I feel flattered, which is making me flustered and lost for words. I carry on eating, not that I'm hungry, far too full of butterflies and adrenaline. This date, the wine, the beautiful man sat across from me. It's all perfect. It's film-star romance. Suddenly, Priya's passion for romance doesn't seem so ridiculous.

We share a Tiramisu as he tells me about his company; how he works for himself repairing computers, laptops and printers.

'How impressive. I wish I was that driven and focused.'

'You've just got a promotion,' he points out.

'Yeah...' I say with a sigh, 'but not for the career I was aiming for.'

'You took a great opportunity. You shouldn't put yourself down.'

Oh no, I wasn't trying to fish for compliments! 'I'll try not to...'

'Good. Can I top your glass up?'

We finish the wine and my head is swimming. We talk until a waiter appears with our bill and a chip and pin machine.

'I'll just get my purse.' I reach down for my bag but a hand is placed on top of mine. My skin tingles as I realise it's Shaun's hand.

'Put your purse away, this is on me.'

He pays for our meal and when I stand up he places a hand gently on my back, guiding me out. We're greeted with dark skies and light rain. Damn, I didn't bring a jacket. I wrap my arms around myself, hoping my hair holds out until I get home.

'Here,' he says, taking off his jacket and putting it around my shoulders. I like the weight of it on me and cling on to it, pulling it tighter. We get in the car and I feel an energy between us that wasn't there on the way here. I pray this is the longest twenty-minute journey of my life, but it feels like only seconds pass until we're back outside my place. I don't want the night to end. He switches the engine off and, reluctantly, I take off my seatbelt. 'Thanks for a great night,' I say, stalling so I can stay sat next to him for a little longer.

'I hope we can do it again soon?' he asks, his voice softer than usual and I swear he leans in a little.

'I'd like that...' and I'd like you to kiss me. It looks like he might, so I wait.

'I'll walk you to your door,' he says and jumps out of the car. Oh.

When we reach the front door, I turn to him. We stand so close we're almost touching and there's that energy again. I don't know what to do in moments like this. I'm sure Kylie would grab him by his shirt, pull him upstairs and have her way with him. I wish I could do that kind of thing but I can't.

'You know, we were right here when we first met,' he says. His voice quiet and just for me.

'I remember. But what made you come back?'

'While I was fixing Priya's laptop, she mentioned you. She said you're sophisticated and smart. Then I saw you, and you looked so beautiful. You're the whole package. I thought, I have to get to know her more.'

'I'm glad you did. I want to know more about you too.' I feel high on compliments, red wine and the smell of rain. All I can think about are his lips, how close they are to me and how easy it would be to kiss him. There'd be nothing wrong with me making the first move.

'What do you want to know?' his lips ask.

I put my hands in his and press my mouth against him. He kisses me back, squeezing my hands lightly.

I pull back. 'Everything. Goodnight, Shaun.'

'Goodnight, Alexa.'

I walk in and don't look back, instead quitting while I'm ahead, hoping it looks completely demure. Once the door is shut, I stand in a state of shock. I initiated a kiss. I kissed a man who thinks I'm 'the whole package', buys me flowers and takes me on romantic dates. In a daydream, I walk upstairs and fall onto my bed, next to a heap of work clothes. A little voice in my head tells me to tidy up, but I don't want to. I just want to lie and enjoy the moment, full of pasta and happiness. But first, I have to ring Kylie and tell her about Shaun.

'Kylie,' I say when she answers, 'you'll never guess what —'

'Hey, you're calling late.'

'I know. I was busy earlier. Which is why I'm ringing—'

'Busy doing what? Oh, it's all right for some. I've had a bloody awful day.'

'Why, what's up?'

'Nothing except I've been bored out of my skull. It turns out, being unemployed isn't what it's cracked up to be and my mum called; I have to go to a meal for Robbie's birthday in a fortnight. I'm dreading it already! An evening of being asked why I'm single and where my life is going looms over me. It'll be followed by a week of analysing everything she's said in a state of post-traumatic stress followed by an existential crisis. So now I'm just trying to watch telly and unwind, but I can't because all I can hear is Lucie doing it with some guy in the next room and they've been at it ever since she allegedly came home from Pilates. Spare me! Tell me about your day; why have you been busy?'

My heart drops. Minutes ago, I was bursting to tell her about my evening and life updates. Now, I'm not sure. I can't just blurt it all out, especially when she's had a terrible day, it would be selfish. I need to focus on cheering her up instead. But first, I need an excuse as to why I was busy. 'Oh, I just got held back at work, nothing interesting.'

'Don't let them take you for granted, Lex.'

'I won't.'

'You should be putting yourself first for a change.'

'I agree. I was thinking, actually, on that note, about how I don't put myself out there enough.'

'What do you mean?'

'I don't know. I was just thinking how I don't take chances, even ones that are right in front of me. I was talking to Priya about romance and I—'

'Ppft, what does Priya know about romance? People put too much importance on the concept of romance. Let me tell you, being wined and dined and whispered sweet nothings to doesn't mean anything.'

Hmm, this is awkward. Telling her about Shaun would be futile. Oh dear. What now? 'You're probably right. I don't know. I was just thinking, anyway.'

'Well, don't stress yourself out. I'm going to bed now, but

don't worry, everything will be okay. We have each other, what else do we need?'

Maybe we don't need anything else, but I think I want Shaun. I get the feeling, when she finally does find out, she won't be too happy about it. However, I can't keep putting this off forever. I'll have to tell her about Shaun tomorrow, regardless of what mood she's in. Yes, I'll definitely tell her tomorrow. I don't know why I'm worrying so much; she'll be delighted by my news. I can feel it.

Kylie

I now have a new reason to hate Mondays. It's no longer a rude awakening back to reality after a weekend off work, but there's still something unpleasant about waking up late with no plans at all. Plus, over-sleeping always makes me feel like I've been hit by a bus.

I've been off work for two weeks. My old routine was to force myself out of bed, get dressed, dash to work. I would be in the office now, typing away, filing this and that, receiving passive-aggressive remarks from Janine. My new routine is to crawl out of bed when it suits me, stay in my pyjamas, plod to the kitchen at intervals to make a cup of tea in-between watching daytime telly. That's what I'm doing right now whilst cradling the biscuit jar, hunting out the bourbons. There's some old z-list celebrities talking about the latest gossip. I started watching it ironically but now I'm fully involved to be honest.

This is what has become of my life. I've been twenty-five for two seconds and I'm already a fully-fledged loser. And I've put on at least 5lbs. My mum would be horrified; she already thinks I'm fat enough as it is. She dreams of me being married with a baby, and here I am married to this sofa and carrying a food baby. I like disappointing her but not when it means disappointing myself.

As much as I hate working; I really do need another job. Finding one, however, is not going to be easy. I don't have much to say about myself besides 'useless degree' and 'five years working in an office until fired'. I'm practically unemployable. I'll have a look on my laptop. There must be someone in this city willing to employ me. The trouble is, a lot of jobs require experience of which you need said job to have the experience. It's a vicious circle. Anyway, I'll check social media first. At least then I can put 'dedicated procrastinator' down as one of my skills.

Oh God, I must be a glutton for punishment. My entire feed is a list of people I know who are more successful than me. Jess has a PHD, Hannah is now a qualified nurse, Joe is in the army, Nat is on a month-long holiday around Asia, and Becki is looking tanned and skinny and feeling 'refreshed' after her gym session. My screen is host to pictures of people enjoying themselves: beautiful dinners, exotic poolside hotels and sunsets. Bloody hell! Alicia has bought herself a brand-new BMW. Just in case I didn't believe her, there's a photo of her smiling next to a car, holding a set of keys. She was an idiot in school as well. One time, I caught her licking scissors. Okay, she was six at the time, but still. Is everyone doing better than I am? How? What's their secret?

I can't sit here any longer and allow myself to turn to mush whilst Alicia drives around the city in a BMW. I'm getting up. I'm going to get dressed and head out to look for a job… any minute now. Just one more biscuit.

Finally, I manage to pull myself away from the sofa and upstairs to get dressed. It's all going well until I pull on my trusty denim shorts and to my horror they feel snug. What betrayal. Leggings it is then, with a longish top. Much better. With the help of dry-shampoo, I manage to look half-decent. Which Lucie confirms as I go back downstairs and cross paths with her.

'Oh, you look nice. Have you been out for a change?'

'Yep,' I lie, 'I'm off out again in a second.'

'I've got some gym friends coming over this afternoon but you're welcome to join us when you get back if you like?'

'An evening of carrots and hummus and comparing six packs? I'll pass.'

'Very funny. There'll be pizza too.'

'Cheeseless pizza?'

'…Yes. But it's still delicious.'

'Don't worry, I'll drop in. Even if your idea of pizza insults my entire belief system.'

'You could invite Alexa. Maybe bring your own pizza?'
'Yeah that sounds like a plan. I'll see you later.'

I leave the house ready and enthusiastic to job hunt. Maybe I'll stop by and meet Alexa from work. In fact, I'll ring her now and see if she's up for it.

No answer. Never mind, I'm sure she'll get back to me. She always does.

Alexa

I've been talking to Shaun through text message since I got in from work. That was about an hour ago.

The weather's going to be really nice on Saturday he says. Hmm. So evidently, we've run out of interesting things to talk about and are down to small talk.

Oh yeah? It's been nice all week. Shame I've had to work.
My sister's having a barbecue. I thought we could go together.
Isn't it too soon?
Too soon for a barbecue? It's the height of summer.
No, to meet the family?
Not unless you think it's too soon? I don't. They'll love you.

Well, I wasn't expecting that. He didn't bring up the weather to make conversation but to bring up inviting me to meet his family. I think things are getting serious. Meeting the family is serious, right? I realise I've taken a while to respond and hurry back a reply, *Okay, I'd love to.*

Good. You can stay over at mine that night, if you'd like...

We haven't slept together but I'm pretty sure we're heading that way. An invite to stay at his seems like an invite for sex. This means I'll be meeting his family, then seeing what his place looks like and possibly sleeping with him all in one day.

Suddenly, the pressure of it all builds in my stomach. I curl up some more to relieve the ache as Priya walks downstairs and into the room. Shock appears on her face when she sees me lying down.

'Everything okay?'

'Oh yeah, period pains,' I say, clutching my stomach for

emphasis.

She looks at me, eyebrow cocked, full of doubt, 'You're early this month then…'

Damn it. 'I guess so…'

'So apart from your uterus, is everything else okay?'

'Usual. Eat, sleep, work, repeat.' I know I'm being vague but I haven't even had five seconds to digest Shaun's offer yet.

'Mhmm,' she says, dragging it out, all the while looking at me expectantly. Then she breathes a sigh of despair, 'I meant how's it going with Shaun?'

'Good, yeah. Really good.'

'Do tell.' She flashes a wicked grin and wiggles her eyebrows. I get the feeling she's going to keep dragging this on until I give in.

'Well, he's invited me to a barbecue. A family gathering…'

'Oh my God!' She plops down next to me, as if the excitement is too much to stand with.

'I know.'

'That's a big step.'

'It is, isn't it?'

'Totally. He wouldn't be inviting you to meet his family if he was planning on ditching you. He thinks you're a keeper.'

Priya's encouraging words give me the confidence to uncurl a little and sit up, 'I'm nervous…'

'Well, don't be. Just be your amazing self and you'll do fine.'

'He wants me to stay at his that night…'

'Oh yeah?' she says with more eyebrow-wiggling.

'We haven't slept together yet. So I'm guessing that will be the night we do…'

'Well it's good to be prepared. You can take your best lingerie, make sure everything is shaved that you want to be shaved.'

Priya is very open about all things related to sex, which she should be, but it always makes me cringe. I decide to skip over the shaving topic. 'I'll be okay as long as I'm well prepared. But that means I'm going to have to cancel my usual Friday catch-up with Kylie…'

Priya shrugs, 'That sounds reasonable.'

'She won't see me cancelling on her as reasonable.'

'Why not?'

'I haven't really mentioned Shaun to her yet.'

'Well, do so. Then you can invite her over to help you with your hair and decide what to wear.'

'I guess.' Except do I want to break my news to Kylie and meet Shaun's parents and sleep with him all in a weekend? That sounds like too much to handle.

The doorbell sounds. 'That's my take-away. Want some?' she leaves to answer the door.

'Yeah that'd be nice,' I say, despite my stomach saying no. It's already too full of nerves about seeing Shaun and guilt about not telling Kylie. I'm the worst friend. Worse still, she called my phone earlier but I was too engrossed in messaging Shaun.

Without hesitating for another second, I call Kylie. She answers straight away, 'Alexa? I've been trying to get in touch with you for hours.'

'Sorry, I did see a few missed calls but I was held up at work,' I lie. 'Everything okay?'

'Yeah, I'm just sitting upstairs. Lucie has some friends over. I was going to join but I saw a bowl of kale and I heard someone talking about their "glutes" so I thought I'd give it a miss. '

'Trendy cabbage and butt-talk? Wise move.'

'How are you? I feel like we haven't seen each other in ages.'

'I'm fine… speaking of seeing each other; I'm going to have to cancel our catch up on Friday.'

'Really? That sucks. I was looking forward to seeing you.'

'I know, me too. I have a work thing and I'm going to be so busy that—' I stop mid-sentence as Priya walks in with take-away boxes.

'Take these pizzas, I'll grab some plates,' says Priya, handing me the boxes.

'Pizza?' asks Kylie on the other end of the phone. 'Does it have cheese on it?'

'Um, yeah of course it has cheese on it. Odd question.' I struggle with the phone and a stack of pizza boxes threatening to leak grease onto my lap. 'Sorry, Kylie, I've got to go. I've got my hands full and I'm starving. Catch up later.' I hang up.

Priya sits down next to me and we load our plates with food.

'Was that Kylie?' she asks.

'Yeah.'

'Is she coming on Friday night to help you get ready?'

'No, she's busy.' Another lie.

'Oh, okay. Well, that's settled it then: on Friday night we'll have a pampering session. You can tell me all of your concerns, I'll try to resolve them and we'll get you ready to meet the family.'

'Really? Thanks, it means a lot.'

'No problem.'

I eat my dinner with a side of guilt at confiding in Priya and not Kylie.

Kylie

My life is now spent lying horizontal or in the fetal position on the sofa or in bed, watching TV or browsing the internet. I have nothing to do and no one to do nothing with. I'm not exaggerating; I haven't seen Alexa all week. She's not usually this busy, or perhaps when I was working and busy myself I didn't notice.

The novelty of doing nothing has worn off and now I would do anything to be busy. My job hunt isn't going so well and I'm scraping the bottom of my overdraft. Only a few weeks ago I was doing just fine. I was going to bars alone. I was dating. Where did it all go wrong?

I'm trying to right some wrongs. I applied for one job online, which was exhausting because they wanted to know the ins and outs of the last five years of my life. Now I'm on the dating app, but it isn't going well. I'm talking to this guy who is displaying the personality of a wooden spoon.

So what are you doing now, babe?
I'm deciding if I should have a bath.
You should.
Yeah? It's been a while since I've had a good soak. I'd like to lather up and caress my body.
I like showers myself. I can't be doing with baths. It's the feeling of bathing in my own filth that puts me off. Like human soup.
What if we had a shower first and then a relaxing bath?
That would be better although I can't see the point.

And I can't see the point in continuing this inane conversation. I sigh and close the app. It's a shame because he's so gorgeous. Or at least, his picture was. You can't tell anything from someone's best photo and their own description of themselves. It won't be who they truly are.

That's the problem with the internet and modern socialising. We've never been more connected to people and yet there's a huge disconnect. I have people I know on social media who I actively avoid if I see in real life. They're not friends, merely associates. Associates who I don't want to associate with. What's the point? I don't want that. I yearn to be close to somebody and I'm not going to achieve that in my bedroom, talking to strangers and people who might as well be strangers. But there's nobody I know who I want to be close to... Except...

Don't do it, Kylie, you're better than this, get a grip, my fingers hover over the phone. Apparently I'm not better than this. I send a message to Harry, *Hey stranger.*

Kylie? What a surprise to hear from you.

A pleasant surprise?

Of course.

Good. Are you in town? I'm not going to beat around the bush.

I'm at Pulp. Come join me.

I pull off my clothes and look for something appropriate to wear. This time, nothing green. Nothing I would usually wear. I'm not trying to be myself, it's not working for me. I find a little black dress and put it on before raiding my underwear drawer for some tights, to no avail. When I find some, they're laddered. I clutch at balled up, ruined tights and roll my eyes at myself: why did I put a laddered pair of tights back into my drawers?

Well, bare legs will have to do, it's not like I'm trying to be modest. I slip my feet into the first pair of high heels I see and look at my appearance. My hair is insane. Well it would be; it hasn't been washed in days. It sits in a tangled mess. I put it in a messy bun and set to work on my make-up, which is littered all over my desk. This room is a dump. It's cluttered, despite Alexa's recent de-cluttering. It's messy and chaotic. I imagine it to look exactly like what inside my mind looks like right now. After I quickly plaster my face in whichever make-up products I can find, it's time to go.

I set off down the darkened street. It's not usually ideal to walk the streets at night, alone, in a short dress. However, I'm in good company. One perk of living in a student area is the streets are littered with people at any given time and often dressed inappropriately as they head out to have some fun. I blend in as I make my way to the city.

As I near the club, I take a deep breath. I can do this. I'm going to have a good time, get what I need, take what I want and go. Be cool, Kylie.

I enter the dimmed room and spot Harry who sits like a beacon at the bar. I'm drawn in, despite everything. Like a moth to a flame and not just because he's hot.

As I approach him I see he's talking to the woman next to him, who's leaned in, eating up all of his charm. He smoulders so casually that it's so clear he does this every day of the damn week. It feels very primal in here. There are predators and prey. The blonde is trying to swoop in and claim my prey, so I stand tall and walk over to the other side of him, cutting the blonde off from her conversation. 'Hey, Harry.'

He turns to the sound of his name being called and smiles when he recognises me. He looks me up and down and seems to like what he sees. It makes me feel good.

'Kylie, you look amazing. Drink?'

'Cocktail. You're buying.' I'm full of faux-confidence. The blonde scowls and leaves.

Harry laughs, 'So, what did I do to get back in your good books?'

He orders me a drink.

'You were never in my bad books.' I lie, suppressing all the hatred and hurt, drowning it with a gulp of Cosmopolitan. 'I think our wires must have been crossed, I'm totally fine.'

'Cool. So, what have you been doing with yourself?'

I've been unemployed, watching daytime telly and eating too many jaffa cakes. 'This and that. Going here, going there, seeing people.'

'Well, I'm glad you could fit me in.'

'My girl friend bailed on me tonight.' This sounds like the

line Harry probably uses except it's the truth.

'You poor thing. We'll have to find something to do instead.' He leans in, and I get a whiff of that expensive fragrance he always wears. It feels strange being face to face with him again. I've imagined it so many times and fantasised about what I'd do and what I'd say. I've thought about strangling him and also running my fingers through his hair and all down his body. In spite of myself, I find the latter desire becoming stronger and stronger.

'I'm sure we can think of a few ideas to pass the time,' I say hungrily.

One drink later and he calls a taxi for us to go to his. We both know the score.

He leads me into his apartment, through to the bedroom. It's vast but empty. He pushes me onto the familiar white sheets and grasps at my dress while I pull at his shirt. It's a very expensive-looking shirt. I might just rip it, like I wanted to the first time.

'Hey, take it easy,' he says, pushing my hands away and unbuttoning his shirt himself.

'Don't you like to play rough?'

'With my £300 shirt? No. With you? Yes.'

I take his shirt from him and throw it to the floor. I hope it's dry clean only. For a moment I remember what Harry did to me, but then he puts his arms around me and suddenly I can only think about what he's doing to me right now. And then I stop thinking altogether.

'That was amazing,' he pants, an hour later. At least, I think it's been an hour. When he pulled me under the covers, time stopped.

We lie side by side, getting our breath back. It's silent except the ticking clock on the bedside table and I feel content and sleepy as he absentmindedly plays with my hair. I didn't think I'd be back here in this bed, in these arms, but it feels good being here, it feels easy. Would I be back here, in his bed, if he didn't feel the same way? 'Harry…'

But then I realise he's stopped playing with my hair and when I look over, he's asleep. I suppose it's for the best.

What was I even going to ask him? If he likes me? If he could see a future with me? If he could love me? It was a stupid idea. Coming here was a stupid idea.

His phone buzzes and after checking he's definitely asleep, I lean over and read it. It's from a girl called Emily. *Hey babe, thanks for an amazing time last night. It's a shame I'm busy tonight, but I was hoping we could meet up tomorrow? I'd love to know more about your plans for skiing this winter.*

Sorry Emily, you won't be hitting the slopes any time soon. It's just a line that Harry tells women like us, so he can reel us in for easy sex. Then again, I suppose I came to Harry tonight for sex. But I'm not heartless like he is. I roll over, away from him and try to give in to sleep. My brain feels fuzzy and my heart hurts. As my eyes droop, I vow to myself to get a job, find a man who really likes me and most importantly, see more of Alexa. I feel like I haven't seen her a lot recently and I miss her. I'd take squashing up next to her on the sofa over sleeping beside Harry in his king-sized bed any time.

Alexa

Shaun's sister's house is a picturesque semi-detached property in a chocolate-box village just outside the city. A basket of colourful petunias hangs by the front door where I'm standing next to Shaun in my cutest dress that gives me a good waist, holding a box of cupcakes. Shaun is holding a crate of beer. Everything about this moment is perfect, but I can't enjoy it because I'm far too nervous. What if my cupcakes give them food poisoning? What if they don't like me? What if they don't like me and that influences how Shaun feels about me?

'Relax,' says Shaun.

I must look as terrified as I feel. 'I just want to make a good impression.'

'You will. Just be you.'

The door opens to a woman who I presume is his sister. She briefly registers me, and smiles at Shaun. 'Shaun! Come in, come in. You're just in time, the barbecue has just been lit.'

Shaun enters and I follow after him like a lost lamb.

'Oh yeah?' he asks. 'How long did it take Dad to do it?'

'Oh, about an hour.'

'That's good for Dad.'

His sister, Amy, looks at me. I can't quite make out how she feels. 'Hi... Alexa?' I see her quickly glance at Shaun and I realise she's unsure of my name. Is she forgetful, or does he bring girls around often? No, Lex, don't go there.

'Hi, nice to meet you,' I say as brightly as I can. 'Your house is beautiful.'

'Oh, thanks. It's getting there, we haven't been in long. Come on through to the back.'

We follow Amy through to the back garden that's full of Shaun's family. I feel like I'm in front of the firing squad. I hold my box of cupcakes up as a shield.

'Everyone, this is Alexa,' says Shaun as he puts his arm around me. I smile, leaning in to him a little, feeling him support me. It feels good.

A woman steps forward and takes my hand, 'Alexa, welcome. Lovely to meet you.'

I presume this is Shaun's mum. She's a tiny yet plump woman with perfectly blow-dried hair and lashings of red lipstick. I take a deep breath, inhale her Chanel No.5 and smile. 'Lovely to meet you too. I, erm, I've brought cupcakes for after lunch.'

'Oh, that's wonderful! I love a young woman who knows the importance of baking.'

'I brought beer for during lunch,' says Shaun. He holds the beer up proudly.

His dad cheers, 'Wahey, that's more like it, son! Come on everyone, the first round of meat is ready.'

'Are you sure they're thoroughly cooked?' asks Amy, wrinkling her nose up.

'Yes, love. Anyway, you should be sitting down in your delicate state. Leave the barbecuing to the men. I'll get Mum to bring you some lunch over.'

We sit at the table in the garden under a giant cream parasol and eat. Shaun helps his dad cook the meat so I find myself sitting next to Amy and her husband. They sit close together, finishing each other's sentences and sharing food. As we talk amongst ourselves I notice Ian put a tender hand on Amy's belly. As someone who doesn't have a close family, it's nice to feel a part of something for once.

After dinner and cupcakes, I insist on cleaning up. Amy has one of those classic rectangular porcelain sinks. I fill it up to the brim with soapy water and as I stand washing dishes in a beautiful kitchen overlooking a beautiful garden, I imagine what it would be like if I had all of this. Maybe I won't have to imagine for much longer. Just then, two arms embrace me.

'Hey, gorgeous, let's get out of here,' says Shaun, briefly

kissing my neck. I feel tingly, and it takes all the self-control I have to finish scrubbing the last plate.

'I've had a lovely time. Thank you so much.' I say as we're at the door.

'Yeah, thanks for the grub, sis. I hope Dad didn't poison us,' says Shaun.

'We'll have to see you both again soon, when the baby arrives.' I get the feeling she is fonder of me now than when I turned up a few hours ago. I can't help but notice that at seven months pregnant, she obviously anticipates me still being around in two months' time.

We get in the car and we make our way to his flat. I've never been before and can't help but wonder what it'll be like. Although Shaun smells nice, wears clean clothes and says he's organised, I have visions of a complete bachelor pad. The type with no food, dirty counters, crumpled bed sheets. Although that sounds like Kylie's place and I manage there.

'You okay?' he asks, 'you've gone quiet.'

'Yeah… I'm just nervous, I guess.'

'Do you still want to spend the night?'

I start to blush at the very mention of spending the night at Shaun's. I was so busy trying to impress his family, I forgot all about it. I'm spending the night at Shaun's. The whole night. 'I do.'

'You don't have to worry with me.' He briefly turns to me with a smile.

Maybe he's right. That would be nice.

The car slows down and comes to a stop outside some flats in an area I'm not too familiar with. He leads me to his place, which is on the second floor of an apartment block. It's modest but not too terrible if you ignore the smell of pizza and cigarettes in the lobby.

He fumbles with his keys, unlocking the door. I realise he's nervous and I feel better knowing it. He smiles and gestures me in. I hold my breath and enter, wondering what awaits me.

It's surprisingly not bad. Actually, it's quite pleasant. It's clean and tidy after all. The furniture is all black and a computer dominates the living room, but I can ignore that.

'Nice place,' I say.

'Thanks. Well, I like it anyway. Drink? I have wine.'

'Wine sounds nice.'

'Sit, please. Make yourself at home. I'll be through in a moment.'

I put my bags on the side and tentatively sit on the black sofa, hovering on the edge of the seat. I feel hot and flustered in anticipation. He's bought wine, I'm wearing my best lingerie; we both know what's going to happen. I wish I could just text Kylie for advice. I'm on my own here, without a wing woman, winging it. I never wing it.

He comes in with two glasses of wine and sits next to me, 'Shall we watch a film? I thought we could watch that one we were talking about the other day.'

'Really? It sounds so soppy. I didn't think men liked romantic films.'

He looks at me bemused, 'I didn't think women didn't! What have you got against romantic films anyway?'

I shrug, 'I don't know. I guess they're just not realistic.'

'Maybe you just haven't experienced real romance before.'

'Maybe…'

'What do you think then? Shall we go with this one or do you want to choose something else?'

'Just this once, I'll put my trust in you.' I can't think of a single reason why I wouldn't. Although Kylie put her trust in Harry and got hurt, I feel like it's different with Shaun. Kylie met Harry in a seedy bar but Shaun and I met by chance, with no ulterior motive from either of us.

We sit side by side in darkness except for the glow of the television. I try to sit in a way that makes me look as slim and demure as possible. All I can think about is that he's sitting next to me. He's never really sat next to me before, only during car rides. We've had two dates but this feels much more intimate. We're completely alone. It's thrilling and terrifying. I feel an arm drape around me, pulling me closer. I let him pull me, willingly, eagerly. I feel at ease sitting here, curled up next to Shaun, watching a movie on a Friday night. Friday nights usually involve me watching television alone and going to bed alone, or going out with Kylie and sleeping on her sofa with her next to me. Right now there's nowhere else I'd rather be but here.

'This is the bit I like the best,' he whispers, turning towards me.

It's an intimate kiss scene, at long last, between the male and female protagonists. If Priya had said that, I would be snarking so hard at her but somehow when Shaun says it it's not so funny.

'I like it too,' I whisper back.

'You want some more wine?'

'No.' I say. I want you, I should say.

'Can I get you anything else?'

'No…'

'Okay. I guess I'll stay here then.' He leans in closer, our lips almost touching. I feel his breath on me, I can smell his skin.

'Good…'

We kiss and he pulls me into an embrace that is all-consuming until we eventually come up for air. I stand up and he leads me to his bedroom. I feel dizzy, through lack of oxygen from kissing for so long and the wine and the events that will unfold.

'I think I'll just go and freshen up,' I tell him.

'Bathroom is the door over there. I'll be in here.'

I go to the bathroom and check how I look. My make-up has lasted and I should be washing my face now but I don't want Shaun to see me without make-up just yet. I run my fingers through my hair. Sexy hair isn't sleek; it has a little oomph. I give it some oomph, and wonder if I have oomph myself. Probably not, but I'm going to give him all I have. It's now or never. I'm in my best underwear and between sucking in my stomach and the dark room hiding my wobbly bits, it should be okay. I wish I could call Kylie, but I can't. I'm just going to have to do this alone.

I leave and enter Shaun's room to find a perfectly nice bedroom and an even more perfect man stood waiting for me. Candles have been lit, and clichéd or not, I love it.

'I er, I just wanted it to be special,' he says, gesturing at the candles. He looks nervous.

'It's perfect,' I say. I'm lost for words although I'm not sure much else needs to be said.

'Come here.' He reaches a hand out. I take it and he leads me to the bed. He unzips my dress and pushes it off my shoulders and watches it slide down my body. I suck my stomach in, horrified.

'You're beautiful, Alexa,' he says, looking at me in a way no one's ever looked at me before. I could get used to that look.

Kylie

'Kylie. Well don't just stand there, come in for goodness sake!' says Mum in one of those frantic whispers that ends up louder than normal talking. She manhandles me in over the threshold.

'What's going on?' I ask, looking around for some sort of disaster that would have caused Mum to lose her mind. But the hallway looks like it always has and the house is silent.

'It's Robbie's birthday dinner tonight, and he's bringing his girlfriend,' she says this slowly, enunciating every word carefully.

I frown, 'So what?'

'*So* she's upstairs and you will be on your best behaviour tonight. Got it?'

'Mmhmm, sure. Why are you making such a big deal?' I follow her through to the kitchen.

'This is an important milestone. He's never brought someone special home. Neither have you, for that matter.'

I sit down, winded from the doorstep assault and my mother's words. She didn't even warm up this evening, she's gone straight in for the kill. Don't take the bait, Kylie. Instead, I smile. 'Well that's great news and I look forward to meeting her.'

Mum frowns, 'Yes well, as long as you act cool everything should be fine. What shoes are you wearing?'

'… Act cool?' Seriously? My own mum thinks I'm uncool and my kid brother has a better love life than I do. Brilliant. Mum stands scrutinising my outfit as I realise it's going to be a long evening.

'Yes. Or if you don't think you can manage it, just try not to speak too much.'

While everyone gets ready, I eat chocolate that I found in the fridge. Mum flaps around being her usual overbearing self.

'Kylie, do you really think you should be eating chocolate so close to dinner?'

I shrug, 'I'm hungry.'

'Well you should have had an adequate lunch.'

'I did!' I protest. I didn't.

She's cleaning around the already-clean kitchen like someone possessed. I keep an eye on her, waiting for her head to do a full 360, Exorcist style. 'Sit down, Mum, you're making me dizzy.'

'I will soon. I'm just wiping things down and then it'll be time to go.'

'Shall I let Robbie and his girlfriend know to get ready?'

'Oh no, leave them be. They're having some private time.'

Ew, what does she mean by that? I don't need that visual. 'Private time?'

'Well, you know, they're just spending some private time together before we leave.'

Hang on a minute. 'Mum...'

'Yes?'

'Is Robbie's door open?'

Mum shrugs with indifference. 'It wasn't when I last went upstairs, no.'

'And you're okay with this?'

'Of course I am.' Mum sounds annoyed now. 'What's with all the questions?'

'Oh! I don't believe this!' I laugh, in shock more than anything. Although, I should have known. Golden boy always gets special treatment.

'What? What don't you believe?'

'I was never allowed boys upstairs when I was his age, and even when I was you never let me close the door.'

'Don't be silly, Kylie. Robbie's sensible.'

'So, I wasn't sensible?'

She stops wiping and looks like she's about to say something, but Dad comes in.

'Hello, love! You look beautiful,' he says to me, smiling. I smile back.

'She'd look even more beautiful if she tamed that mane once in a while,' says Mum disapprovingly.

I'm about to get annoyed but then I catch Dad rolling his eyes at her. 'She has beautiful hair,' he says, 'it's just like mine was back in the day.'

'You were hardly a style icon, Pete.'

'Well, I was no John Travolta but I had a little something.' He starts dancing and we laugh until Robbie and his girlfriend walk in. How come the latest sixteen-year-olds are so much more mature and glamorous than the sixteen-year-olds of my time ever were? At sixteen I had nothing but store-brand foundation, a few sticks of eyeliner and a collection of Tammy tops. It's not fair. I suddenly feel self-conscious.

'Robbie! Happy Birthday!' I say, smoothing down my hair.

He grunts at me. Ah, teenage angst. I remember it well.

Mum goes up to Robbie, fussing him. Poor boy. 'You look lovely, darling. Kylie, doesn't he look lovely?'

'Oh yeah, very handsome. Like a young Josh Hartnett.'

Robbie frowns, 'Who?'

'Right then, are we ready?' asks Mum, cutting our conversation short. Probably for the best.

'I'm ready,' I tell her. We all stand up to leave and head out.

Mum stops me, 'Kylie, aren't you going to take your jacket?'

'No, it's warm out and I'll only take it off in the pub and probably lose it or something.'

'So, you're going like that?'

I give her a look and decide to ignore her. I look perfectly fine in what I'm wearing. I did as she asked and came dressed up, in matching shoes even. I'm not biting, not tonight. I'm not in the mood and I want this dinner over with as soon as possible.

We arrive at the pub and it's quite nice with warm lights

and inoffensive background music. I follow everyone to the restaurant bit at the end and sit down. It's quiet here, and a little too intimate for my liking. Whenever I dine with family I like the place to be busy and noisy so that I can pretend I can't hear everyone speak and eat my dinner in peace. Instead, I'm going to have to make small talk with the family. The horror.

I'm at a restaurant for Robbie's birthday dinner. The family small-talk is killing me, Lex, but the burger I've ordered will be worth it!

'Kylie,' says Mum, 'must you be on your phone while we're all at the table?'

Yes, I must, because otherwise I will be bored out of my mind or worse, subjected to questions from you about my love life.

'No I suppose not,' I reply through gritted teeth. Never mind, the waitress is approaching with my dinner. She puts a plate down in front of me, on which sits the biggest burger on the menu. It's photo-worthy, but Mum is still glaring at me so I slip my phone in my pocket and turn my attention to food. It takes both hands to pick the beastly burger up, but when I do, I take the biggest bite I can, accidentally squeezing ketchup out of it. It splats back onto the plate.

'Kylie, couldn't you have ordered something a bit more sensible? Something you could have eaten with a knife and fork?'

'Let the girl eat, Marie. She's got my appetite, haven't you, love?' says Dad.

'That's right.' I smile at Dad, between chewing. Mum rolls her eyes as Dad stifles laughter. I'm always grateful that he's on my side.

By some miracle, I've managed nearly an entire dinner without an interrogation from Mum. I tuck into a rather large Sundae that Dad persuaded me to order and feel content.

'So, Kylie, anything new to tell me?'

I swallow a big lump of ice cream in shock and give myself brain freeze. 'Sorry, what?' I ask, with my hand to my head.

'For goodness sake, Kylie, eat with a little grace. I was asking if you have anything new to tell me. How are things in your life?'

'Oh… everything's good,' I shrug.

She rolls her eyes in exasperation 'Good? Could you please elaborate a little more, Kylie? Is it too much to ask? Or do I have to look on your google page if I want to know how you're doing?'

That'd be ideal, really, 'No,' I say 'sorry, Mum. There's not much to report. Alexa's good, Lucie's good, work is good…'

'Well, that's good then. You've been in that job for a long time; I keep waiting for you to tell me you've been promoted but it never happens.'

'I'm happy as I am, Mum.' Or at least, I was happy, until about a minute ago…

'Well of course you are, but you need the push to better yourself. Maybe I could call them or something. No, that would be unprofessional. But my friend Helen has connections to your office, I could give her a call and see if she can—'

'No!' I shout, alerting everyone around me. They all watch, waiting for me to speak next. Brilliant. 'I mean,' I think of a reason why I wouldn't want Helen putting a good word in for me, 'I want to do it on my own. Or I won't feel I've earned it.'

Mum considers this and I watch on, studying her, on the edge of my seat, waiting for approval. Finally, she nods, 'Okay I understand where you're coming from.'

What a relief. 'Thanks, Mum.'

'But if you haven't progressed in a few months, I'll be calling her. You can't be afraid to accept help, Kylie.'

Despite everything, I start to feel a little warm towards Mum for a change. She cares about me. She's looking out for me.

'Especially when you need more help than most. I always worry about you.'

'Oh…' so she's looking out for me because she thinks I'm

pitiful and incapable of being a successful adult. Great. I finish my ice-cream, no longer hungry but needing something to fill the void in my stomach. And then the ice-cream threatens to make a reappearance as the bill arrives and I see the total of my dinner. There's every chance my card could decline. Why did I order ice-cream? Why did I come out at all?

'Oh, put your money away, darling,' Mum says to Robbie's girlfriend. 'It's my treat, and Robbie's because it's your birthday, of course. Kylie, your total comes to—'

'Never mind that, we're paying for Kylie.'

'Oh, Dad,' I protest, 'you don't have to do that,' except you literally might have to unless the restaurant will let me wash pots to pay my way.

'Nonsense. Your mum and I wouldn't have it any other way, would we, Marie?'

Mum looks annoyed but I know she won't put up a fight with Robbie's girlfriend present 'That's right, love. Dinner is on us tonight, Kylie.'

'Well, if you insist. Thanks, Mum.'

'Don't thank me, thank your dad.'

'Thanks, Dad,' I say as Dad smiles back at me. It makes me feel even worse. As well as feeling like shit, I now feel sorry for Dad for having me as a daughter. I'm a failure.

As I leave, my phone buzzes and I hope it's Alexa but instead it's Jason, *Hey Kylie, it's been a while. How have you been?*

I've been emotionally drained now that I'm unemployed and have no prospects. *Pretty good, how's the band?*

We're doing okay. So, I hardly got to hang out with you that time we met. You free tonight?

I am free. But I'm still not sure I want to hang out with Jason. After all our first date was disastrous. But why do I think so bad of Jason for it? Because he isn't the man I see myself with? I know how that feels now. The truth is Jason is nice. Nicer than Harry, nicer than I am.

Yeah, let's hang, I reply.

Meet me at the Fox and Duck – this time I'll buy.

Alexa

The sound of my alarm going off wakes me like it does every Monday morning, but when I open my eyes, I'm not in my bedroom and for a moment feel confused. I turn the alarm off and sit up to find Shaun asleep next to me, in his bed. He's an attractive sleeper and I admire him a little before creeping out of bed to the bathroom. I leave the door unlocked as I undress and step into the shower.

The water hitting my body is rejuvenating and I feel refreshed despite very little sleep last night. We were up until the early hours talking and doing things that didn't require talking, if you know what I mean. It's easy to lose hours with Shaun for company and it would be easy to go back to bed and skip work. But I shouldn't, and won't. Instead, I hop out of the shower and get ready for the day.

I didn't bring a hair dryer, so with no choice but to let my hair dry naturally, I use the time to make coffee and breakfast. The plan is to put everything on a tray and surprise Shaun in bed. I tiptoe into the bedroom. 'Good morning'.

Shaun opens his eyes and smiles, 'Good morning, gorgeous.'

'I brought you breakfast.'

'You didn't have to do that, thank you.' He kisses my forehead. 'Morning breath,' he explains.

I perch on the edge of the bed and sip the last of my coffee, 'I have to go.'

'Can't you stay?'

'No…' I say with a sigh, 'but you can pop by my work at lunch time if you're in town?'

'Try and stop me.' He puts my cup down and pulls me in for a hug.

'I'll see you later.' I miss him already.

I catch the bus to town and float to work, feeling lighter than air. Everything feels surreal, but also completely normal. It's like I've always known Shaun. It's effortless. It's blissful.

Which is why it feels hard to tell Kylie about it all, given her predicament. Priya wants us to go on a double date with her and her boyfriend but I've said not until Kylie meets Shaun. It wouldn't be right; Kylie comes first. I really need to see her soon and tell her everything. I'll message her tonight, I promise.

I get to work ten minutes early, which is how I like it. It's enough time to grab a drink and settle down for the day ahead. As my computer loads up, I think I'll message Kylie saying good morning.

But then there's a knock on my office door that makes me jump. I sit up straight and smooth my hair before saying 'come in' in case it's Shaun. Instead, it's my boss.

'Morning, Chapman, you sound chipper today.'

'Do I?' I feel myself begin to blush.

'You do. Any changes that would make you so happy?'

'No, can't think of any...'

'Really? No mystery men who send you flowers?'

'Is it that obvious?'

He smiles and hands me some folders. 'Don't worry, as long as you keep doing your job well, it's fine by me. It's nice to see you happy.'

'Thanks, John.' I take the folders. He nods and leaves my office, closing the door behind him.

He's right; I am happy. Everything is going great. I push through my workload, keeping my eye on the time, knowing Shaun will walk in soon. I keep checking my appearance, making sure I'm sat perfectly, which is exhausting but we're still in that part of the relationship where you pretend you don't have bad breath in the morning to the extent you get up early to brush your teeth in secret. It's taking up my concentration so much that I'm pretty sure I've messed up a few of these documents, which isn't like me. Get a grip, Alexa. I'm like a girl with a school crush. I might as well be writing my first name and his surname in my notebooks. Alexa Abbott. It has a nice ring to it.

Kylie

I feel like I've been hit by a bus. Emotionally and physically. Physically, because I overslept and possibly because I have been consisting on crisps, crackers, Nutella and biscuits. Emotionally, because I slept with Jason last night and I'm not even attracted to him. I was vulnerable after my encounter with Mum at Robbie's birthday dinner and he was the only person I had to turn to. I met him at the Fox and Duck and this time he bought me drinks, gave me attention and I just wanted to feel good, which I did, but now I feel groggy and kind of gross. And not just because of him but because I'm basically out of money and every time I think of asking Dad or Alexa for money, I hear Mum's humiliating words about how I need more help than most. The weight of my shitty life choices is weighing me down, crushing me, and if I don't get up now I never will.

I crawl out of bed, peel my God-knows-how-many-days-old My Chemical Romance top off and pull on jeans and a top. I hobble downstairs, grab some shoes, open the door, wince at the sunlight and set off to town to find a job.

The only problem is, damn it, my printer's all out of ink so I only have five CVs to my name. But I have a plan; I'm going to sneak up to Alexa's work office and borrow their printer.

I make my way to her work building and take the elevator to her floor. But as I enter the room, I see someone else at her desk. Who is this woman? Where's Alexa? 'Hey,' I say, 'I'm looking for Alexa? Alexandra Chapman?'

'You want the third floor,' the mysterious woman says.

That's odd. Has she had a move around? I could have sworn she worked on the second floor.

I set off to the third floor. It's nicer on this floor and quieter and that's how I know already that she definitely doesn't work up here. She always complains that she's cramped at work like a caged hen.

Then I see her, through a big glass window, in an office where she's sitting behind the desk. When did she get promoted? She would have told me. Maybe I forgot…

As I set off to meet her, I see a guy enters the office and walks up to Alexa. I wait, not wanting to disturb a colleague. They might not want me using their printer. But then, hang on, what… I don't believe my eyes. The guy leans over her desk and kisses her. She kisses back. What's going on? Everything becomes white and time slows down as I watch Alexa, as she laughs and tenderly touches this man who I've never seen or heard of before. The scene doesn't compute in my brain. It's all wrong. I watch and it feels like I don't know her at all. What else is she hiding from me, and why? I turn and leave, feeling sick and reddening in the face like I've been slapped. I feel like I've seen something that I shouldn't have, like I'm a peeping Tom. Suddenly I feel angry because I shouldn't be shocked at seeing Alexa kiss someone. I should know who he is. I should know every little detail. I thought we were best friends.

Alexa

I'm walking through town with a spring in my step, excited to see Kylie. I haven't heard from her in a week, which must be some sort of record because even that time I was struck down with the worst flu of my life we were still in touch daily. At one point I lost my voice, and staring at a bright phone screen to text was unbearable, so we communicated via emojis. This week, however, she's missed every call I've made and hasn't replied to any message. I know she's okay because she's been somewhat active online. Perhaps she's been busy herself. Maybe she's found a new job, or a new boyfriend. Hopefully some good news for her sake and for mine as I'm going to be sharing my own good news today.

Nervousness creeps in, as I still don't know how I'm going to word it, because the simple truth is: 'Oh, Kylie, I'm with this guy, he's really great. How did we meet? Oh actually, we met on my front doorstep'. No, it doesn't sound right. Kylie will just laugh in disbelief, and then tell me it's creepy just like I thought it was, way back then.

I slow my pace as I try to focus. Do I mention that I met Shaun weeks ago? Or do I say he's a new boyfriend? He's not even officially my boyfriend; we haven't asked each other out or mentioned it but it feels like he's my boyfriend. Maybe when you get to a certain age, you don't have to clarify things like this. After all, asking someone to go out with you sounds terribly juvenile. Maybe I should just mention that I'm seeing a guy and we've had a date. Okay, that's the plan. I take a deep breath as I reach the cafe and head in.

As I enter the cafe, I see she's already there. 'Kylie! You're early! I hope I didn't keep you waiting.'

Kylie says nothing.

'Shall I get the drinks? Then you can fill me in.' I go to walk by her to the counter, but she puts her hand up to stop me. I look at her and notice she looks terrible, on the verge of tears.

Oh God, something terrible has happened.

'How about you fill me in. Have you changed jobs? Got a boyfriend? Anything a best friend should know?'

Her eyes meet mine as a knot gathers in my stomach and now we're both on the verge of tears. 'How do you know?' I ask, sitting down. My legs can't carry me right now.

'Does it matter? Why are you hiding such huge things from me?'

'I, err... look it's just...' I take a deep breath. It wasn't supposed to go like this. This wasn't the plan. 'It's not like that, Kylie; the timing was all wrong. You'd just been fired and dumped. You were fragile. I didn't want to rub your nose in it.'

'Bullshit!' shouts Kylie, her voice cracking. 'You could have told me. I thought we tell each other everything.'

'We do! We did! I was going to!' Even as I speak I know it's not good enough. Why didn't I tell her sooner? All I can tell her is the truth '...I didn't want to upset you.'

She shakes her head and I look down in shame.

'You think I'm so pathetic and self-centred, that I can't enjoy your success when I'm such a failure?'

'Not at all! Please, Kylie, let's just—'

'I'm going.' She stands up and the chair scrapes backwards making a piercing noise that cuts through the room.

Everyone's looking, I know they are. But all I can see is Kylie get smaller and smaller as she walks away from me.

'No, stay, please!' I choke.

'No. Don't let me get in the way of your fabulous life.'

The door slams shut and my world falls apart.

Kylie

My heart beats faster and harder than ever before, and not just because I stormed out of the cafe quickly. I look back, and although my vision is clouded with tears, I can see enough to know she isn't behind me, so I slow down and stumble along my street. I didn't mean to storm out, I had so much more to say, but now all of the unsaid words are stuck in my throat, choking me up.

Maybe it's for the best because I'm not sure I want to hear her answers. What could she possibly say to justify lying to me about important life changes? I guess she didn't want me to know that she's some big shot at work with a boyfriend who visits at work just to kiss her. Maybe she's moved on from the unemployed and unlovable. Well that's just great. I will my legs to move faster, but my brain and body aren't in harmony which is fitting; there's nothing harmonious about anything in my life right now.

What's upsetting me the most is Alexa finding me pitiful. It was inevitable I guess. She's always been better than me. She carried me through university. Let's be honest, she carries me through life. I've always known she was going to be more successful, but I've never been bitter or jealous. It hurts that she felt the need to hide things from me. She says she was protecting me but maybe she's embarrassed by me. Oh God, she's embarrassed by me. As realisation hits, I trip over my own feet as I scramble to the front door. I need to get inside and shut the world out.

It's hard to have an epiphany while you're trying to find your house keys, yet here I stand at my front door rooting through my bag. I pull out fistfuls of junk; lip balm, tissues, a broken phone charger, five chocolate bar wrappers but no keys. I feel like Mary-bloody-Poppins. Where the hell are my keys? Sod it, I'll use the emergency key under the porcelain tortoise. Thank God I decided to buy it. Alexa was furious when she found out. She said it was stupid, a burglar's dream and in an emergency I could just get my spare key from hers. Ha!

I go to my room, shut the door, curl up on my bed and close my eyes. Despite the silence, my mind is too loud, full of questions that have been going through my mind since I saw Alexa in that swanky office kissing that guy, whoever he is. Despite stalking social media for him, I still don't know who he is. I hate that fact almost as much as I hate this whole situation. Who is this man that has dared to come between us?

I could find out, if I dare to answer the incoming call from Alexa. I take a deep breath and answer, 'What?!'

'Kylie, please, I don't want us to fight. Let me explain it all.'

'Explain how you've moved on in life and think you're better than me? Oh, I've figured that out on my own, don't worry.'

'It's not like that at all! You have to realise that—'

'No, Alexa, I've already realised it all. I've realised that you've been lying to me and you were quite happy to do so and to kiss men in offices without telling me a word of it. I realise you're only calling me because you got found out and you feel bad. Well maybe you should feel bad. Don't call me back!' I hang up as all of my emotions bubble to the surface, spilling out of my eyelids. It was a stupid idea to answer her call. I want to know, but I'm not ready. Relieved that Lucie isn't in, I head to the bathroom to wash this hideous day off me, plus the mascara that has streaked down my face.

A stream of bubble bath hits the running water and fragrant bubbles form. This bubble bath was a present for my birthday, before my life turned to shit. It's fitting really as bubbles and happiness are both temporary things. Eventually all you're left with is the diluted memory of what once was.

Before I undress, I push the laundry basket against the

door. Damn it, I really need to get a lock for the door. I undress and get in the bath, letting the hot water cleanse me. It's comforting, but not enough to distract me from my problems. It's a shame I can't go back in time and start all over again. Even if I could just go back to the day after I turned twenty-five when I last had a hot bubble bath but when I also had good friends and good boobs. Now I only have a hot bubble bath and at twenty-five it's only downhill from here, for my boobs, and for me.

Alexa

I'm on my fourth coffee and still exhausted from a night of not sleeping. I tossed and turned but every time I closed my eyes I saw Kylie's face from the cafe, full of hurt. Hurt that I caused. Since dawn I've sat in the kitchen, working out how I can fix this.

Kylie, I need to explain everything and tell you just how sorry I am. Please.

It's 11am, so she should be up. I'll just message again: *Kylie talk to me.*

Nothing. What the hell do I do now? But then, my phone buzzes, *What do you want from me?*

Can I come over? Please?

No. I don't want you here.

What about at our bench? Please, Kylie, give me a chance.

Fine. Meet me there in thirty minutes.

Thank you! I jump up and head out before she changes her mind. Okay, I'll tell her about my job first, then I'll move on to Shaun. Oh God, any second now I'll see her. What do I say? Racing down the street towards our bench, I realise I haven't grabbed my bag, or phone. Damn. She better be there. As I approach the bench my stomach churns. Kylie isn't there. I sit down, check my watch, glance down the road, check my watch again. She's always late, but what if she isn't coming? Double damn. I sit on the bench, holding my hands together and wait...

A pair of feet appear next to mine. I take a deep breath, 'I'm sorry.'

She doesn't reply. I look up and she looks back at me with bloodshot eyes and doesn't seem pleased to see me. 'Who is the guy?'

I look back down and play with my hands again, 'His name is Shaun...'

'How did you meet him?'

'He was repairing Priya's laptop and was leaving the house when I came home from work. He came back and gave me his number.'

'Why didn't you tell me?'

'I promise you I was going to, that night I found you in your bed. You had been fired, and dumped and it just didn't feel right.'

'That was ages ago. You could have told me at any point since then, but you didn't.'

'It was never the right time.'

'When would the right time have been? In a wedding invitation?'

'I know.' I look up at her, into her eyes, pleading with her, 'I fucked up. And I'm so, so, so sorry.' There's a cold look in her eyes that I've never seen before. I feel like it isn't even Kylie on this bench with me.

'Why have you moved up a floor at work?'

'I got promoted.'

'When?'

'A while back...' I already know there's no way this will come across well.

'Before Shaun?'

'Around the same time.'

'So you've been living some sort of double life. One life as my best friend like always and another in a big office with a new boyfriend and whatever else I don't know about—'

'Kylie, honestly, it's not like that. I'm still me, I'm still your best friend nothing has changed except yes I got a promotion and I have a boyfriend.'

'No, everything has changed. Because now you see fit to keep huge life events from me.'

'It's not like that. It looks bad, I know...'

'Why are you even fighting for me when you've clearly moved on? Or do you just want it to look like you tried to keep the peace with me and so when we fall out you can put all of the blame on me?'

'What? No. Come on, Kylie, we aren't—'

'Everything you do is so meticulously organised and choreographed. I used to think it was OCD or some sort of quirk but I can see it's really clever manipulation.'

'What are you talking about?'

'You wanted to build up your career and relationship at the same time as tying up loose ends with me so you can unveil this new lifestyle, this new Alexa and it will be seamless.'

'No, Kylie. You're so wrong on this.'

'Then give me one good reason you wouldn't tell me about your new job and your new boyfriend?'

Blood rushes up my body, reddening my cheeks and suddenly I feel dizzy. I came here with clarity, having spent hours planning what to say, but Kylie has put a weird spin on everything and it's throwing me off. Words come out without me okaying them first, 'I don't know, I just felt sorry for you!'

'You feel sorry for me? Really, Lex?'

'No, I didn't mean—'

'This is like the second guy to show any interest in you since we met and suddenly you're sorry for me?'

'No, I'm not—'

'You get a minor promotion and suddenly you're sorry for me?'

'I just mean—'

'You suddenly thought that now you have an office and a boyfriend you're better than me? Who is this man that you barely know? Do you love him?'

'No! And I don't think I'm—'

'So why is this man coming between us? Or is it that now you have a man, you don't need me. You were just using me until the first man looked your way.'

'I was never using you!' My voice is raised, and people are looking.

'You were using me, and if you want to feel sorry for anyone, try feeling sorry for Shaun. You're going to use him like you used me.'

'I'm not going to sit here and be called a user! You're acting out because I upset you, fine. But there's a line, Kylie.'

'There is a line. Lying to me and using me and pretending it's all for my own good is crossing it. You're a coward, it's pathetic.'

My voice cracks, 'You're being unreasonable and I'm going.' I get up and leave, blinking away emerging tears.

'Yeah, you go,' Kylie shouts so I can hear as I walk away. 'Go and take your pity elsewhere! Go and run home to Shaun, tell him all the terrible things I've done!'

I run home, to nobody, and the tears come.

Kylie

So that's that.

I met Alexa at our bench to talk things through and we had a fight. A justified one, I might add, because as discovered, she's been living a bloody double life for months. Lies upon lies. So we fought. I admit that I said some things I didn't fully mean and in the end she walked off, hurt and angry. Why did she get to be the one to walk off? I was the one who was lied to, used and worse – pitied. She pitied me. I thought Alexa was on my side, but maybe she never has been.

That was three days ago. Apart from going to the toilet and grabbing snacks, I haven't left my room. If it weren't for telly, it'd just be me sitting here, alone, in silence. Then again, at this point, Netflix is just about my only friend. I could die in here and the first person to know would be their finance department when I stopped paying my subscription.

I'm scraping the last of the Nutella out of the jar when someone knocks on my door. My heart drops, what if it's Alexa? I don't want to see her.

'Who is it?'

'It's Lucie. Can I come in?'

I look around my room, properly, for the first time all weekend. It's a mess. There's a strange smell that could either be me or the bed. Or the pile of dishes on the side. I don't feel like seeing people but seeing as I live with Lucie, it's inevitable. I sigh, 'Fine'.

She comes in, 'Good God, Kylie. This is bad, even for you.'

I shrug, past caring.

She looks at me, trying to figure it all out. 'Have you been in here all weekend?'

'Yeah.'

'What's happened?'

'I've fallen out with Alexa, we aren't friends anymore...' It's the first time I've admitted this out loud and it breaks my heart all over again. I sink lower into bed. I'm never leaving.

Lucie sits down at the end of the bed. 'Why? You guys have never fallen out.'

'That's because we've never lied to each other before. She was keeping things from me, big things.'

'Why would she do that?'

The very same question I've been trying to figure out myself.

'I don't know. She said she was trying to protect me but I have my doubts. If you ask me, I'd say she was just covering her tracks. Alexa never likes being the bad guy. She's never had the guts to stand up for herself; I always had to do it for her. So when it came to ditching me, she didn't know how to do it alone.'

'Are you sure it's as bad as this? Are you sure you're not being dramatic?'

'She's in a relationship, Lucie. With a guy I've never heard of. And she has a new job. She's changed her entire life and managed to keep me out of it all. We're clearly and obviously over as friends.'

'Shit.'

'Shit, indeed.'

Lucie sighs, taking it all in. She doesn't know what to say but she doesn't need to. Besides, 'shit' summed it up well. Things are well and truly shit.

'How long were you best friends for?' she asks.

'Seven years. We met on the first day of university. I thought we'd be friends forever.'

'So did I.'

'I don't even know how to make new friends. How do you make new friends at twenty-five?'

'At work? Speaking of work, have you found a new job?'

'No.'

'Well, as insensitive as it is because I know you're hurting;

you need to find a job.'

'I know.'

'Let me know if you need any help. I'm off to work but I'll catch up with you later.'

'Come up and see me when you get in.'

'Will do.'

She goes to leave but then stops and turns to me.

'You know, I'm your friend. And when you find a job, you'll make new friends. You make out like at twenty-five you're old, but you're still young. Maybe losing Alexa is the push you need to make something of yourself. Maybe it was just time you went your separate ways.'

'Maybe. It's not like I have a choice.'

I wonder if she's right. If she is, am I capable of going it alone without Alexa? She said that I make out that being twenty-five is old. I thought it was, but suddenly I find myself having to start over. I have to find a new career, a new job, new friends and a new purpose. Suddenly twenty-five is the new fifteen. Hopefully without the hormones and dodgy Myspace poses.

'You should take up Thai Chi. Research has shown it to have a powerful effect on the mind. It increases focus, boosts cognitive skills and reduces stress. It's also a great physical exercise. I have a DVD if you're interested.'

'Er, no thanks you're all right.'

'Well at least do something. Why don't you clear up in here? You could read up about Feng Shui—'

'Do you get paid commission every time you suggest a sport to me? You know I'm not the sporty type. I was never Sporty Spice; I was always Ginger Spice. Curvy and unapologetic about it.'

Lucie sighs, 'Feng Shui isn't a sport it's a state of mind.'

'My state of mind right now is annoyed. But I don't need to rearrange my furniture, I just need you to stop bringing up Asian things because it's making me crave Chow Mein and I'm broke.'

Lucie sighs, 'If you do something productive, I'll buy you Chow Mein on the way back from work.'

I jump out of bed, 'Very well done, Lucie, you know nothing motivates me like food.'

'See ya tonight.'

And with that she leaves, shutting the door behind her.

I suppose it couldn't hurt to get out of bed, I was becoming one with the mattress. Hungry for Chow Mien, I look around for things to tidy. I put my laundry in the hamper, fold the not-quite-dirty clothes and lay them over my chair, take dishes downstairs and put things that are inexplicably on the floor back where they belong. But as I'm smoothing a pile of books, I come across that stupid framed inspiration quote Alexa bought me for my birthday, 'Behind every successful woman is herself'. The gold foil text gleams at me, looking very smug indeed. I hate inspirational quotes because I think they're a load of nonsense. I hated it when Alexa gifted me it, and I would have thrown it away if it hadn't been for her. I suppose I can throw it away now, but I can't, because it would be like throwing away one of the last pieces of Alexa I still have. I read the text again: 'Behind every successful woman is herself'. It's funny… up until now I've had Alexa behind me, and now all I have is myself.

Alexa

Alexa? Are you there?
 Alexa? Is everything okay?

Six missed calls and several concerned texts fill my phone, all from Shaun. I'm not answering, and not just because I'm in my rubber gloves on my hands and knees as I scrub out the kitchen cupboards.

'Alexa, your phone keeps going off,' says Priya, entering the room.

'I know.' I look at my phone which is lit up and buzzing to itself. I should have switched it off.

'Are you going to check it?'

I carry on scrubbing the cupboards. I won't feel satisfied until every inch is spotless. 'No' I reply. I can't bring myself to talk to him. Everything with Kylie feels so raw, and also I can't help but feel like Shaun is the reason we fell out. The truth is, I'm the reason we fell out, but that's because I lied about Shaun. As a result, I feel guilty about being with him. Everything is a big old mess, so I'm cleaning. Cleaning always makes me feel better.

She sighs and looks at the phone screen. 'Shaun has been calling all day!'

'I've been really busy, cleaning.' Which is the truth but I don't feel like telling her why.

'Have you two fallen out?'

'No.'

'So you're ignoring him because you feel guilty about Kylie?'

I sigh, and look up at Priya, 'You know me too well… '

Priya folds her arms and looks like she's about to chastise me, 'I do. I know that it'd be just like you to sacrifice your happiness and sabotage something great in the hope that it'll make someone else feel better. But it won't make Kylie feel better, will it?'

I carry on cleaning, this time with a pout. 'I doubt it. We're not talking, anyway.'

'Are you likely to make up?'

The question itself hurts. The truth hurts even more. 'I don't know.'

Priya unfolds her arms and sounds softer this time, 'So why are you throwing Shaun away for her?'

'I'm not. I don't know. I don't know what I'm doing.'

'I know what you're doing; you're punishing yourself, only you're not just punishing yourself; you're punishing Shaun.'

'I don't know what to tell him.'

'Just tell him the truth.'

'I fell out with my best friend because we're going out?'

'Tell him an easily digestible version of the truth.'

'None of this is easy to digest. I've lost the best friend I ever had. I messed up.'

'Oh, Lex, things have a way of working themselves out.'

'Is that your answer for everything? Love finds a way; friendship finds a way…'

'All I'm saying is… what's the phrase? If you love someone, set them free. If they come back, they're yours. If they don't, it was never meant to be.'

I roll my eyes at her, 'You're like one of those pull-string dolls. One that just says cheesy, generic phrases.'

'How about this phrase: Call Shaun.' She picks up my phone and holds it out to me.

'That's not very generic…' I say light-heartedly, but Priya doesn't crack a smile. She stands there, just holding my phone. Priya always gets her own way.

I roll my eyes and try to look sincere. 'When I've finished cleaning, I will.'

'You better. I'll see you later. If you feel like stalling any longer, I have some laundry for you to do.'

I wait for Priya to leave and then take off my rubber

gloves. The whole house is spotless, and I don't feel any better. But I can't ignore him any longer. When I pick up my phone, there's another message.

Are we okay? Did I do something?

How could I make Shaun feel bad when he's done nothing wrong? Apparently I won't be satisfied until I've alienated everyone around me. Well that's changing from now on. No more lies, no more alienating people. I'm going to put everything I have into giving Shaun and me a chance.

Everything's fine, you did nothing. Want to come over? I'll tell you all about it.

Kylie

I'm dressed for the first time in five days, as I've finally run out of snacks. The plan was to pop out, get food, and come back, but my financial situation is so dire that I need to look for a job. So I've done my hair, meaning I've brushed it and set it with some spray, and I'm looking pretty presentable. I just need some shoes and I can head out. The shoes I've been wearing recently are the black and white pair from Alexa. A present to help me remember my youth, which now serve as a reminder of what I need to leave behind. I put on some grey flats instead and make my way towards the city centre.

I have little work experience under my belt; the office job from which I was fired, and a Saturday job washing dishes in a restaurant during college. With all this in mind, I have no idea where to even start looking for work. I take a deep breath and walk into what is clearly a high-end boutique, although once inside its décor gives off more of a high-class brothel vibe. Intimidated but desperate, I approach the pouting sales assistant, 'Excuse me, do you have any vacancies?' She looks at me with a pained and mildly disgusted expression as though I'm something on the bottom of her shoe.

'No,' she replies. Shocker.

As desperate as I am to find a job, I'm pretty relieved and leave as quickly as I can. Not before accidentally knocking over a display item. Mortified and clearly unable to pay for anything broken, I run to the next shop, not looking at what it is. I get inside and catch my breath before looking around and when I do, the whiteness of the walls and furniture almost blind me. Then I see what's on the racks and rails and wish I was blind: it's a baby boutique. I make my way to the counter, past the wicker baskets of metal rattles and rows of pink booties. Some of the booties are diamanté encrusted and I nearly choke when I see the price tag. Babies don't even bloody walk!

'Excuse me, do you have any vacancies?' I ask the middle-aged woman behind the counter with a poof of auburn hair and large glasses that are hanging from a chain around her neck. She puts them on and peers at me.

'Do you have retail experience?'

Oh dear. 'Yes,' I lie, 'I also have a degree.'

'Do you like children?'

'Of course. Babies are adorable,' I lie again.

'Do you know the difference between a muslin cloth and a burp cloth?'

Crap. 'No,' I admit, 'but I'm a quick learner.'

'Do you know what an iCandy is?'

'Is it the latest trendy gadget?' What has this got to do with babies?

'Sorry.'

So apparently you have to be an expert in something to sell it now.

It's been hours, and so far, an entirely fruitless venture. I've gained nothing, and I'm about to lose everything. On top of it all, I really shouldn't have worn these shoes. My feet hurt now as well as my brain and my heart. My life is officially buggered. I have five pounds left to my name. I was going to buy as many custard creams as I could, but seeing as my life has turned to shit and I have no other options but to go back to my parents, fuck it; I'm going to buy a stiff drink. A send off, if you will.

Because the universe hates me, the first bar I come to is the one in which I met Harry. I walk past it as quickly as possible, despite my blistered feet, and take refuge in the next one I see.

It's not as stuffy or dark in here as some bars I've been in. It's light and fresh, with art on the walls and rustic wood. In the seven years I've lived here, I still haven't been to half of the places in this city. A pang of regret and sadness hits me as

I realise that this won't be my city for much longer.

'Kylie?' someone calls my name. I recognise that voice... Alicia.

'Alicia?'

'Kylie! Wow, long time no see. Come sit with me! How are you doing? What are you doing here?'

I take reluctant steps to Alicia and sit down at the bar. What am I doing here? I can't exactly tell her the truth, 'I'm on my lunch break.'

'You are? But this is a bar...'

Why would I be in a bar on my lunch break? Think, Kylie, think. 'I've had a really hard day.'

'Oh really? Well, I guess being a psychologist can be draining. That was your degree, right? How's it going?'

It isn't. It went nowhere. A bit like me. I'm going nowhere except back to my parents' spare bedroom. 'Oh, you know. Fine. Draining.'

'But rewarding?'

Financially? No. Emotionally? No. My degree is a very expensive piece of paper, 'Absolutely.'

'Brilliant. Aww, I'm so pleased for you. I'm just here for a quick glass of fizz to celebrate picking up an excellent client. It's the highlight of my career actually! There's a surprise party for me later organised by my colleagues, not that I'm supposed to know, but I couldn't resist a quick toast to myself. Grab yourself a drink, on me, and we can have a toast together.'

'Oh, sure.' I smile and curse the universe. As if I wasn't already having a terrible day, fate has struck me with Alicia. She looks exactly the same as she did at university; still as thin, damn it, and with salon-fresh hair. This time she has tousled ombre curls that fall on her tanned shoulders. She smiles her pearly-whites and clicks her fingers in the air.

'Barman! A white wine for Kylie.'

Alicia talks on and on about herself, but I've stopped listening and instead I'm watching the barman make my drink. He's gorgeous. Not your normal type of gorgeous, but Jared-Leto-circa-2012 gorgeous. His hair is better than mine and his eyes are so blue and inviting that I'd love to dive right in. He puts the glass of wine in front of me.

Suddenly, Alicia's phone begins to ring, 'Oh, can you pay for that? I've got to take this.'

'That'll be £5.50.'

Shit. I look to Alicia to ask for change but she's already gone. I hand him a crumbled up five pound note and search through my bag and pockets for 50p in a state of panic. I feel myself turning red. This is no send off. I'll have to admit I haven't the money to Alicia and die of embarrassment. I would ditch her right now but the barman is standing opposite me, waiting. 'I don't have the 50p,' I tell him, 'it's lost, like my will to live.'

The barman smiles in amusement, with thin lips but a perfect cupid's bow framing pearly whites. 'Take the drink.'

'Are you sure?' I ask, feeling like a charity case. Although I suppose I am.

'Yeah. Don't worry, I won't tell your... friend.'

I thank him and he nods. I take a sip of the wine, just as Alicia comes back. 'I've got to go, business calls.' She knocks back the last of her drink, 'enjoy your lunch break. We've got to catch up soon okay? I'll message you.'

'Oh, such a shame. Yeah, message me and we'll get together,' I say with absolute certainty that we won't get together. For starters, I'll be avoiding her at all costs. I never did like Alicia very much. She's richer now with good hair and tinted eyebrows, but she's still the same annoying Alicia. I watch her leave and I don't know if it's that fact or the alcohol but I feel much more relaxed.

'So, where is it?' asks the barman.

'What? I don't know, I don't really keep change on me I guess.'

He laughs and I suddenly feel less relaxed.

'No,' he says, pouring a drink for someone nearby, 'your will to live.'

'Oh. That went ages ago. Probably around the time I got fired and dumped simultaneously and then lost my best friend.'

'Wow, that's rough.'

'Yep. And now, I have to finish this drink and go home defeated. I can't find a job. I am out of money and options. I'm going to have to leave the city, my home, and go back to my parents and live miserably ever after.'

I can imagine it now; turning up at my childhood home, wheelie suitcase in hand. Mum would invite me in politely, but the throbbing vein in her neck that appears when she's particularly furious would give away how she really feels. She'd take me to my old bedroom, which was changed into an office the second I left for university, and I would leave my stuff next to the blow-up bed. She would last until dinner where passive-aggressive comments would trickle out somewhere between shepherd's pie and apple crumble. Eventually a lecture including phrases like 'not getting any younger' and 'why couldn't you have tried harder?' would ensue. Before I know it, she'd have found me a job that I'd have no option but to take. Slowly but surely, I'd settle into mediocre village life and start looking forward to church bake sales.

'I wouldn't give up just yet.'

He's now sitting opposite me behind the bar, close enough that I can smell him. It's enough to distract me from my thoughts.

'Why? It's hopeless.'

'It's only after we've lost everything, that we're free to do anything.'

'Well, that's not entirely true.'

'Okay but you can't just give up your life here and go back to live with your parents. This is your life, and it's ending one minute at a time.'

'And I thought I was depressed before I came in here.'

He stares at me in amazement. He's really starting to annoy me, regardless of his looks. 'Have you seriously never seen Fight Club?'

'No,' I admit. Great. Now I'm uncultured. Unemployed and uncultured.

'Go home and watch it, and then come back here

tomorrow 9am, Kylie.' He gets up to see to a customer.

What? 'Are you setting me homework?'

He smirks and shakes his head. 'Yes. Come back tomorrow, 9am sharp and tell me how much you loved the film and then your next homework will be learning how to pull a pint.'

I stand, dumbfounded. He's offering me a job, unless I'm mistaken. A great sense of relief kicks in, but I suppress it. I shouldn't be too hasty, considering what happened the last time I was promised a job. 'Why should I trust you?'

He looks over from where he is, 'I'm not saying you should trust me. Be here, tomorrow, 9am and find out for yourself. What do you have to lose?'

Nothing is the answer, although I don't reply. Lost for words, I nod and quietly shuffle out of the bar and set off for home. Home! Maybe I can still call the city that after all.

Alexa

Shaun strokes my hair, which is something I've always loved. It soothes me somewhat but I still feel wretched as I curl up on the sofa, staring at the television but not watching it at all.

'I can't stand to see you like this.'

Neither can I. 'I'll be okay. It was my own fault anyway.'

'I don't think it's as black and white as you lying and her being hurt. You must have lied for a reason; you must have felt you had to lie.'

He gets it, he gets me, and I feel better for it. I look up at him, 'I didn't want to hurt her.'

'Exactly,' he smoothes the hair around my face, 'you made an error of judgement, fine. But Kylie blew it out of proportion.'

'I guess…'

'You know what I think? I think she's lashing out at you because she's jealous of how well you're doing. She said some terrible things to you, but has she called you to apologise?'

'No.'

'So she hurt you, after you went to sort things out, and she hasn't called? It doesn't sound great. Maybe, one day, you'll look back and realise it was right you two fell out.'

Could he be right? I don't know. I hope not. But he's right about one thing: Kylie hasn't called. I've even looked online to see what she's been up to. Alicia Combs tagged her saying 'Good to see you, must meet up soon to have a proper catch up'. When did they become friends? I thought Kylie couldn't stand Alicia, and yet apparently they're hanging out. She's clearly moving on. Maybe I should too.

'Don't worry,' he says, kissing my forehead, 'everything will work itself out. You've got me.'

I force a smile, although I am happy Shaun's here. If only it wasn't under these circumstances. 'I do. I'm lucky to have you. It's just so weird not having Kylie in my life. I mean, the only reason I decided to stay here after university was Kylie. She is, or rather, was, a big part of my life. We used to talk all day and call each other after work.'

'Well, I'll call you every day after work.' He runs his fingers through my hair.

'Tomorrow is Friday, and we always meet at the café to catch up. As the days go on I'm finding Kylie-shaped-holes in my life. Maybe I should just move back to my home town…'

'No! You can't leave! You'll have to find new people and new traditions to fill those holes.'

'Who? I see enough of Priya already. Besides, we don't have a lot of shared interests.'

'No friend from your university days?'

I shrug, 'None I've kept in touch with, or want to reunite with. Except a few mutual friends who will no doubt be Team Kylie.' In fact, I'm surprised the witch hunt hasn't already begun.

'What about work colleagues?'

'I don't know any of them. There's Emma in accounting, we share a hello and a smile if we bump into each other in the staff kitchen. But she's quite a bit older than me.'

'You're an old soul, it's worth a try. I bet it'll be great.'

'You think?'

'Absolutely! Go in tomorrow, find Emma and strike up a conversation that goes beyond "hi, nice weather we're having". Get yourself out there.'

'It's not a bad idea…'

'Have you cheered up yet? My hand's getting tired,' he says referring to the fact he's been stroking my hair this whole time.

'Nearly, just one more minute?' I really do love it.

'For you, one more minute.'

Kylie

With all this running I do, you'd think my body would be used to it. But as I run to work with breakfast threatening to make a reappearance, it appears that's not the case. I arrive with minutes to spare, make a mental note to Google what a heart attack feels like, and head in. Oliver, the guy who hired me, and a girl called Zara, are already there.

'Morning, Ky,' says Zara. She's taken to calling me Ky and I don't know how I feel about it.

'Morning, Zara, Oliver… am I late?'

'Nope, you're right on time. Zara just came in early to pester me into letting her favourite band's music play in the bar.'

'They're going to be huge on the indie scene. You'll be thanking me one day.'

Oliver frowns, 'If they're going to be huge, won't they go mainstream not indie?'

'I hope not. What a hideous thought.'

'But don't you want them to succeed? Don't you want them to break into the charts?'

'Being in the charts isn't the definition of success, Ollie. Who even cares what's in the charts? You are so old.'

Oliver rolls his eyes, but I can tell he's amused. I feel just like he does.

'Being in the charts isn't the definition of success, but it can't hurt to be popular, can it? It didn't do Panic! At The Disco any harm…'

Zara looks at me, and I don't know how but I've managed to say the wrong thing. Oliver busies himself and Zara rolls her sleeves up and washes her hands. 'Are you ready then, Ky? You take that side, I'll stick here closer to the door.

Hopefully I'll take most of the customers and you can take it easy.'

I know that she has no choice but to let me take it easy, because I have yet to come to grips with everything involved in this job. Who knew that bar work wasn't simply a case of pouring drinks and taking money? It makes me feel bad, like I'm letting her down, but I don't show it. 'That's so nice of you. I'm getting the hang of it, I think.'

'You're doing fine, it won't be too busy this time of the day anyway.' She reaches a toned arm up to run her fingers through her silver hair, oh so nonchalantly. As she does this, her shirt rises, and her hips show. No muffin-top in sight. I pull my own top down over my decidedly bigger hips and tuck my hair behind my ears, just as people start trickling in. Soon the flood will come.

'Two pints please, babe,' says a grubby looking man in his thirties.

'Excuse me can I get some service here?' says a mean-looking girl around my age.

Someone else leans over the bar, holding out a drink, 'I ordered diet coke and vodka and this is full fat.'

'I'm so sorry,' I say, taking the definitely-diet-coke, and replacing it. Oliver has told me before that the customer is almost always right and it's easier to just replace drinks. 'Here you are.'

'Excuse me, service please?' says the mean-looking girl again. She has an attitude so I've put her to the last of my priorities.

'Two pints coming up.' I pour the pints, ignoring the mean girl for as long as possible. She stands with her money in her fist, looking like she'd rather do something else with it.

'I know bar tenders don't need qualifications but you'd think they'd be remotely competent.'

I grit my teeth and turn to her, 'Can I help you?' I ask. That is, if I were 'remotely competent'.

'Two pinot grigios.'

She takes the drinks and flounces off.

'You're welcome!' I hiss.

'Don't worry about it, Ky,' says Zara who is now behind me.

'It's just so rude and unnecessary.'

'I know. I get it all the time from those types of people. They think they're better than us. They think working in an office is everything and it's not. I'd rather have no job, frankly.'

Hmm. It's a close call, but unemployment was no fun.

Zara carries on, 'And they're so generic. Walking suits with no original ideas. Completely vapid.'

'At least they've gone now,' I say.

'When does your shift finish?'

'In an hour.'

'Me too. I can't wait to get home.'

'Oh same. I'm going to stick the telly on and do nothing.'

'I don't own a TV.'

'Seriously?'

'No. They only put on what they want you to watch. Think about it.'

'I guess you're right…'

'I'm going to read a bit and then write. I'm writing a novel.'

'Really? That's amazing!'

'It's probably not going to get picked up. It's a dystopian anti-establishment piece where medicine has been exposed as ineffective. Publishers don't like to take on controversial books no matter how compelling.'

'Wow.' Most of what Zara says goes right over my head, but I understood enough to know that she's smart and thinks outside the box. She does things people only dream of doing. 'I wish I could do something like that.'

'I believe you could do it. You seem more than capable.'

'Maybe I could. I should. This is my life and it's ending one minute at a time.'

Zara sighs, 'You've been listening to Ollie too much.'

I'm not going to watch telly when I get in. Zara has inspired me to do something productive, although I'm not sure what. Maybe I should read more, and then I'll be able to keep up with her on an intellectual level. Until then, I'll try to keep up with her behind the bar.

Alexa

I don't know whether it's just me, because I'm still in a funk, but today has been thoroughly underwhelming. Work dragged on and on and I found myself watching the clock. When it was time to go home, I didn't feel relief but indifference. Why would I be relieved to go home so I can sit alone, eat alone and go to bed ready for another day of monotony? It's just one of those days. I might have an early night and get it over with.

As I turn onto my street, there's a noise. When I snap out of my thoughts I realise it's my phone ringing. 'Hello?'

'Hey, it's me,' says Shaun.

'Oh hey. Everything okay?'

'Yep.'

'Oh. Why are you calling then?'

'I said I would call you after work.'

'Oh.' I can't believe he remembered and actually followed through with it.

'Is that okay?'

'Of course it is.' I realise I'm being aloof. 'Sorry, you just caught me off guard. I'm actually still walking home.'

'What are your plans when you do get home?'

'I don't know. I guess I'll find something to eat and have an early night.'

'That sounds nice. Anything in mind in terms of what to eat?'

'I haven't thought that far ahead yet,' I say as I enter my yard. That's actually a little white lie. I plan on raiding the fridge for leftovers and finish off with a snickers bar I've been saving. But there are some visuals a girl keeps to herself. 'Any ideas?'

'How about Coq Au Vin?'

'That sounds delicious but I don't think I'm up for making a big meal.'

'Not a problem.'

'What?' I go to put my key in the lock, but instead the door's already ajar. As it opens, I see Shaun in my apron looking at me, smiling. The oven is on, things bubble inside pans on the stove. Garlic, onions, wine and many other smells permeate the room. I have so many questions and exclamations inside my head, but the first thing that comes out is, 'How did you get in?'

Shaun laughs, 'Priya let me in. Is that okay?'

'Of course it is. Sorry, it's just such a surprise.'

'A good one, I hope?'

'Absolutely! I can't believe you're here. And after the day I've had…'

'Come and sit down, tell me all about it,' he says, pulling out a chair. 'Wine?'

'Yes please. I bet I look an absolute mess. I haven't looked in a mirror since this morning.'

'You look beautiful. But if it makes you feel better, go and change into something more comfortable and I'll dish up dinner.'

I dash upstairs, changing into leggings and a casual dress. There's no point dressing up after he's just seen me stumble in from a nine-hour work-day. When I come down, Shaun's sat at the table with our dinner, waiting for me. 'This is too much,' I sit down, 'you really didn't have to do this.'

'I wanted to.' He pours wine into two glasses. 'How was your day?'

'It was fine. It's much better now.'

'I'm glad.'

'This meal is incredible. No one's ever cooked for me. Except Priya. But not like this.'

'Did Kylie ever cook for you?'

'Oh no, she can't cook at all.'

'Well, you've got me now. I'll cook for you.'

We talk some more and eat and it fills me up so much that

there's no room for any funk. In a weird coincidence, Shaun gets a phone call as I finish my last sip of wine. He takes it to the living room and I jump up to clear the plates, pans and many utensils lying around the kitchen. It turns out Shaun's a messy cook.

'Are you sure you don't want help washing up?' asks Shaun, coming back in as I'm scrubbing my best pan.

'No, absolutely not. Go and sit down, you've done enough.'

He admits defeat and goes to sit down. It's true, he has done enough, but that's not the only reason I'm washing up. I have a system. But I can't tell him that for fear of sounding insane. Speaking of insane, I came home after a hard day's work to a home cooked meal. What a time to be a woman!

'So I was thinking we should go away sometime soon,' Shaun shouts through from the living room.

'Where?'

He breezes back into the kitchen, 'What do you think of Paris or Rome?'

'Really? When?'

'This weekend? I don't have much business this weekend so I figured we should make the most of it.'

A holiday with Shaun? It sounds like heaven. 'Wow, that's such a nice idea. Although, going abroad just for a weekend. Would it be enough time?'

'Take Thursday and Friday off then.'

'I can't do that. I can't just take time off.'

'Of course you can. Ask for some leave. Call in sick.'

'I could never call in sick. I could ask for leave but I haven't prepared to go away. It's all a bit rushed. I don't know, maybe we should reschedule for a later time.'

I feel two arms wrap around me, pulling me into an embrace. 'Go on. For me? Look, could it hurt to be spontaneous?'

'Spontaneity isn't really my thing.' I carry on washing dishes, pushing down my rising anxiety.

'Think about it.' He snuggles into my neck, kissing it. 'You and me, a beautiful view, red wine, relaxation.'

I consider his offer, 'I have always wanted to see the Pantheon.'

'Then we'll see the Pantheon, together. What do you say?'

A beautiful man wants to whisk me away on a romantic mini-break and I'm washing dishes and worrying about work. Wasn't I just moaning to myself about the monotony of work? Plus, it'd be nice to escape from the Kylie drama and unwind. I lean back into him, letting him support me. 'Let's do it.'

Kylie

Oliver shutting the front doors signals the end of my first night shift. Thank God. It's been an eye-opening night, being on the other side of the bar. Firstly, I've realised just how annoying drunk people are and secondly, I've realised how many types of drunks there are. There's a whole spectrum from happily tipsy to giddy, to inappropriate or emotionally unstable. Not forgetting mean drunks, like this ogre of a man earlier who Oliver had to tell to leave.

It was fascinating seeing Oliver as an intimidating presence. He's usually quiet and passive, preferring to listen in and only commenting occasionally if not just smirking to himself. He's inoffensive and unassuming, or so I assumed. You wouldn't have thought that an hour ago; he had protected me against a mean drunk who leaned over the bar and shouted at me. Until Oliver stepped in, I thought I was going to crumble on the spot.

And now I'm about to crumble again, because I've been on my feet for hours and I'm shattered. Never mind, it won't be long before I'm home.

'Ollie, do you mind if I take off?' says Zara.

'Where could you possibly be rushing off to at this time of night? Besides, there's still ten minutes of your shift left.'

'What's ten minutes between friends?' Zara puts on a faux puppy-dog face until Oliver rolls his eyes.

'Fine,' he concedes, 'get out of here. Kylie can help me finish up.'

Shit. Cheers, Zara. I'm officially dead, why can't I leave early instead? Then again, I suppose I'm not in a position yet to do so. Zara heads out through the back before Oliver has a chance to change his mind. And now, we're alone together.

Oliver squares up tables, and I know this is my cue to put stools and chairs where they belong. I haven't done this yet and although it's simple enough, I feel awkward in the silence with my boss watching my every move. But as I venture out into the room, I realise I haven't fully appreciated the finer details of it. The wall lights look vintage, and the art looks real. I figured they were all mass-produced prints bought from a wholesaler, but as I push a chair back against a wall, I notice the painting has a signature. 'Oliver Caverly,' I read out loud.

'Yes?' says Oliver, suddenly behind me. He's so quiet it's like he can glide or something.

Shit. I didn't mean to say it out loud, or at least I didn't mean to say it loud enough for him to hear. Why couldn't I have gone home early? I take a breath and turn around, trying to look casual. 'Oh, I was just reading the signature on this painting?' I ask, 'is it yours?'

'Yes, it is. It'd be a huge coincidence if I'd have bought art from another Oliver Caverly.'

'I guess. Coincidences happen though, that's why there's a word for it. You could do business with another Oliver Caverly, stranger things have happened. I don't know another Kylie Lee but I'm sure there are some out there.' I'm rambling. Stop, Kylie. Jesus.

He stands, doing nothing, as if waiting for me to carry off on another tangent. When it's clear I'm not, he smiles. 'Do you like it?'

'My name? It's okay, but I mean it could be bet—'

'No,' he says with that infuriating smile that makes me feel foolish, 'do you like the painting?'

I look at the painting again. 'It's nice…'

'Nice?'

'Great. The swirls and stuff, they're great.'

'Thank you,' he says. 'But it's not just, as you put it, swirls and stuff.'

'Oh?'

'Look beyond your first impression, look past its exterior and you'll see so much more.'

I look at the painting again and squint my eyes and look harder, but it's still swirls and stuff. Oh God, I'm going to offend him. 'Well, I do see flicks and dots and other things.'

'You're looking at parts of a whole. Look at the whole thing, but beyond that.'

What? 'Like, through the other side of the canvas?'

Oliver actually laughs at this. 'I like your raw spirit, Kylie Lee. There might be another Kylie Lee, but there's only one you.'

I feel embarrassed, confused and flattered all in one go. Not knowing what to say to this, I busy myself with putting chairs back and end up staying well past the end of my shift.

Alexa

'I'm not certain we'll be heading to the coast, considering the short time we'll be there, but I want to be prepared. Besides, there could be a swimming pool at the hotel or a jacuzzi.'

'It's better to be safe than sorry,' says Priya 'what about this lovely two-piece?'

'Do I look like I wear two-pieces?' I ask.

'Why not? It's modest. The bottoms are high-waisted.' She puts the two-piece against her own body for demonstration. 'See?'

'I do see. And I'd like swimwear in which you can see less of me, actually.'

Priya sighs and puts the two-piece down. We're in my favourite clothes shop, trying to get everything I need for my mini-break with Shaun this weekend. I walk by rails of clothing, touching items gently as I go and eye up well-dressed mannequins. I wonder how I'd look in those outfits. I want to look sophisticated and classy, if possible.

'What about this one?' asks Priya, holding up a swimming costume. I go over to inspect it. With my figure, I can't afford to be anything but critical about swimwear.

'It's quite nice,' I say, feeling the fabric, 'but aren't horizontal stripes fattening?'

'No, I think they decided vertical stripes are more fattening. But that's irrelevant because you're not fat.'

I am fat, but I'm not going to sit and argue about it in public. I hold the two-piece in my hands, frowning at the lack of tummy-control panel and how low cut it is. 'Hmm, I don't —'

'The colours are lovely,' Priya insists, talking over me. 'Very on-trend right now.'

'Are you sure?' I ask, although I know Priya is always sure and will persist until I give in. Still I can't help but think, 'maybe black is a safer bet.'

She sighs, rolls her eyes and grabs a black costume from a rail nearby. 'Let's get both, and you can decide when we finish. What's next?'

I tick swimwear off my list. 'I need a nice day dress. There's a nice one by the doors.' I turn to where the dress is and freeze. Someone walks into the shop, with tousled hair, neither brilliant blonde nor deep brown. I can hear my heart pound; it thumps so hard I bet Priya can hear it. It sends blood rushing up my body, it must do, because suddenly I feel faint.

But my heart starts to settle as the girl with the tousled hair looks up at something, and I see with relief it isn't Kylie. I couldn't face her, here, as I shop with Priya for holiday clothes. It's not betrayal, we're not friends, but it feels like it.

'Okay, lead the way then,' says Priya who didn't notice my near-heart-attack.

I walk to the dress and pick out my size, holding it against me. 'It's nice, right?'

'It's lovely.'

'Is it too short?' I ask, feeling doubtful, 'will I need tights? But will it be too hot for tights?'

'Alexa, you are over thinking this. Buy the dress, it's not too short. Take tights just in case. Take them off if it gets too hot. You have great legs.'

'You're right,' I say, in which I mean right about over thinking things, not the legs. 'I'll get it.'

'Good. Come on, my lunch break's nearly over.'

I look at the time. 'Shit. Let's head to the counter.'

On the way there, Priya nudges me, 'Do you need any lingerie?'

'I don't think so.'

'What about to wear in bed?'

'No, I have plenty of night wear. In fact, I bought a pair of short pyjamas last week.'

'I don't mean pyjamas. I mean something special for bed.'

'Why would I do that?'

'Don't you want to be able to go to bed, in Rome of all places, looking sexy?'

'I hadn't thought about it.' I stop by a selection of nightwear, which are sheer and delicate instead of my usual cotton ones.

'What about this one?' Priya picks up a tasteful semi-sheer black nightie, with lace edges.

'It's quite nice,' I say, uncertain. But time isn't on my side right now. I have to be back in the office in ten minutes. 'I'll take it.'

Priya smiles, she loves to win. 'You won't regret it'. We walk on to the counter.

At the counter, I go through my list. 'I think that's everything. I'll just need to pop to the chemist after work for travel-sized toiletries.'

'Use the hotel's stuff.'

'I guess I could.'

'Are you excited?'

'Yeah, it'll be nice.'

'Nice? Are you kidding? You're being taken to Rome by your boyfriend. It's more than nice.'

'It is, isn't it?'

'It's ridiculously good. Hold on to Shaun, he's one of the good ones. He's almost too good to be true.'

'What if he is, too good to be true?'

Priya ponders this for a second, and then shakes her head. 'No way, he's totally genuine. I've thought about this, actually, and could list at least ten different reasons why I think you two are a perfect match and meant to be. One, you met organically. It wasn't forced, through an awkward match up or blind date. Two, you went at your own pace, you didn't go on a date for ages and he didn't get bored or...'

I smile. Priya enjoys a good argument and loves backing up her opinions with facts. I enjoy countering her arguments, but I think I'll let her win this one.

Kylie

I'm in leggings, which have a small hole in the crotch but are so comfortable that I have resisted throwing them away, and a cosy long-sleeved top that I've dug thumb holes in over the years. And no, the top doesn't cover my bum nor the hole in my crotch. This isn't going out attire, but it's perfect for sitting crossed legged on my bed and listening to music, which is what I'm doing right now. I'm home alone and have nowhere to be. It feels a little lonely, but I'm trying to be at peace with it.

My phone lights up in the corner of my eye. Excited, I pick it up, only to see that it's Mum calling. Disappointed, I sigh and answer, 'Hi, Mum.' I have a feeling I'm not going to be at peace with anything by the end of this conversation.

'Kylie? I'm on the personal computer, and Robbie has showed me your profile on the Google,' she says with pride in her voice.

I stifle a laugh. Mum has always been hopeless with computers. She isn't even that old, not really. She's just stubborn and resists change, even refusing to get a mobile phone until just about everybody and their dog had one. 'Oh right that's cool,' I reply.

'I thought you'd want to know that it says you work at a bar. Have you been hacked? I've heard about people getting hacks. You can't click on those Google pages offering free things. Robbie told me that, after last time. Like always in life, if something sounds too good to be true that's because it probably is.'

'No, Mum, I haven't been hacked.'

'What do you mean?'

I sigh. It's time. Here I go. 'I got a new job, in a bar.'

Silence.

'I don't understand. You got a second job?'

'No. I replaced my existing job.'

'You quit a respectful, stable job to work in a bar?'

'It wasn't the job for me. That's all that needs to be said.'

More silence. Then muffled sounds. Possibly the sounds of Mum having a stroke or a my-daughter-quit-her-respectable-job induced aneurysm.

'Well, darling, I just don't know what to say. Did you at least leave your old job on good terms? You didn't burn any bridges did you?'

No, but I wouldn't mind setting Janine on fire. 'No I didn't, but it's irrelevant because I'm not going back. I'm happy, Mum.'

'You can't pay the bills with happy, Kylie.'

'I'm paying them just fine so far.'

'Well sure, while you rent a room in a house, but you can't rent a room forever and you can't work your way up in a bar job. This is completely irresponsible. What did Alexa say? She's a sensible girl, she can't have agreed to this.'

Alexa was understanding, and compassionate about what really happened with my job. In all my anger I had forgotten how good she was to me during that dark time. 'I didn't ask her permission... I can make my own decisions.'

'Look I've got to go, but please talk to Alexa about this: she's always helped you make good choices in the past. I just worry about you, darling, in a big city on your own.'

'It's true that I live in a big city full of strangers, crime happens daily, you don't know what's waiting around the corner...' or on the other side of a phone call, 'but I'll be fine. I like my new job, it pays enough, and I'm doing good.'

'Hmm, yes, well we'll see. Speak to you soon.'

I hang up. Why does every interaction with her leave me feeling so terrible? I could scream! Instead, I get up and pace around, trying to work off the pent up frustration that I feel. In the past, whenever I felt frustrated by Mum or anyone, I would turn to Alexa. Now I have no one, not even Lucie because she's out somewhere overnight. I sit down, defeated.

I just wish I had someone who would hold me and listen to me. For a crazy moment I yearn for Harry. And then I realise there's someone better who I can turn to.

Hey, can I come over?

Alexa

'Hi, er, buona sera... we have reservations? Alexa and Shaun Abbott.'

'Alexa Chapman, that is,' I add. He shoots me a puzzled look and I shrug apologetically. I'm being pedantic, but he made it sound like we share a surname and it was instinct to correct him.

We're given keys and I follow Shaun as he carries our bags up to the hotel room. At long last we've made it to Rome. I'm exhausted. So is Shaun, and I can carry my own bag but he insisted. He opens our hotel room and puts the bags down.

I walk in, tired and in need of a shower but neither of those factors are enough to distract from how beautiful this room is. It's full of character, save for a modern bed with brilliantly white sheets. It looks so clean! Usually, I don't like the idea of a hotel bed because of how many people sleep in it but this bed looks like it's brand new.

'So, what do you think?' he asks.

'It's stunning,'

'I agree. It's a beautiful room, looks just like the photos on the website.' He walks across to the window and looks out, 'It looks like it'll be a great view when it's daylight.'

'I can't wait to explore Rome.' I join him by the window, looking out at the darkened view 'thank you for bringing me here.'

'Thank you for coming with me.' He turns and kisses me against the backdrop of sleepy Rome. It feels magical. I might be tired from travelling but I feel exhilarated.

'Shall we go to bed?'

'You read my mind.' He kisses me again, putting his hands

on my waist.

'Is it okay if I freshen up first?' I break away from him. I know what he wants, but I really want to wash my face and get into clean pyjamas.

He smiles, 'Of course. Go and freshen up, I'll be waiting.'

The bathroom looks like it could be in an interior design magazine. I make a mental note to take pictures of it tomorrow, along with the rest of Rome. It's such a beautiful place to be. However, when I look in the mirror I see travelling has taken its toll. I rid my face of make-up, hoping I won't scare Shaun. We're still in that stage where we pretend we look perfect and smell nice every second of the day, but I don't want to smudge foundation and mascara all over the hotel bedding. It's a risk I feel I have to take. When I'm changed into pyjamas (the nice ones I picked up when I went shopping with Priya), I head out to find Shaun already in bed.

'You look beautiful,' he says. I blush. I'm not used to be being told I'm beautiful at all, let alone bare-faced and showing more flesh than I care to. He pats the bed and I know that's my cue to get in. I don't know if it's because I'm so tired, but it's the most comfortable bed I've ever lain in. He gestures me to lie in the nook of his arm and I do. As I lie there in Shaun's arms, I feel a rush of happiness and calm. For a moment, I can't remember the last time I was this happy. And then I remember, and feel a flood of guilt. I shuffle uncomfortably as it threatens to consume my body.

'What's wrong?'

'I just... I can't help but feel bad. That I'm so happy, when I made Kylie so sad and—'

'Don't be silly,' Shaun soothes.

'It's just weird how things turn out. I don't feel I deserve all of this.'

'Of course you do. Now, I don't want you to worry any more about Kylie or anything else while we're here. Let me look after you, okay?'

'Okay,' I say as I settle back down. Shaun strokes my hair as I succumb to tiredness.

Kylie

I knock on Jason's door and wait. But I don't have to wait for long and soon enough he opens the door. 'Come in,' he says quietly. I step into his house.

'It's dark in here,' I say as I look around. Although even in the darkness I can tell it's messy and dirty. I shiver in the open doorway, wondering if I should have come at all.

'Everyone's chilling in their bedrooms.' He gestures me in and shuts the door. 'Do you want a drink?'

'No thanks.'

'You seem quiet tonight.'

'Sorry.'

'Don't be sorry. Come on, we'll talk in my room.'

I follow him upstairs and into a bedroom. It's more cluttered than mine by miles, but not half as cosy. I sit on the unmade bed and Jason sits next to me.

'What's up then? You don't seem yourself at all.'

'My mum rang tonight,' I pick at the thumb-holes in my top, 'and I had to tell her that I've got a new job in a bar. She was horrified and disappointed. I'm used to disappointing her but... I fell out with my best friend recently. With Alexa by my side, not much bothered me. But now I have no one. I'm a disappointment and I'm a failure and I'm alone.'

I feel an arm drape around me. Jason pulls me closer. He smells slightly of body odour, but he's warm and I let him hold me.

'You're none of those things,' he says gently.

'I am. I'm twenty-five and I don't have a solid career or a boyfriend or even a friend. For once my mum's disappointment seems valid.'

'You'll find your feet. And in the meantime, you have me.'

'Jason…'

'Yeah?'

'Can I stay here tonight?'

'Of course.' He squeezes me tighter for reassurance.

I sigh with relief and start to relax. 'Thanks. I just need to be with someone.'

'I'll be here for you. Don't worry about a thing.'

I lie back against Jason and he holds me tight. It feels nice. We lie in the quiet.

'Will you stroke my hair?' I whisper.

'No. But I will fondle your boobs if that would help.'

'Goodnight, Jason.'

I close my eyes and try to sleep. Jason puts his hand on my waist, which feels a little too close to my boob region so I gently nudge him away and his hand settles on my arm. He plays with a few stray curls which I enjoy until his arm drops and I hear him begin to snore gently but it's rhythmic and rather nice. But just as I start to fall asleep, I'm jolted awake as Jason removes his arm from under me and rolls over. And then I lie in the dark, alone.

Alexa

I wake up alone, the space Shaun occupies is empty with the covers pushed away.

'Good morning, gorgeous,' I hear. I roll over and see Shaun standing there with a tray.

'Morning. I didn't hear you wake up.'

'I sneaked out quietly to order room service,' he says as he puts the tray down on the bed. An array of pastries, succulent fruit and aromatic Italian coffee. I've never seen anything more beautiful. This is the second day Shaun has woken me up with breakfast. I could get used to it, but tomorrow we're going back home and I'll be back to making myself muesli before work.

'I almost don't want to eat it. I'll ruin it.'

'It's there to be eaten, silly.' He kisses me on the head. 'Enjoy it; I'm just going to jump in the shower.'

I watch him go to the bathroom, hear the shower turn on and turn my attention to breakfast. I wasn't kidding about not wanting to eat it, it's magnificent looking. I take a photo of it with my phone and post it to social media, to preserve its memory. Some scoff at the notion of photographing good food, but in history people went to the trouble of making extravagant oil paintings of their food. I sip the coffee, which has a smooth taste unlike any coffee you'll find back home, and check social media. My old friend Clair from school comments that the breakfast looks heavenly. She also commented on a photo of me and Shaun at the Pantheon yesterday, saying what a perfect couple we are. Sarah agreed. I look at us standing together, side by side with Shaun's arm around me, and smile. We really do look like a perfect couple.

I put the coffee down and pick up a pastry as the shower turns off and Shaun steps into the room with a towel wrapped around his waist. Apparently I don't have to leave my hotel bed for a nice view.

'So where shall we go today?'

'I was thinking we could go to the Sistine chapel, and then maybe look around town and buy some souvenirs… if that's okay?'

'Of course it's okay, babe. I'll take you wherever you like.' He gets dressed while I finish my pastry and help myself to grapes.

'Can we get some Gelato?'

'Definitely.' He sits down next to me, takes a grape and looks at what I'm looking at, 'Hey I like that photo.'

'I like it too.'

'Can I send it to my mum?'

'Sure.'

'She's going to love it, you look beautiful.' He smiles at me, just like he's smiling in the photo. Maybe as well as looking like the perfect couple, we actually are one.

Kylie

I'm standing atop a pile of clothes, unsure of what to wear. Zara has invited me along with her on a night out and I should be setting off soon, only I'm still in my pyjamas. If I'm honest, I'm nervous. I love a good night out, but this won't be my idea of a night out. Zara will put her own cool, edgy spin on it.

With that in mind, I need to put a cool and edgy spin on my outfit. I wiggle into a black dress and nearly break my arm as I contort it around my back in order to zip it up. I'll never understand who thought it was a good idea for dresses to zip up at the back. I've decided to keep my hair wild and with a sweep or three of eyeliner, and one last look in the mirror, I'm ready.

It feels weird stepping out into the night, stone cold sober, dressed to the nines. Usually Alexa comes round and we have pre-drinks before walking side by side to town together.

When I reach work, where we're supposed to meet, Zara isn't there and I wonder if I should go in. It's a choice between that or standing outside alone. I go in. Oliver sees me and stands looking amused, like always. I hate that I can't read him.

'Kylie, damn, you scrub up well,' he says without a hint of sarcasm.

'Thanks, so do you,' I say without thinking and fumble to correct myself. 'I mean, you probably do. Erm, I'm just waiting for Zara.'

'She'll be late. She always is. Have a drink on me. White wine?'

His light-hearted dig isn't lost on me, 'Yes please. I can't afford to turn down a free drink.'

'So, where is Zara taking you tonight?'

'I have no idea. Do you?'

'Oh I'm guessing it will be somewhere unimaginably pretentious with music you've never heard before.' He passes me a glass of wine.

'Come on, she's not that bad.'

'Well, you can tell me all about it tomorrow on your shift.'

'I will.'

'You can tell me about all the men you've pulled.'

'I'm not going out to pull men!' I say, feeling my cheeks flush.

'Hey, it's not my business. Maybe you'll go to some hipster bar and see a guy across the room. You'll be taken aback by his man-bun. He'll come over and ask you how you feel about Palestine and you'll want to rip his plaid shirt off.'

'Shut up. I'm just going to have a nice night out with Zara. Nothing weird is going to happen. I'm not going to rip anyone's clothes off.'

'Rip whose clothes off?' asks Zara, who suddenly appears next to me.

'Oliver's. I can't get enough,' I say, smirking at Oliver. He shoots me side eyes and a hint of a smile and makes himself busy. Do I see a touch of embarrassment?

'Come on, let's go.' Zara sets off to leave and I down my drink and get up too. 'See ya, Ollie. Don't put any shit music on while we're away. I know you.'

'Have a good time, ladies.'

The air now feels cooler than when I was last outside and it contrasts with the warming alcohol inside me. I'm fixated on Zara's outfit, which is a crop top and short legged dungarees. Oh, and a black choker that I haven't seen the likes off since the early noughties. I'm not going to lie, the look wouldn't suit many people but she looks amazing from the tip of her Doc Martens to her hair while usually dyed grey, is an array of pastel colours and tied up in pigtail buns.

'Right then, shall we?' she asks.

'We shall.'

'Come on, I know the perfect place.'

The alleged perfect place is a small terrace building that has been transformed into a night club. It has an odd choice of décor for a club and it's dark and gloomy, lit only by candles and dim wall lamps. Zara tells me she will buy me a drink and I watch her go to the bar while I stand feeling thoroughly out of place. There isn't enough room to dance at all. People stand in corners huddled together looking like they're having serious conversations, and I have no idea what music is playing. I hate Oliver for being right.

'Here,' says Zara as she hands me a small glass of clear liquid. I take a sniff. Ugh. Vodka.

'Where's the mixer?' I ask, masking my horror.

'Mixers are empty calories.' She shrugs.

'Delicious calories,' I say. Delicious calories are the best kind of calories.

'They're full of sugar. Sugar's a carcinogenic you know.'

'Oh...' I don't think that's true, but I have no desire to get into scientific discussion. I have a desire to get drunk and dance.

'What do you think of this place?'

I think it's bizarre and a little intimidating. But I can't possibly say that. 'It's cool,' I say instead, 'what band is this that's playing?'

'The Violent Femmes.' She doesn't pause to think before answering.

'Ah, of course.' By which I mean, I have no idea who they are, of course.

'Come on, I've found some people I know. You'll like them.'

She takes me through another room that's even gloomier than the first, and up some stairs. It's quieter up here and I try to take it all in as I follow her, apparently out of the building onto a roofed terrace. The warm night air is cooled by the atmosphere up here.

'Zara,' says a solemn looking Goth upon seeing us.

'Blair, didn't know you'd be here.'

'I know. I don't usually come out on Fridays.'

'Oh, why's that?' I ask, trying to make conversation.

'It's far too predictable,' she says, looking sorry for me that I had to ask.

'This is Kylie. She's a friend from work.' She turns to me. 'This is Blair, Gus and Rudy.'

'Kylie?' asks Gus. 'Is that your actual name?'

'Yeah,' I reply. Oh, here we go, here comes the stifled laughter and references about how I should be so lucky.

'It's a great name.'

'Yeah,' agrees Rudy, 'it's like so basic but 90s basic, which actually makes it darling and retro now. It's future vintage.'

'I still can't believe the 90s was over twenty years ago,' says Zara.

'It's going to blow people's minds that we were born before the turn of the millennium.'

'Or before the death of Kurt Cobain,' Blair remarks. Everyone reacts. Except me.

'How old are you, Kylie?' asks Rudy.

'Erm, twenty-five,' I say, finishing my vodka. I need the buzz.

'I can't wait to be twenty-five,' says Gus.

'Me too,' agrees Rudy, 'it's thoroughly masochistic being twenty.'

'Oh yes,' says Gus, 'as a twenty-two-year-old, let me confirm it gets worse. The happiness of finishing education and feeling free is short lived until you realise that you're anything but free, but about to join the rat race.'

'I know what you mean. It's the boiling frog theory,' adds Blair.

'Totally,' says Gus as everyone nods in agreement.

'Anyway, we've monopolised you guys for long enough. I'm going to take Kylie to Hinge.'

We say goodbye, I smile and no one smiles back. We walk back through the rooms of sullen people, all standing motionless, listening to another song I don't recognise.

'God, it's great in there,' Zara says as we leave.

'It's not quite what I was expecting.'

'Good,' she says in all seriousness. 'There's nothing worse

than something ordinary.'

I don't have anything to say to this so instead I focus on keeping up with Zara. We walk past 'ordinary' party-goers and I wonder what awaits me next.

'What's The Hinge like?' I hope there's room to dance.

'Oh, it's not The Hinge, it's just Hinge. It's nice. It's chill but upbeat.'

I don't know how somewhere can be both chill and upbeat but I let her take me there to find out.

'I'll get the drinks,' I tell her when we arrive but immediately regret it. This place is weird. Even in the roughest clubs, with hen-parties and mean-looking men in polo tops, the atmosphere is never this hostile. It looks and feels like an outdated doctor's waiting room. Or a really eccentric wake. I need a drink. 'Vodka?'

'Yes. I'll be over there.'

'What do you have that's fruity and mainly sugar?' I ask the bored looking bartender. He looks both surprised and annoyed by my question.

'Sugar's a carcinogenic,' he replies.

Why do people keep saying this? I roll my eyes at him, 'Well I have to die eventually. Hopefully soon if people keep denying me sugar.'

I see a glint of amusement on his face at my comment, 'How about an Old Fashioned?'

'That and a Vodka please.'

I take the two drinks to Zara who's found two guys with man-buns to chat to. They look identical, down to the plaid shirts.

'Thanks, Ky.' She takes her drink. 'What have you got? An Old Fashioned? Ah very nice.'

'There's so much sugar in that you know,' says the man-bun next to her.

'So I've heard.' I knock the drink back. It's okay, no Cheeky Vimto, but okay. Could do with being sweeter.

'Sugar really is evil. One day we'll be sugar free and look back in horror at how much we consumed and how it ravaged our bodies. Like cigarettes.'

'I miss cigarettes.'

An upbeat song comes on. I don't recognise it but it's catchy and I feel the urge to dance. 'Zara, I love this song, let's dance!'

'No one comes to Hinge to dance, Ky.'

We stand and talk and don't dance until finally Zara leads me out. It's 11pm and I'm hoping it's a respectable time to call it quits.

'Onwards!' says Zara once we leave and are on the street.

'I'm so tired, had such an early start,' I add a fake yawn for good measure. 'I think I'm just going to grab some food and head home.'

'Oh? Yeah, let's get some food. I can't remember the last time I ate.'

We head back together until I come across my favourite take away.

'Here!' I say, 'let's get food here. I love this place.'

'Okay sure. Shall we share?'

'Yes! Do you want to go halves on cheesy chips? I absolutely love cheesy chips.'

'I'm vegan.'

'Really?'

'Yeah. I'm sorry, I just can't bear to hurt animals.'

'Oh, well... cheese is just made from cow's milk. I don't think it hurts them.'

'Cows are raped so they will have babies and produce milk. Then their calves are ripped away from them so we can steal the milk for our own frivolous consumption.'

'Really?'

'I'm afraid so. There are just things more important than personal enjoyment, you know? We can get plain chips, though.'

Plain chips? Just when I thought this night couldn't get any worse.

We walk home sharing a tray of plain chips. They're not as good as cheesy chips but they fill my stomach and soak up the booze and by the time we reach my street I'm practically sober again.

'Well, this is my place. I had a great time,' I lie. 'Do you want the chips?' I hold out the tray.

'No, take them. I'm full. Well, see you at work, Ky.'

She hugs me and I hug back, clutching my tray of cheese-less chips. As she turns to leave, I run into my house and ditch the chips in favour of sugary, evil, carcinogenic snacks from my cupboard, which I take to the sofa and curl up watching telly. Well, that was a night out with Zara. It was strange, underwhelming and not what I'm used to. We're just a little too different I guess. Zara lives in a world where chocolate and cheese are evil and dancing is forbidden. It was kind of a buzz kill.

I should just go to bed seeing as no one is staying over but I'm always drawn to the sofa after a night out, although it feels like something's missing. I fill the void with chocolate digestives and switch on my laptop to check social media. Boring, boring, boring, oh and a nice selfie that Zara took with me earlier. Wait. I've just scrolled past a photo of Alexa, and that guy. I scroll back up, my nosey nature getting the better of me. Apparently they're in Rome. She looks gorgeous and thinner than ever. Her boyfriend looks nice. They're standing outside some impressive looking building, arms around each other, smiling. They look happy.

Alexa

Rome was a dream come true. But now it's back to reality with a rude awakening. No one covered for me while I was in Italy and even though I only missed two days of work, the backlog that sits before me on my desk is unbelievable. I try not to think about how at this time yesterday I was in a beautiful hotel room eating pastries and drinking Italian coffee. Instead, I drink staff-room coffee while replying to an email from an odious client of John's. I need to put my assertive cap on this morning.

'Morning, Chapman.' My boss pops his head into my office.

'Good morning, John.'

'How was Rome?'

'It was great.'

'I'll bet.' With a nod and a smile he leaves, which is good because I'm not in the mood to chat after a whole long weekend with Shaun. I need a break to get over my break.

But alas, I have work to do, lots of it. I type up the assertive email and send it, hoping for minimal backlash and press play on the answering machine. I take notes as I finish my coffee. There's several phone calls I have to make today, but it can wait until I tackle this mountain of paperwork. Most of it will be pretty straight forward and if I keep a good pace I can get it all done today.

Suddenly, Emma bursts into my office, 'Alexandra!'

Oh no. 'Hi, Emma.' I force a weak smile and try to carry on.

She walks in and sits down at the chair opposite my desk. 'I hadn't seen you in the staff kitchen recently, so I asked Joanne where you were and she said John said you had gone on a mini-break. Rome, I heard. Is that right?'

'Oh, yeah. I went away with my boyfriend.'

'I bet it was wonderful! I brought you coffee, I thought you might be needing one.' She puts the coffee mug down on the table, without a coaster.

'Thank you,' I say, trying my best to ignore the lack of coaster.

'Which landmark was the best? The Colosseum or the Pantheon? Oh, it's got to be the Sistine Chapel, right?'

'Hard to say, they were all beautiful.'

'Yes I saw a photograph online. You and Shaun look the perfect couple.'

I nod, smile and carry on working. I don't mean to be rude, but I really need to get on with it.

To my relief she stands. 'Well, I better go. Are you free after work for a catch up?'

'Oh, I'm not sure. I'm very jet-lagged.' But also I'm dying to go home and unwind.

'Nonsense, you can spare me one drink. I'm dying to know all the details.'

Absolutely not, sorry, not tonight, I think. But then I remember what Shaun said about making new friends. So instead I put on a smile, 'That sounds nice. I'll let you know if I feel up to it.'

She puts a coffee on my desk. 'I'll pop by later, just in case.'

I take the coffee and put it on a coaster, finally. Emma leaves and I set to working again but before the door even shuts, it opens. I'm about to get annoyed but then see it's my boss. 'Chapman, I know you're swamped right now, but I need this by lunch time.' He hands me a wad of papers.

I groan and take the papers, 'Okay no problem.'

'I know, it's a big ask with you already being busy, but my hands are tied. It's the price you pay for getting whisked away on holiday. Lucky.'

'It's okay. I'll have these done by lunch.'

'I know you will.'

This is the last thing I need. I put the answering machine

notes to one side, and the backlog of paperwork to the other side, of my desk and get started on my new task. I'm walled in by paperwork. I'm drowning. It can't get any worse.

Then the phone rings, and it's Amy, Shaun's sister. Will it ever end? 'Hello?'

'Hi, Alexa, it's a bit cheeky to call at work but I just wanted to say welcome back!'

'Thank you, Amy.'

'Did you have an amazing time?'

'Oh yeah, Rome was great.' Apparently that's the only adjective I know today.

'I bet. I looked online but you've only posted one or two photographs. Can you email me them when you have a chance? Before lunch preferably. I'm dying of boredom.'

I sigh. I have a thousand things to do before lunch, which I'll be eating at my desk while I work. I have better things to do than to show you photos where I'm smiling and pretending to enjoy Italy. I should say, instead of, 'I'll try, although I'm so busy this morning.'

'Oh, please? Can't you make an exception for a heavily pregnant and very hormonal woman?'

'…Yes.' I say in defeat, looking around for that assertive cap. I could use it right about now.

Kylie

I'm finally in a good rhythm at work. I know what I'm doing, nothing surprises me. It would be easy to feel complacent but Oliver, Zara and my other colleagues keep me in good spirits. I don't know what it is… maybe it's that I haven't messed up an order today, or that it's pay day tomorrow, or that I'm comfortably wearing my skinniest jeans, but I feel great.

'Kylie, it's getting busy out there. Can you do the stock check later and go help Zara?'

'Sure.' I put down the clipboard and head out to the bar. Oh no. Well, I was feeling great until the bloody ghost of Christmas past decided to show up. It's Harry. Shit. I freeze as I watch him walk towards the bar. He hasn't seen me but I see him and God he's more gorgeous than ever. I can't be here. I can't serve him.

I back out of the bar into the store room. The air feels thick in here and suddenly I can't breathe, but have nowhere else to go. I can't go back out there and serve the guy who I gave everything to, the very one who decided I wasn't good enough for him.

'Kylie?' I jump as Oliver speaks. 'Didn't I ask you to go help Zara?' he asks.

'You did. Sorry, I'm just looking for something.'

'What are you looking for?'

'Erm,' I stall. What am I looking for? My dignity? 'We're all out of napkins.'

Sometimes I feel he can see into my soul. Especially when he looks at me like he is now. He keeps looking and then he frowns, 'you're hiding'.

There's no point pretending with Oliver, 'I am.'

'Why? Who from?'

I peep out of the doorway and check to see where Harry is. He's standing at the bar. I gesture Oliver closer and whisper to him, 'you see that guy out there? I'm hiding from him.'

'Why? Do you owe him money?'

'Is that really what you think of me?'

He looks amused, and goes to say something but then stops for some reason and instead says, 'Why are you hiding?'

'He's my ex. Well, he's kind of my ex. We were dating. Then out of nowhere he ditched me, said I wasn't the type of girl he saw himself with. If he sees me behind this bar... it's just...'

'It's just that... you think your new job is a step down from your old one?'

'Well... technically, I guess. I mean, I'm happier now. I love my job.'

'I didn't have you down as someone who cares what people think.' He looks disappointed and it bothers me.

I look down in embarrassment and shame. 'Well, I guess I do... I'm sorry.'

'Don't be sorry. And don't be ashamed of your life. Especially not to him. If you ask me, you should paint on a smile, go out there, serve him a drink and hold your head up high.'

'You think?'

'Yes. And when you pass him his drink, lean over a little and remind him of what he let go.'

I nod my head after Oliver's little pep-talk. 'You're right. I'm going out.'

Before I can talk myself out of it, I let my feet carry me to the bar.

'What can I get you?' I ask Harry, acting like I don't recognise him, which is hard. I want to reach over and punch him, and then rip his clothes off. It's very conflicting.

'Hey, can I get a...' He stops, looking stunned and confused, 'Kylie?'

I try to act casual, and a little bored. 'Yes? Sorry can you order quickly, there's a queue.'

He looks behind him, and sees there's no one waiting to be served. 'Scotch on the rocks please.'

I go to prepare his drink and see Oliver from inside the stock room. He nods encouragingly and pushes his shoulders in. I stand taller and accentuate my chest. I've got this. When I pass Harry his drink, I lean over and linger. He looks, I know he does. 'Anything else?'

'That's it for now.' He hands me cash.

'Until some poor girl comes by and then you'll be buying her a drink,' I mumble to myself.

'What was that?'

'What? Oh, nothing.'

He stays at the bar and I serve customers. I feel his eyes burn into the back of me as I try to pretend I'm not bothered he's there. It's distracting but I need to keep my cool.

'So, I'm glad you got a new job,' he says suddenly to me.

No thanks to you, 'Mmhmm.'

'It suits you.'

'What does that mean?'

'Just, you look happy. That's all.'

'I am happy. Now.'

'Good…' He downs his drink and sits shaking the glass, letting the ice cubes clash against each other. Suddenly he looks serious, 'look I'm sorry about what happened between you and me.'

'It's forgiven. Forgotten.'

'That's real cool of you, Kylie.'

'I'm sorry about what happened between you and me too.'

'Oh yeah?'

'Yeah. I'm sorry I degraded myself to being one of your bar-victims, and falling for your charm.'

'Kylie!' shouts Oliver from the store room, 'I need you.'

That's my cue. I leave Harry stunned and speechless and leave the bar, feeling victorious.

'I did it!' I tell Oliver.

'You did. And damn, remind me not to break your heart.'

'Did I do well?' I feel elated and giddy, full to bursting with adrenaline.

'You did. You did yourself proud.'

'I did, didn't I? Right I'm going back out.'

'Stay here for a few minutes. You don't want to over-do it.'

'Okay.'

Oliver sits on a crate and pats the space next to him.

'There's nothing wrong with working in a bar, you know.'

'Oh, I know. I'm sorry, I didn't mean to offend you. I love working here.'

'That's okay.'

'Have you always worked in bars?'

'Pretty much. My real passion is art but there's no money in it unless you're lucky. These days people expect artists to pay the bills with exposure. I started working in a bar during uni but I hated the manager and then I moved to a different bar but I had trouble with the manager again. When I graduated in Fine Art, my family expected me to make a career out of it but I knew all along it would be unlikely. So, when I could I bought my own bar. It meant I could have excellent management, aka myself, and a career.'

'When did you finally get your own bar?'

'Three years ago. I was twenty-seven.'

I wonder if in two years I will have done anything half as impressive? Probably, definitely, not. 'That's incredible,' I say, 'you're incredible.'

He smiles and looks bashful, 'Well, you're not so bad yourself, Kylie. Now get back to work.'

When I enter the bar again, Harry is still there and… I don't believe it! He's actually chatting up a woman. Right in front of my eyes. He's offering her a drink and I go over to serve him, feeling amused.

'What can I get you and your latest bar-victim?'

'I'm sorry, who are you?' asks his victim, with a look of confusion.

'A survivor. What can I get you two?'

'Actually, can we be served by somebody else?' asks Harry, looking uncomfortable. I'm ruining his game plan. My heart bleeds for him.

'Sure,' I say with as much nonchalance as I can fake. On the inside, I'm screaming at my own audacity. 'Zara!' I call.

Zara comes from the other side of the bar. 'Yes?'

'Customers for you.'

I give Harry one last smirk and move to the other side of the bar. I've never understood the need for closure before, but that interaction with Harry made me so satisfied. Before long, Zara comes up to me, 'What was that about?' she asks, 'who's the Suit?'

I glance at him again, drinking a Scotch on the rocks, sitting next to a woman who has no idea what's about to hit her. I feel sorry for her, and I feel sad for him. This is all he has. It feels like I'm seeing him with fresh eyes, and it's eye opening. 'Nobody worth bothering over.'

Alexa

I got in from work an hour ago, and I'm still waiting for Shaun to ring. He usually has by now. Priya is working late tonight, so I'm home alone. Fed up, I pick up the phone and call him.

'Hello?'

'Shaun? It's me, Alexa.'

'Oh, hey. How's it going?'

'It's going good… I thought you were going to call me.'

'Sorry. I forgot. What are you up to?'

'Not much. Priya's not in until later.'

'Well come over if you want.'

'Yeah?'

'Of course. I'll see you soon, babe.'

'Okay, I'll make my way over.' I hang up, finish my cup of tea and head over to Shaun's place.

When I get to his apartment, the door is locked and I must buzz three times before he answers. He greets me at the door in jogging bottoms and an old top, 'Hey beautiful, come in.'

I follow him into the apartment and make myself comfortable. Football is on. He gives me a quick kiss and continues watching the game. It's clear he doesn't want me to interrupt. I suppose we're at that point where we're comfortable enough in each other's company not to have to make a special effort, and I guess that's a good thing. Or at least it would be, if it didn't mean I have to watch digital men run around a digital football pitch. How can he do this over and over?

'Do you play football?' I ask. I can't believe I don't know the answer to that.

'What, like for real?'

'Yeah just as a hobby or something.'
'Not really, not anymore.'
'Do you wish you did?'
'Nah, I'm too busy really.'
'You're not busy now.'
'I beg to differ.' He looks at me, smiles and pats my thigh. 'Besides, this way I can do it with you right next to me.'

We're sitting on his black leather sofa, side by side. He returns his gaze to the television and I'm back to being ignored. I remember the first time I came to his place and sat here, full of butterflies and anticipation. Now I'm full of chicken korma and boredom. I get up and walk around for something to do. Upon inspection, Shaun's living room isn't as clean as I had thought. Dust lines photo frames, magazines lay crumpled on the floor beside the sofa and the waste-paper bin's overflowing with empty crisp packets and chocolate bar wrappers.

'Where's your cleaning stuff?'
'What? Oh, in the kitchen under the sink.'

I head to the kitchen, noticing a photo of us from Italy stuck on his fridge and find the cleaning supplies. I'm going to clean every inch of this house, and maybe then he'll be done with his game and we can have some quality time together. I'm going to start with something that's been bugging me the whole time I've known Shaun and that's his hallway mirror. I make my way to the hallway. I wipe down the mirror and arrange letters to sit neatly on the side table by the door. The side table has drawers. I look inside, curiosity getting the better of me, and find nothing. Not one thing. That's odd. Maybe it's because I only have one room but I utilise every drawer and every nook and cranny available. Come to think of it, a lot of Shaun's flat is empty. The cloak cupboard has two coats and an old vacuum cleaner, most of the kitchen cupboards are empty and his bedroom has only basic furniture. I open the bedroom windows to let in some fresh air, smooth down the curtains and dust the tops of his drawers. Suddenly, there's a tap on my shoulder. I jump out of my skin and make a noise that sounds like a pig being stepped on.

'Sorry, I didn't mean to scare you.'

'Oh, you didn't. I was just in a world of my own.'

'Oh yeah? Are you having fun?' He looks amused and it's then I realise how sad I might seem, cleaning for pleasure.

I cringe at him, feeling silly 'Yes. Is that bad?'

'No, it's not bad. I'm sorry I've been leaving you out. I'll switch off the game.'

'It's okay, carry on. At least until I finish.'

'If you're sure?' he asks, and I nod, 'okay then.'

As he heads out of the room I say, 'You have so much space you know. I wish I had all this room.'

'Yeah, I know. I chose this flat for the space but I've never quite managed to fill it. You should fill it.'

I was hoping he'd say that. My mind starts flooding with all the online browsing I'm going to be doing later. 'Oh yeah? I'll gladly help you pick out some bits. Some soft furnishings maybe.' And some fairy lights for over the bed! No, he'd never agree to that.

'No,' he says, putting a stop to my thoughts of shopping. 'What I mean is, you should fill it. You.'

'Me?'

'You said it yourself, you wish you had all this room. So have it, and move in with me.'

'Oh, I mean that's such a nice gesture. I don't know what to say.'

'Say yes. Oh, and have you eaten?'

'No…'

'Neither have I. Do you think you could put something together for us?'

'Sure.'

'Cheers, babe.' He leaves and I stand in his room in a state of disbelief, clutching a spray bottle and a cloth and trying to process what just happened. When I said I wish I had all this room, I didn't exactly mean I wish I could move in with Shaun. I don't know what to do. It's all a little overwhelming for a Wednesday evening. I put the spray bottle down, and head to the kitchen to make dinner.

Kylie

Does anyone else get overwhelmed shopping for food? I go in with good intentions, but come out with ready meals, a multi-pack of crisps and a sense of shame. This results in having nothing substantial in and having to run to the corner shop at the last minute for an essential item.

I used to go with Alexa when possible and she always guided me. If she was here I wouldn't be halfway through the aisles with just a frozen lasagne, three packs of bacon because they were buy-two-get-one-free and a bag of oranges that I won't eat anyway because I don't like oranges. I bought them because I have a cold coming on and I was hoping maybe somehow the vitamin C will permeate the room and be absorbed by myself. Anything is worth a try to keep the sneezing at bay. Which reminds me, I need tissues.

I find the tissues and spot a box saying 'man-sized' on them. Man-sized? What the hell does that mean? I pick the tissue box up and place them in my basket with defiance. You don't get to tell me what to do, tissue box! I'll enjoy blowing my woman-sized nose on them later. That'll show them.

'Kylie!' someone calls. I look around and spot a green-haired Zara.

'Oh hey,' I say, 'small world.'

'Yes, of all the eight billion people in the world, here we are bumping into each other.'

I never quite know how to take Zara, so instead I smile and take a moment to appreciate her outfit. It's a strange choice of attire with high-waisted jean-shorts and a jumper that looks like something my nan would knit, tucked in.

'I'm just getting some food in,' I tell her, as if it wasn't obvious from the fact I'm in a supermarket carrying a basket of food.

'Oh, that's cool.' I see her quickly glance at my basket. Is that horror on her face? Oh right, she's a vegan. It'll be the bacon she's recoiling from. And the lasagne.

'I don't usually shop here. With my diet being plant-based and me preferring organic, I try to stick to local grocers. But I'm staying at Oliver's tonight and I can't not have cashew milk in my morning coffee. So here I am.' She gestures to the cashew milk in her basket.

'Oliver's?' I spit out, my heart sinking.

'Yeah, he's the guy I met last week at that gig, the one I told you about. Don't you remember?'

I scan my memory for mention of an Oliver, and then with relief I remember she did tell me about meeting a guy called Oliver. 'Oh, of course. Cool.'

'Wait,' she says, laughing, 'did you think I meant Oliver at work?'

'I did for a second...' and may we never talk about it again.

She laughs some more, 'Can you imagine?'

I can. That's the worst part. 'I'd really rather not,' I lie.

'Me either! Fuck, that's funny. Anyway, I better be going. See you tomorrow.'

We're on shift tomorrow evening. 'Seven pm, it's a date.'

She sets off walking and then stops, 'You know, processed meat takes years off your life. Not just that, but cows are actually really smart. I don't want to lecture you, so I'll message the names of some great documentaries. Okay?'

'Oh, okay. Sure.'

She leaves and I set off down the chocolate aisle, picking up five chocolate bars and two packets of biscuits along the way as I head for the checkout. I leave with the shame that I once again bought nothing of substance, that I'm apparently taking years off my life, that cows are smart and that for a moment I was worried Zara was seeing Oliver. It was much easier when I went shopping with Alexa.

Alexa

I shuffle my way into the passenger seat of Shaun's car, holding a gift basket wrapped in clear polystyrene tied with a large pink bow.

'You didn't have to go to all this trouble, babies don't need gifts you know.'

'It's expected to bring a gift when visiting a newborn.' I say, frantically tugging at the seat belt because he's already started the car.

'I know but you could have bought it a teddy bear or something.'

'Well I did buy *her* a teddy bear, as well as a few other things and something for Amy.'

He drives on without a further response.

'How long do you think we'll be here?' I ask.

'Not long. Do you want to come back to mine after?'

'Sure.'

We come to a stop outside his sister's house and he gets out of the car, making his way to the door whilst I struggle alone with the gift basket.

'By the way, my parents are inside,' he says as I catch up with him at the doorstep.

'What?!' I'm not appropriately dressed. I completely dressed down today as I thought we were briefly stopping in to congratulate his sister who will almost definitely be in her pyjamas.

The door opens, with his mum on the other side. 'Shaun!' she embraces him and kisses him on the cheek. 'Come in, come in, the baby is beautiful! Oh hi, Alexa, lovely to see you again.'

'Lovely to see you again too, Mrs Abbott.'

'Oh please, call me Gillian.'

I trail behind Shaun and Gillian with the gift basket to the room where Amy sits, not in pyjamas as I thought, but looking as polished as the first time I saw her. She cradles the baby in her arms.

'Hey, sis, congratulations. Let's have a look at her then.' Shaun peers over the baby. 'She looks just like Dad.'

Amy shoots him daggers, 'Shut up, you. She's beautiful.'

'I'm only kidding. Anyway, what did you call her?'

'Amelia,' says Amy. She looks down at the baby and sighs blissfully. 'Little Amelia Rose.'

'It's beautiful name. I've brought a few gifts for you and Amelia.' I gently place the basket beside Amy, scared to startle the baby.

'That's so kind of you, thank you.'

'Yeah, just a few things from us,' lies Shaun, who smiles at me without shame.

'Thanks, Shaun. It all looks so nice.'

We sit, with tea, and cake with pink icing and watch baby Amelia. Amy tells us all about what it's really like giving birth, which was something that up until now I was blissfully unaware of. I had it down as a beautiful moment like it's portrayed on television; an inconvenient passing of water followed by a few huffs and puffs before a baby appears. As it turns out, that's not the case. A beautiful moment, it is not.

'But it's remarkable all the same,' says Amy, 'I wouldn't take any of it back. Not the pain nor the stitches. It brought me Amelia.'

'You're a trooper, sis.'

'Yeah, Amy, you've done so well. She's lovely.'

She gets up and puts Amelia down in her Moses basket. 'She's asleep. Shall we go and talk in the kitchen? I don't want her disturbed.'

Once we're all in the kitchen, Shaun shuts the door and clears his throat. 'Now that the baby talk is over, everyone, we have an announcement.' He walks over to me, putting his arm around me.

'Oh my God, you're pregnant!' says Gillian.

'No, I'm not!' I want to say, but instead the words won't come. Paralysed with fear, I stare up at Shaun wide-eyed, looking for help. What is he doing?

'No, it's not that. Alexa's moving in with me.'

Suddenly, Amy and Gillian are hugging me and congratulating me and 'welcoming' me to the family. I think I'm nodding and smiling, but I'm not certain. I'm also not certain I agreed to move in with him.

'Well, that's quite the surprise, Shaun. But a good one, you two are great together. I think this calls for another cup of tea.' Gillian collects everyone's cups. Just then, Amelia starts to cry.

'Brilliant,' sighs Amy, 'excuse me.' She makes her way to the other room.

'Babies are so needy,' jokes Shaun.

'You have it all to come one day.' Amy turns to me, 'do you want kids, Alexa?'

I can feel everyone's eyes on me. 'Yes…' I begin, 'maybe, I don't know!' What a question to ask. 'One day, I suppose.'

She smiles, looking relieved. 'Shaun has always wanted kids, haven't you, Shaun?'

'What? I guess so.'

'He has,' says Amy, coming back into the room. 'He even told me I couldn't use the name Lily.'

'That was a long time ago.' Shaun glares at his sister.

'What about you, Alexa?' she asks, 'what names do you like?'

'Oh I don't know. Nothing too common I don't think. No obvious celebrity names either. Kylie would never forgive me.'

'Kylie?'

'My friend. Well…' No, better not get into that. Why did I even mention Kylie? It just came out. 'She hates being named after a celebrity, that's all.'

'So, nothing too common and no obvious celebrity names. That's a tough one. As long as it's not too weird, like Apple or something.'

Everyone laughs.

'It's good enough for Chris and Gwyneth.'

'Who?' Gillian asks and then scoffs. 'Oh, the Coldplay guy. Terrible band. I don't know which is worse, the band or the name Apple.'

Everyone laughs again. I smile, aware that everyone's attention is still on me. Help.

'Don't worry, Alexa, we're getting ahead of ourselves anyway. Shaun has got to pop the question yet.'

'And on that overbearing note, we really have to go.' Shaun gives me an apologetic look before saying his goodbyes. 'It was nice seeing you, sis, and little Amelia.' He hugs his sister and kisses the baby before leaving. I follow him, relieved. It was getting a bit claustrophobic.

The door shuts and Shaun lets out a sigh. 'Jesus, I'm so sorry. My family can be a nightmare at times.'

'That's okay, they were fine.'

'They weren't, they were unbearable.'

'It was a bit much,' I admit. 'The baby naming stuff made me a bit uncomfortable.'

'Did it?' he asks, but walks ahead of me to the car without waiting for my response. I follow him and we set off for his.

It's been a good while and we still haven't spoken to each other. I glance at him and find him watching the road, which is good, but there's a look on his face that's not so good. He looks tense, annoyed. I wonder if it's something I've done or the encounter with his family.

As he opens the door of his apartment, I dare to break the silence, 'What shall we order then for dinner?'

'Oh anything,' he says as he kicks off his shoes and goes into the living room, 'just not pizza'.

'Chinese?'

'Yeah, whatever.' He walks to switch the telly on, turning it over to the football and sitting down on the sofa.

This isn't really how I imagined spending my Saturday night.

'Or I could just go home?' I offer.

'What? What do you mean?'

'Well, you just don't really seem like you're in the mood

for company. I don't mind going home.'

He looks at me properly, for the first time today. 'No, stay. I'm sorry. Don't go home. Besides, I want you to start thinking of this as your home.' He takes my hands in his and looks at me again with his puppy dog eyes. I'm a sucker for that look.

I sit down next to him, 'Only if we don't have to watch football all night.'

He smiles, 'Okay. Order a take-away, anything you want, and we'll choose a film.'

'Shaun…'

'Yes?'

'I like the name Lily.'

'Oh yeah?' He pulls me in, wrapping his arms around me.

'Or maybe something a little less commonly used like Lola.'

'Just not Apple.'

'Nothing fruit-based.'

'Agreed.'

Kylie

It's 2am and I'm sneaking in my front door so as not to wake up Lucie. It's something I'm not very good at, my late great grandma once described me as having 'all the grace of an elephant'. But it's so late that I have to try, not just for courtesy but she'll kill me if I wake her. She might be seven stone wet through but Lucie has a wrath unrivalled when her solid eight-hour sleep is interrupted. I tip-toe in on tired feet, but as I pull my boots off and wriggle my freshly liberated toes, they feel a little better. The last hurdle is climbing the stairs to the finish line that is my bedroom door. Each step feels laborious but I make it and fall into bed. Finally, I can relax.

I need to get undressed and changed for bed, at least pull my jeans off. After a few minutes willing myself to move, I do, promising myself that the moment I'm done I can get back into bed. Finishing so late means I'm hungry but it's not really an appropriate time to eat, or cook. Once again my stash of snacks comes in handy.

I munch a biscuit in the glow of my lamp and can hear every chew. It's like everyone in the city is asleep except me. It's that curious time of night, what's it called? The witching hour? That mysterious time separating night and day. Actually for me, it's when I feel most alert and I've always been a night owl, however, there's nothing to do at 2am. I used to get home after working at the office in the evening and my night would consist of talking to Alexa on the phone, making dinner and winding down with some Netflix. But now my life is made up of different things. My job dominates my life, which is fine because I actually enjoy working now. But it's times like these, when I'm not distracted with work, that I realise I wish I had someone to hear how my day went and to put their arm around me when I need support.

But there's no way of meeting men. Harry has put me off picking men up in clubs and the dating app was a terrible waste of time. In fact, I lost more than time, I lost a little faith in humanity. Other than that, I don't know how anyone would even come across potential dates. I can't exactly date customers at work and I can't date Oliver, partly because he's out of my league and partly because he's so annoying with his wry smile and his bizarre sense of humour and the fact he's always right. He drives me crazy. Although right now, crazy would be better than utter boredom and loneliness. But no, I can't message Oliver. But maybe…

Inspiration hits me. I finish my biscuit, pick up my phone and type out *Are you awake?*

Only just. What's up? replies Jason.

Nothing. I've just got in from work. Feeling a little lonely. Over-thinking things.

What kind of things?

It feels embarrassing to admit. *How I come home from work, to be alone.*

It's not so bad being alone. There's less drama, and you don't have to share your food. But if you want someone, I'll be that someone, babe.

Goodnight, Jason.

But I don't just want someone, anyone. I wish I did; life would be easier if he could fill this void. I put my phone on the bedside table and pull the duvet tight over me. He's right that being alone means less drama and not having to share your food, but drama is passion and passion means you care, and sharing food is a great diet aid. Some things are just better done with someone by your side to do them with.

Alexa

The door knocks and I can tell from the knock itself that it's Shaun.

'Come in.'

The door opens and there he is, looking excited to see me. He walks slowly, clutching my laptop bag and carefully places it on my desk. I try not to laugh, but his level of respect for my laptop is as funny as it is endearing. 'Is everything okay with it?'

'This is one of the tidiest laptops I've seen,' says Shaun sounding impressed. He sits down on the other side of my desk.

'I thought so; I generally keep on top of it but I just wanted your expert opinion.'

'Well, in my expert opinion, it's perfect; like you.'

'Can I get you a coffee?'

'I have to be with a client in ten minutes.'

'Okay, well that's good actually because I'm really busy. I've been waiting on getting this laptop back.' I take the laptop out of its bag and switch it on.

Shaun stands and leans over to kiss me, but as he does I let out a gasp of horror.

'What's up?!'

'You've... changed everything.' I try to push down the panic in my voice.

Shaun looks puzzled and reaches to see the screen, 'I've just rearranged your desktop files so they look better. What's the problem?'

'You've changed the background.'

'Well it was just an old one of you and that girl.'

'Kylie.'

'Yeah, Kylie. And I thought a photo of us would be better, no? But nothing's really changed.'

'Right, I suppose not.' But everything has changed. A knot gathers in my stomach as Shaun's face stares back at me, where Kylie's once was.

'Anyway, I've got to go, babe.' He leans in again and kisses my cheek. I watch him leave and try to avoid looking at my laptop. I need a coffee.

'Alexandra! Glad I've caught you,' says Emma as I walk into the staff kitchen.

'Oh?' I ask, grabbing my mug from the cupboard and selecting cappuccino from the coffee machine. The machine moans and groans and I urge it to hurry up.

'This is Louise, the one I was telling you about.'

Any mention of Louise is drawing a blank in my memory. When I turn and see Louise, I still have no idea who she is. 'Oh, of course, hi, Louise.'

'Hi, Alexandra. You're John's assistant, right?'

'I am.' I smile and will the coffee machine to work faster. I can smell the dreaded small-talk coming. When my coffee is good to go, I make a run for it. 'Anyway, I was only here to —'

But Emma stops me in my tracks by standing in front of me. 'So, like I told you before, Louise runs beauty parties and they're amazing.'

'That's right,' says Louise, 'it's just a little side job mostly because the freebies are excellent and also to get out of the house away from Richard and the baby and have a bit of "me" time. I come to your house, do demonstrations, give out samples, that kind of thing.'

'It sounds brilliant, doesn't it, Alexandra?' gushes Emma.

'It really does,' although I'm very particular about my make-up, 'but actually I was—'

'So, I was saying to Louise you'd probably be up for a party at your place. Louise has spaces next month if you're interested?'

'Oh, well, it sounds really nice...' I pause while I try to think of an acceptable way to turn them down.

'Brilliant! Louise, when are you free?'

'What I mean is, is it sounds really nice, but I don't know where I'll be next month.'

Emma frowns, 'What do you mean?'

'Well it's just, I might be moving in with Shaun.' Even after a week to digest the idea, I still feel uneasy about it, especially saying it out loud. The words feel reluctant to come out and I kind of resent Emma for making me have to say them.

She clutches my arm excitedly, 'Oh my God! That's amazing! Did he ask you? Is his place nice?'

'Er yeah he did ask me and his place isn't bad at all.' I wriggle free from her grasp.

'Oh, but you can make it better. You'll be able to decorate. Is it a house? Does he own it?'

'An apartment, but yes he does own it.'

'Brilliant! The world's your oyster! You'll be able to totally transform it!'

'I guess...' I say, rubbing my shoulder and thinking about the possibilities. I never considered I'd be able to decorate an entire apartment.

'Well, when you're settled in we'll organise a beauty party. You can send Shaun out for the night and tell him you're having the girls over.'

'I don't really have any girl friends...' I say, thinking out loud. 'Oh! Except you, of course. And Priya,' I carry on, worried I've offended Emma, 'and possibly a few old university friends...'

'Well, now you have Louise and, oh look, here comes Alice and Victoria. Ladies! Come and meet Alexandra she's new on this floor. She's having a beauty party next month, if you're interested.'

I watch the door longingly as Emma tells Louise, Alice, Victoria and two other women I don't recognise all about my weekend in Rome with Shaun.

'Oh, Ryan hasn't taken me on a long weekend in forever. It's just not a priority when you've been married for this long.'

'Yes well, it's always on the cards, isn't it? But then the car breaks down or the boiler packs in.'

'How old are you, Alexandra?'

'She's twenty-five.'

'How young! To be twenty-five again…'

'Don't be fooled, Michelle; Alexandra's an old soul.'

'Most twenty-five-year olds still act like teenagers these days!'

'Not Alexandra.'

'I always see girls in their mid-twenties coming home from nights out together, stumbling down the street in a state of undress. It's appalling.'

'Well, I hope they enjoy their fun while it lasts. They won't be able to get away with crop tops and take-away forever. One day they'll wake up and they'll be thirty and overweight and all the good men will have been taken.'

'At least you don't have to worry about that, Alexandra,' Emma says to me. I'm surprised I'm even a part of this conversation with how they're all talking like I'm not here. Although I do wish I wasn't. I continue to watch the doorway longingly.

'Oh yeah,' agrees Victoria, 'you've already found your man. How lucky. You don't need to dress up like that and go out on the town hoping some man will rub up against you.'

'Nope. Now you can spend time with your man or just come out with us.'

The women talk around me, planning my future. I drink my coffee and admit defeat. This is my life now, and it's fine, it's fun even. But going out, getting drunk, dancing and stumbling home with a tray of cheesy chips was also fun. Will I never do that again? So much is changing. And another thing that's changing is where I get my coffee from in future.

Kylie

'But what about the proletariat?'

'Exactly, anyone who has read The Communist Manifesto wouldn't have any hesitation in agreeing.'

I'm at Zara's place. She invited me to come to her 'thing' which at the time I thought was code for 'I'm too cool to use the word party' but now I realise she called it a thing because there's not really a word for what this is. It's not that I don't like Zara, but we aren't the same kind of people. Her kind of people like to stand around and have long discussions, which I do and I've lost many hours talking to Alexa about all kinds of things but none of those things were communism or gentrification. I suppose I could open my mind and try and join in, but whenever I have in the past it's resulted in awkward silences or worse, laughter.

Then again, maybe an awkward silence would be worse than actual silence, which is what I'm getting from Jason as he sits next to me. I brought him along for company and support, but it turns out he's good for neither so I'm counting the fairy lights tacked to the ceiling while I wait for time to pass. Fifty-two lights and thirty-minutes until I can leave. Fifty-three lights, twenty-nine minutes and fifty-nine seconds until I can leave…

'I should have brought a guitar,' says Jason.

Oh God, I don't need to add strangled-cat music to this disaster of a night. 'Maybe you should have.'

'Do you want another drink?'

'No, it's between gin or craft beer and I don't know which is worse but neither are good.'

'Okay. I'm going to grab a drink. You okay here on your own?'

'Sure.' Rather, okay as I can be. It'd help if I was drunk, but gin tastes like detergent. Then again, I'd rather drink bleach than sit here much longer.

Jason comes back in the room. 'Kylie,' he says, 'I've just met this amazing bunch and they're off to another place. Are you coming?'

'Where is it?'

'No idea. Some place about twenty-minutes away. We're all going to share a taxi.'

I groan, 'I'm not going in a taxi to a strange place with people I've never met. Can't we just stay here? We can go soon, and grab a pizza.'

'Come on, it'll be fun,' he pleads. He looks so pitiful but I'm not going. It's irresponsible. Besides, all I want to do is go home and get in some warm pyjamas. I'll just have to hold out here on my own.

'You go, have a good time.'

'Are you sure?'

'I'm sure. Go.'

'Okay. See you around, babe,' he says, dashing off without looking back. I watch him leave with indifference. I'll be fine on my own. I'll be even better when I can finally leave, but until then… fifty-four lights, fifty-five lights, fifty – someone hovers by the door, looking at me. It's Oliver. He beckons me over.

'I didn't know you'd be here.' I try not to sound too pleased but I'm thrilled to see a familiar face.

'Zara told me to pop over if I had the chance. So I did.'

'When did you arrive?'

'Just as your boyfriend was leaving.'

I feel confused, and then realise with horror he's talking about Jason, 'He's not my boyfriend.'

'Did you break up? You don't look happy.'

'No, he never was my boyfriend. And I don't look happy because I'm not.'

'Is that because you wish he was your boyfriend?'

'No. Can we stop talking about him now?'

'Okay,' he says as he walks to the kitchen. I follow him,

annoyed by the interrogation but still grateful that he's here. He begins to go through Zara's cupboards and I stand and watch and try not to check out how great he looks in those jeans.

'Are you sure you should be doing that?'

'I'm just looking for something, she won't mind. Also, she won't know.'

'What are you looking for?'

'Something to drink.'

'There's gin and craft beer over there.'

'I know that. I'm looking for something to drink that isn't foul.'

'Hallelujah!'

'What's your poison?'

'I'd kill for a Cheeky Vimto.'

'Jesus, Kylie, really?'

'Yes. It's delicious and makes me feel eighteen again.'

'Who would want to be eighteen again? Well, I've found some port but I can't see there being any Blue Wkd in the fridge.'

'You can't go in her fridge!' I tell him as he does just that.

'Well, how can we have a Bourbon and Coke without the Coke?' he asks, pulling a bottle out of the fridge with a grin. I watch him pour Bourbon into two glasses and top them up with Coke. He pushes one glass my way. 'It's not a Cheeky Vimto, but it'll sort all of your problems.'

'Why? Is it a time machine?' I knock it back, expecting the worst but discover it's not so bad, and has a sweet aftertaste that lingers. He pours another round and sits down next to me. He smells of men's fragrance, musky but clean and the air around us smells of alcohol. Every time I'm alone with Oliver, I become very aware of my senses. Something about him being in close proximity makes me feel uncomfortable, but I can't put my finger on why and I don't want him to leave. I focus on my glass, circling its rim with my finger.

'So, what's up?' he asks.

I shrug, 'Nothing.'

'I know when something's up…'

'I guess I just don't really fit in here.'

'Does it matter?'

'I suppose not. But I feel out of my depth. They talk about things I don't understand or care about and it makes me feel stupid.'

'You shouldn't measure yourself by other people. You can only be you.'

'But I could be a different version of me.'

Oliver shrugs and finishes his drink. 'I like this version.'

'Well, you're about the only one who does…' I wonder what Alexa would think of me if she saw me here. She'd probably think I'm more pitiful than ever. I bet she doesn't go to house parties anymore; she's far too sophisticated for that now. Memories come to me of Alexa by my side on many nights out, tipsy and giggling away and I drink to wash them away. It's too painful.

'Maybe they don't see what I see…'

'You don't have to be so nice to me, especially out of work.'

'I know.' He cocks his head to catch my eyes and I dare to glance at him. I really shouldn't have, because now all I can see are his piercing blue eyes. The alcohol must be hitting my system, because I suddenly feel hot and fuzzy and nice and all I can think about is how his lips would feel on mine. And then I realise where I am and who I'm with and I manage to break away from his gaze and see it's past midnight.

'I should be going.' I force myself to get up, 'I have work tomorrow, as you know.'

He gets up too, 'I'll walk you home.'

'Oh, you don't have to do that.'

'No, but I want to.'

'I wonder what Zara thinks of chivalry.'

'It's not chivalry. I'll be a staff member down on short notice tomorrow if you're mugged on your way home.' He leads me out the house and we set off into the darkened street. Chivalry or otherwise, I'm glad to have him by my side.

Alexa

'Are you staying at Shaun's this weekend?' Priya enters the living room, having come in from work. I can tell by the shoes.

'No, I fancied a weekend at home.'

'It's not your home for too much longer.'

It's true, and my choice, but the words hit me in the gut and I feel winded 'I know…'

'What's up?' she sits down on a chair. I'm on the sofa, curled up under a pink blanket.

'I don't know. I'm going to miss this place… And you.'

'Thanks for adding me on as an afterthought.' She throws a cushion at me in protest.

I sit up and hug the cushion to me tightly, 'Sorry. I think I'll miss you most of all actually…'

'That's more like it.'

'You or this sofa, it's a toss-up.'

'I didn't know you felt so fondly about this sofa. What's wrong with Shaun's?'

'It's leather and cold… and it doesn't have cushions…' as I hear myself speak, I know I sound petulant. Priya confirms this by rolling her eyes.

'So put a throw over it and take some cushions. What's up with you? Your perfect boyfriend has asked you to move in and you're pouting, why exactly?'

I don't know why I'm 'pouting', as Priya put it. Everything is changing, everything is moving at light speed and I can't keep up. Work, Shaun, the fall out with Kylie, Rome, moving in with Shaun; life has been a rollercoaster recently. And I know that's the most cliché thing that could ever be uttered, but it's true. And frankly I feel dizzy and want to get off and take a nap on this sofa which is soft and gentle, unlike Shaun's. 'I'm just tired.'

'How was work?'

'Work was fine...' mostly because I managed to avoid Emma and the beauty-ladies.

'Good.' She stands up and I stretch out. 'I'm going upstairs to get ready. I have a date, so don't wait up.'

'Sounds fun, have a good time.'

Priya leaves the room just as there's a knock at the front door. I'm not expecting anybody, not even a phone call despite Shaun once promising to always ring me after work. So I stay in my blanket-cocoon, and continue to pout. But then I hear Priya coming back in to the room. 'She's in here, feeling a bit down I think, but I'm sure she'll feel better now you're here, Shaun.'

Oh no.

The door opens. 'Babe? What's the matter? Are you not feeling well?'

'No.' It's the truth in a way.

'Is there anything I can do?' He closes the door behind him and then sits at my feet. I hug the cushion tighter, wrapping my arms around it fully.

'No, I'm okay. Don't worry about me. Why are you here?' I try to sound casual but a hint of accusation slips out.

'I came to drop off some more boxes. How's the packing?'

'Not well. I've been at work,' I say. But the truth is I've been putting off packing.

'Is work going okay?' He tenderly strokes my leg, his face full of concern.

'Yeah, it's fine.' I offer him a weak smile.

'Have you been making an effort to talk to people? Have you been talking to Emma?'

'Yeah. I've made a few friends. They want me to host a beauty party.'

'What's that?'

'Louise comes to your house and tries to sell you beauty products.'

'Oh, that sounds fun. You could have them round on a Friday night once we're settled at the flat.'

I suppress my lips forming into a pout again and force a smile, 'Mmhmm.'

But this time he catches me out. He looks at me and cocks his head. 'Doesn't it sound fun to you?'

'I guess it's not my idea of a fun Friday night.'

'What is your idea of fun?'

'I'm more used to hitting clubs, dancing and coming home with take-away.'

'I know, but your clubbing days are behind you, really.'

Why does everyone keep saying that? 'Are they?'

'I would have thought so. Girls only hit the kind of clubs you used to go to for one reason.'

I sit up and cross my legs, out of his reach. 'That's not true.'

'Really? Girls like Kylie don't dress up and go out to pick up men?'

'You don't even know Kylie!' Shaun talking about Kylie triggers something inside of me and a surge of anger rushes to my head. I can feel my cheeks redden and my pulse race.

'But I know girls like her.'

'You can have fun with girls like Kylie without also picking up men.'

'Sure.' He says this in a tone I don't like.

'I'm not saying I want to go out and pick up men. Of course I don't. I just didn't realise I couldn't go out anymore.'

'I just figured you wouldn't want to, especially now you and Kylie aren't talking.'

On the surface, I feel that Shaun has taken the privilege away from me but the fact is I can't go out to drink and dance and come home with cheesy chips anymore whether I want to or not. Not without Kylie. I shrug, defeated.

'I know you're sad that you and Kylie fell out,' he soothes. 'It's the end of an era. But Emma seems nice, more mature. She's taken you under her wing. I know it's different but you're lucky you have her and her friends.'

He inches as close as he can to stretch out and put an arm on my shoulder.

'I'm starving,' he says, 'were you planning on making food?'

'Not really…'

For a while, we sit in silence. Shaun gets out his phone and busies himself with it. Then he puts his phone away and stands. 'You don't look well at all, you don't seem yourself. I put the boxes in the kitchen but I'm going to move them to your room and then let you get some rest, okay?' He leans down and kisses me. I swallow the lump in my throat and kiss him back. He goes to leave and I feel relief.

'I hope you feel better soon.'

'Thanks.' I give him a little smile.

'I think you'll be happier when we're finally living together. I can make you happy… I love you, Alexa.'

I think this is what people describe as an out of body experience. I feel my eyes widen and then I feel my body freeze up and then I see myself frozen to the spot above myself and I see Shaun at the door. I see this scene that is me curled up on the sofa and Shaun, who has come to help me pack up my single life to share a life with him, fawning over me and telling me he loves me for the first time. Written in a novel, or in a movie, it's the epitome of romance. In real life, however, it feels overwhelming and yet underwhelming at the same time. He stands, waiting and I know I need to react before it gets awkward.

I choke out the words, '…I love you too.'

He smiles and I smile back, hoping it looks sincere. As I watch him leave my side, my smile is replaced with a frown. Suddenly I have everything I wanted: good job, a boyfriend who loves me, and soon a two-bed apartment in the nice part of town. But, I don't remember saying I wanted any of that. That was Kylie's insistence, when she was talking about the 'wrong side of twenty-five' nonsense and having some sort of quarter-life crisis. Everything was going fine until she decided it wasn't, and now I don't even know what I want. I delve deeper under my blanket and hide.

Kylie

I place my bag on my peg at work as Zara enters the room. 'Hey, are we on shift together or are you just leaving?'

'I've just arrived so it looks like it's you and me tonight.'

Zara grins and cries, 'Yes!' I feel a sense of pride and achievement. Especially considering how awful I was at my job when I started working here.

'Are you ready then?' I ask.

'Let's go.'

We each take a side, no fussing over who goes where because I can handle whatever comes at me now. I'm Zara's equal behind here and it feels good. I watch her, on the other side, tying a black apron around her waist and running her fingers through her mermaid-green hair. I used to feel insecure and self-conscious standing next to her, but recently I've started to feel at peace with who Zara is and embrace who I am too. Her looks don't invalidate mine. I can only be me. And I'm not so bad.

The bar gets busy fast and we find ourselves serving customer after customer. Two regulars come in and sit at the bar like they always do. They're young and smartly dressed, a fine pair of men neither of which I'd kick out of bed. I serve them drinks and linger nearby, slicing lemons and pretend to be busy so I can hear their conversation.

'I can't stay long, I have to get to Kim's on time or she'll kill me.'

'Why are you at Kim's tonight?'

'She needs me to look after Millie, she has a work meeting.'

'So you're leaving me early to watch Teletubbies and heat up spaghetti hoops?'

'It's not easy being a single dad, you know.'

I can't believe he's a dad! I've been hearing him mention Millie for weeks, but I never caught the full conversation and figured she was his girlfriend. Just then, someone calls for attention and I have to put a pause on eavesdropping. When I turn around, I can't believe who it is.

'Kylie?'

My blood runs cold, 'Alicia?'

'Oh my God, do you work here?'

What could I tell her? I know the manager? I'm conducting a psychological experiment? But why would I care to impress her? I read online she bought a new car last week, which she affords from having a successful big time job. But so what? I hold my head up high and smile, 'I do.'

She frowns, 'Did you work here last time I saw you?'

'No,' I reply, 'I was on the other side of the bar with you.' As I remember fondly… not!

'I remember. How odd. Oh, a glass of white wine please.'

I get a glass and begin to pour. Hopefully she'll go and sit elsewhere. But as she slumps her tiny but expensive bag on the counter, it doesn't look promising. She's making herself comfortable.

I put the glass in front of her, 'That'll be £5.50 please.'

She opens the tiny bag and then a long purse containing various credit cards. With a long, manicured finger she picks one out and swipes the card reader that I'm holding. To my surprise, but not hers, the machine beeps and the word Declined reads across the screen.

'Oh, I'm sorry, it's er…' I begin.

'Oh, shit.' She takes her manicured finger and picks out another card. This time it accepts. I smile and go back to slicing lemons, but with disappointment I see the two men have gone. It must be time for Millie's spaghetti hoops. Damn.

'So, did you have enough of psychology?' says Alicia from where she's sitting.

'Oh?' I ask, but then remember she thought I worked in psychology, 'Yes. It was just… what's the word? Draining.'

She nods at me, 'I totally get that.'

'But I love my new job, so it's all worked out well.'

Alicia holds up her drink, 'Well, cheers to that! It's not as easy as people think, finding a job that makes them happy... some people look like they have it all but actually they have nothing.' She falters at this, shakes her head, downs the drink and looks back at me with a pearly-white smile. I smile back, hiding disbelief.

She gets up, 'I better dash. Call me; we really ought to meet up soon. At a different bar! With a different credit card... My treat.' I watch her stagger away.

'Absolutely,' I lie. I can't think of anything worse than making small talk with Alicia while she 'treats' me on one of her many credit cards. 'See you soon.'

Alexa

What I've learned from spending time at Shaun's is that I don't enjoy cooking as much as I enjoy Priya cooking for me. Apart from that one time Shaun cooked Coq au Vin, I've been persuaded to be the one to cook when we eat together. There are worse things, but after a day of working the last thing I feel like doing is peeling potatoes while Shaun plays computer games. The sound of shooting drowns out my thoughts as I stand over a chopping board.

'Alexa?' calls Shaun, 'your phone's ringing.'

I dry my hands but as I put the towel down, Shaun comes in with my phone to his ear. 'Hello? No this is Shaun, Alexa's boyfriend, who's this? Sam? Sam who? What do you mean you didn't know Alexa had a boyfriend?'

Annoyed, I reach up and snatch the phone. 'Hello? Alexa speaking.'

'Alexa? I thought you sounded a little masculine before. It's Sam.'

'Sam? Oh hi!' We haven't spoken since Kylie's birthday. I make my way to Shaun's bedroom for some privacy. Shaun's lingering was making me feel uncomfortable. He makes his way back to the sofa as I shut the door behind me.

'I was just calling to check you're still alive. It's like you've fallen off the face of the earth.'

God, have I really fallen off the face of the earth? It's true, I haven't seen anyone I used to hang out with in ages. 'Sorry. I guess I've been keeping to myself recently.'

Sam sounds concerned. 'Is everything okay?'

'Everything's fine,' I say as Shaun pops his head into the room, 'good actually. How are you?'

'I'm great. So I was calling because we're going out next

weekend and I wanted to give you plenty of notice.'

'Going out where?' Did I imagine it or did Shaun just frown?

'All over I guess. Who knows!'

'In town?'

'Yeah.'

'Is Kylie going?'

'No, she has to work. I'm surprised you had to ask.'

It stings that I had to ask. Kylie's working, and she's choosing it over going out and my mind is racing with questions like where does she work? How is she finding it? I shouldn't care but I do. I can't go into it now, though, not with Shaun hovering by the door and listening in. 'Oh, right, sorry my mind is elsewhere.'

'It sounds it. So, what do you say?'

Yes I'd love to, I say in my head. 'No,' I say to Sam, 'well, I mean it sounds great but, I'm in a serious relationship now so you know…'

'…So what? I'd say bring them, but it's a girls only night. Tell them you'll bring them back some cheesy chips and that drunk Alexa is the best version of Alexa.'

'Oh, I don't think they'll care for that…' I say with more honesty than intended.

'Well, have a think and let me know, okay?'

'Okay then, talk to you later.' Sam hangs up and Shaun stands, waiting for some kind of explanation. 'Oh, that was Sam,' I tell him, hoping it's enough.

'I gathered that. Who is he?'

'Sam is a girl, and just a friend.'

I see relief on his face, and then, what I think is suspicion. 'You've never mentioned her before. Is she from work?'

'No, she's an old university friend.'

'Cool, what did she want?'

Why does it feel like I'm on trial? He hasn't done or said anything, but I can't shift the feeling. 'Oh she just wanted to invite me out next week,' I say, hoping it comes across as breezy.

'Out in town?'

'Yeah, she was only asking.'

'Oh, that was nice of her. You'll have to have a girly day some time instead.'

I don't appreciate being told how I should spend time with my friends, and besides, I can't even imagine having a 'girly' day with Sam, but I keep this to myself. What would be the point in telling him that the only real time I socialise with her is at clubs or bars? We live different lives but always go for a drink now and then. Or, we used to, before things were different. 'I better get on with making dinner.'

Kylie

Today is a day to truly celebrate. Fellow procrastinators, join me in celebrating not later but now. Let this day forward be a national bank holiday in celebration of I, Kylie Lee, fixing the bathroom lock.

I'm going to celebrate in the only way appropriate: having a bath in absolute guaranteed privacy. I turn on the taps and reach for my own full tub of bubble bath and pour in a liberal amount. Bubbles form and keep on forming. I want a big bubble bath that lasts as long as possible and nothing will get in my way. The door locks with a satisfying clink and I undress, eager to get into the hot water. It burns my legs a little, but I'll get used to it. I sit down as the water reddens my pale calves and let the bubbles embrace me. This is the life.

It's Friday and I've had the day off but I found myself with nothing to do and no one to do it with. I feel Alexa's absence all the time but never as much as on a Friday. Every time I pass a café or any of our old haunts I'm reminded of what I've lost. She did a bad thing, lying to me, but it wasn't worth falling out over. I was wrong to be so callous to her; I let my emotions get the better of me. But I try not to dwell because every time our lives cross on social media through mutual friends I see how happy she looks and I shouldn't get in the way of that. Instead, I should move on, and I have to an extent but I don't feel the same connection with my work friends as I ever did with Alexa. Which is weird because we've never had much in common and we probably wouldn't have been friends if we hadn't both been late on the first day of university. Fate brought us together and some unknown energy kept us together. But then I fucked it all up. And now

I'm fixing bathroom locks out of boredom and pretending that having my life together equates to being happy. Wow, that got deep fast.

I lie back and try to think of other things but it's no good. The plan was to drag this bath out for as long as possible because there's nothing on telly tonight. I thought a bath would be soothing and the more bubbles there were, the better I would feel. But as the bubbles evaporate so does the illusion of happiness.

Alexa

I'm supposed to be going over to Shaun's, but he's just called me and told me that I'm having a drink with Amy first at a café, which has completely thrown me off and has me feeling a little apprehensive because I associate cafés with Kylie.

I head over to the café, as instructed. Shaun also told me she's bringing the baby, which surprised me because I didn't think she'd be up to going anywhere so soon but Shaun said she's taking it all in her stride. She's a better woman than I am, clearly, because I'm freaking out over a change of address and she's made a living person that she has to take care of for the next eighteen years. When I get to the café, an aroma of coffee greets me as well as Amy. She waves from a table for two as she sits holding Amelia.

'Alexa! I bought you an Americano, Shaun said that's your favourite.'

It's not. 'It is,' I smile, 'and thank you, that's so sweet. I should be the one getting the drinks.' I sit opposite and notice with a heavy heart that she has a latte. 'How are you?' I ask, sounding bright, 'how's Amelia?'

'I'm fine. She's fine,' she says with a contended smile. She looks better than fine, she looks great. She's glowing. I'm only glowing thanks to highlighter.

'How are you finding parenthood?'

'It's hectic and I'm breast-feeding around the clock but she sleeps next to me so that makes it easier. It's all rather blissful, actually.'

'Seems it. She's beautiful.'

'It's your turn next.'

I nearly choke on my Americano. 'Well, I mean not for a while.'

'Oh, well of course. Get settled in first. Are you nearly ready?'

'No, not yet...'

'Shaun's excited. He's made room for you. I told him that it won't be good enough and you'll want to rearrange everything. You'll want to redecorate, no doubt. I warned him of all this so don't worry, I've got your back.'

It feels nice having Amy as my friend, and for someone to have my back again. 'Oh, I appreciate it.'

'It's no problem. I think you're great together. And you're so lucky. He's my brother and I know he can be a pain in the arse, but he's good and he loves you. What more could a girl need?'

I smile and sip my coffee. Amelia lies in Amy's arms without a care in the world. She's the lucky one here. I try not to think about the very question I have been asking myself since Shaun asked me to move in. What more could I want? Nothing, really. But something niggles at me and it's not just the hit of caffeine.

'Oh, look at your face, bless you! It's normal to feel nervous. It's a big deal, of course. It's life changing, in fact. It's a commitment. This is it now. You'll carve a life out together, save for a house, marry, have kids. Then you'll work less, maybe stop altogether, and have different priorities. It will all come together naturally though and you'll never look back, only to wonder what you were so worried about.'

'Did it make you nervous? Starting a life with Ian?'

'Oh, totally. I was twenty-four, so younger than you, and an absolute mess. I felt sick from a mixture of excitement and nervousness. That was seven years ago, and I feel like a totally different person.'

I wonder what kind of person I'll be in seven years if I'm still with Shaun? I'm not perfect by any means, but do I want to be a totally different person to who I am now?

We finish our drinks and Amy looks like she's about to offer me another when a smell emits from Amelia and she decides she should probably go. We leave the café and part ways as she goes home and I make my way to Shaun's home. I walk with heavy feet, weighed down by Amy's words. Is moving in with Shaun really so life changing? Will I lose my identity and gain a new one with different outlooks and priorities? I suppose so. People grow and change all the time, but seldom so instantly. I have one week left and then in one swift move, in an instant, all the major factors of my life will change. I feel sick. I'm about to be reacquainted with my Americano. Only, unlike Amy, my reason for nausea feels very decisive. No excitement; all nervousness.

I arrive at Shaun's home with surprise. My feet carried me here without much instruction from my brain, which was preoccupied. As I walk in, I hear cheers and whistles and realise with disappointment that he's watching football. Again.

'Hey,' he says as I enter the living room, 'did you have a good time with my sister and Amelia?'

'Oh, yeah. It was nice. Amelia's getting big.'

'Yeah, I bet she is,' he replies, putting his hand on my lap and giving it a squeeze as I sit next to him. But his eyes don't leave the direction of the television.

'Shall we get on with measurements then?' I ask. After all, it's why I'm here.

'Can we do it after the game?'

'How long is it on for?'

'An hour.'

'Seriously?'

'It'll fly by,' he soothes, putting his arm around me. I sigh and watch the men run around the field. On Shaun's screen they look to scale. It's obscene. I've never noticed before but his television is huge.

'Do you think the television's too big for this room?' I ask.

'What do you mean?'

'It's just... really big. It dominates the room.'

'Yeah, that's the idea. You can really immerse yourself in what you're watching.'

'I know, but with your computer set up in here too the room is a bit tech-heavy.'

He looks at me and smiles, 'Amy said you'd be wanting to move everything around.'

'Well, it was just a thought.'

'I get it. It's fine, I'll put the computer stuff in the spare bedroom. I'm not sure about the telly though, that might be a compromise too far.'

He smiles and then goes back to gawping at the television. I can't sit here any longer, doing nothing. I get up, 'I can't just sit here; I need to do something.'

'Why don't you pop out and choose something for dinner?'

'Oh, okay,' I say. He smiles and carries on watching television. I grab my coat, take my annoyance out on the door a little and with a slam, I set off. At least with all these stairs every time I want to leave or enter the flat, I'll get great calves. My regular supermarket isn't anywhere near Shaun's place, I'm going to have to settle for a different one, which is another compromise.

But I feel bad for resenting having to compromise, because they're just petty problems and does it matter if Shaun's television is big? Does it matter if I have to change where I shop? Shaun's letting me into his life, and home, and putting his beloved computer in the spare room. He's compromising plenty without a fuss. I enter the supermarket and pick up a basket with a sigh.

Even dinner will be a compromise, every day. I'm used to eating what I want and yes sometimes Priya and I share meals but if we don't feel like it we simply don't. But couples share meals, don't they? Shaun won't be my housemate, but my other half. It's not a case of changing addresses, I'm not swapping Priya for Shaun; I'm about to commit myself to Shaun. To a life of compromise and togetherness. Is love always so suffocating or am I just being cynical?

I furrow my brows and scour the aisle, trying to decide what we'll eat tonight. Sushi calls me from the refrigerated section, but does Shaun like sushi? He doesn't seem like a sushi guy. There's so much I don't know about him. I ditch the sushi idea and pick up a red bell pepper and an aubergine. A light pasta dish will be nice, at least I know he likes pasta.

Maybe I'm over-thinking it. There's a lot I do know about Shaun, such as he's nice and thoughtful and caring. I know he likes pasta because he took me on a date, to the place his parents fell in love, and then he took me to Rome. I know enough about Shaun. I'll find out the rest over time.

I pay for the pasta ingredients and head to what will soon be home. With each step I try to be more positive. I can do this, can't I?

As I get into the apartment, I put the bag down in the hallway and tell Shaun, 'I'm back,' and hang my coat up. He doesn't reply, probably because he's still watching television. 'I'm just popping to the bathroom.'

But when I open the bathroom door, I hear a noise and with a gasp I glimpse Shaun on the toilet, trousers around his ankles and newspaper in his hand. I see a flash of horror in his eyes before I shut the door. Oh God, I can't un-see it.

Feeling flustered and eager to get away, I pick up the bag of shopping and take it to the kitchen. I start preparing vegetables and put water on to boil for the pasta. I know Shaun likes pasta, I know that about him. But there's a lot I don't know, that I haven't seen. And I don't know if I want to.

Kylie

The bed; not just made, but with crisp clean sheets, is a feature in the room and sets the standard for which everything else in the room can be measured. Space is available at every turn and the floor is free of clothes and other miscellaneous items that used to reside there. Over by the window sits a desk, equipped with pads of paper and pens that are gathered neatly in a pot. Cushions add a sense of comfort and lighted candles permeate a delightful scent. Who lives in a room like this?

Me, apparently. And I hate to say it, but it feels good. I can't help but think how proud Alexa would be right now, after all the times I questioned her on her need to be excessively clean all of the time. The only motivation I've ever had to clean my room is if expecting company, but it hadn't had a clean since Alexa came over when I was pining over Harry and it had accumulated an embarrassing amount of crap, like the room itself had imploded. Every nook and cranny was cluttered and dusty and the almost-clean clothes pile that usually sits on my chair was spilling off said chair and all over the floor. The clothes were like lava and the floor was engulfed. My bed was the only safe place. It looked like the inside of my mind: full to bursting with interesting things, but in need of some clarity.

So, on my day off last week I started to tackle the clutter and it took me all weekend to get it to an acceptable standard. Ever since then I've been adding to my room with a cushion here and a cute storage box there. It's snowballed and now my room is… really nice actually. It feels like an epiphanic moment in my life. I haven't exactly found God but it's still pretty enlightening.

Despite all of my personal achievements recently, or maybe because of them, I'm officially boring. It's my day off, and I've already managed a successful food shop in which I took a list, and came out having ticked off every item on there. I heaved my bags home with a sense of pride. Now I'm sitting on my bed eating an apple, doodling on a notepad. I had every intention of writing a best-selling novel but it hasn't come to me yet. Then I thought I would learn to draw but it's not as easy as it looks. Feeling inspired is exhausting. Just when I thought some sort of adult gene had kicked in, what with me tidying my room and all, I realise that I'm pretty skill-less.

I sit and doodle and carry on eating my apple. What a riveting life I lead! There's a knock at the door, but I don't move, Lucie can answer it. She's downstairs practicing yoga in the living room. I have no urge to interrupt her downward-dog position. How does she bend like that, anyway? It's not right.

'Kylie, it's for you!'

Who could it possibly be? I close my sketch book, sit up and put my apple on the side as the door opens... and Oliver walks in. 'Oliver?' I say, horrified. What the hell is he doing here?

'Hey,' he says, 'I hope it's okay I popped by. Your housemate sent me up.'

I glance around the room, looking for things that I don't want him to see. I think I'm safe, except the stack of CDs on the side that is showcasing some of my guilty pleasures, which I'd rather he didn't know about. I'm sure Oliver listens to nothing but music of substance, not pop-punk of the noughties. I'm sure he doesn't need to know I have every Paramore album and three copies of Three Cheers For Sweet Revenge. Oh well, maybe he won't notice. I sit up taller, and hope I don't look like I've lain on my bed for two hours. 'No, it's fine. What's up?'

He shuts the door and makes no attempt to disguise looking around the room. I watch with bated breath, suddenly feeling exposed and vulnerable.

'Nice place, although not what I expected.'

'What did you expect?'

He's walking around now, taking further inspections, without shame. Unbelievable!

'I don't know,' he says, 'it's just very... organised. And clean.'

'So? What are you trying to say? That I'm neither?'

He pulls a wry smile at this and I want to throw my sketchbook at his head. 'No, I guess it's just a little too organised and a little too clean. It's not how I had imagined.'

'Really? How often do you imagine my bedroom?'

This comment throws him. His eyes narrow but he's smiling, he nods in a way that I know means 'touché, Kylie' and says, 'Just the once, when I wondered how this would look in it.' He puts his hand in a bag, that I only just notice, and pulls out a large, square object wrapped in brown paper, and hands it to me.

'What is it?' I ask.

'Open it.'

I peel off the brown paper and discover a canvas that has been painted with vibrant swirls of orange and yellow with red splodges and white flicks. The colours look like they're jumping and leaping to their own tune. In the corner, it says Raw Spirit by Oliver Caverly.

'Is it for me?' I ask.

'Yes.'

'It's beautiful. Thank you.'

'A beautiful display of swirls and stuff?' he asks, smiling.

'Something like that.' I look at the painting again, and Oliver's writing. 'Raw spirit...' I read out loud.

'That's right. It's you.'

'I love it.'

'And so you should. I better be off.' He heads for the door, opens it and pauses, 'You should put it on the side by your CDs. It'll feel at home next to Sum 41 and Destiny's Child.'

'I will,' I say, and with that he leaves. I set the canvas down on my chest of drawers, leaning it against the wall and stand back to admire it. It looks nice. It adds a little something. Although Oliver's right, my room is way too clean and organised. But why was he here? He could have given me the painting at work, but instead he came to my house and now he's been in my room. It all feels surreal. I stand in a haze until I hear the front door shut.

I scramble to the window and peer out to see Oliver leave. To my horror he catches me, and gives a little wave. I jump back, knock over a stack of CDs and they fall into a heap.

Alexa

I sit on the floor, applying make-up from a cardboard box. It's frustrating to look for my favourite eye shadow palette and coming across everything but, along the way. Finally, I find it, squashed next to my summer foundation, a rogue brush and a nude lipstick. It's not supposed to be like this.

Where will I apply make-up in Shaun's place? It's one of the many questions I have yet to find the answer to, like where will I put my books? Will they sit next to his, split half and half, or mixed up as to order if they're lined up alphabetically?

And what about the rest? The contents of this room are an accumulation of the last seven years, which makes up my whole adult life. As I dismantle my whole adult life, memories surface like concert memorabilia, novelty slippers, notebooks full of nonsense. Things I forgot I had now sit in a pile in the corner, waiting to be packed. And then things that have no place except a place in my heart, things you keep to yourself, lie around with an uncertain future. I'll no longer be just myself, but myself and Shaun. I'll be we and us, no longer just me. And I'm not sure I'm comfortable with Shaun seeing certain versions of myself, so I'll have to be on my best behaviour at all times. No more plucking stray hairs whenever I see them, no more watching my guilty pleasure television. I'm trading it all in to have Shaun by my side, all day every day.

There's a knock at my bedroom door and I freeze: he wasn't supposed to be here until much later. But then the door opens and Priya pops her head around. I let my body thaw and feel every muscle relax a little.

'Only me,' she says, 'morning.'

'Morning.'

'It's the big day.'

'I know.'

'Oh, don't look so worried. It'll be fine. I'll come and visit all the time. Don't go thinking you've got rid of me that easily.'

I try to swallow the rising lump in my throat. Priya has been the best housemate. She's clean, has great taste in décor and makes a mean omelette. I'll miss her mum's famous curry and our movie nights and the life we've shared for so long. I smile and choke out the words, 'I'll miss you.'

'Me too.' She sits on my bed. 'But you'll be fine with Shaun. He'll look after you. He loves you, and you love him, right?'

It's something I've been wondering myself in secret. But if anyone can shed some clarity on love, it's Priya. 'How do you know when it's love?'

She shrugs, 'It's all consuming. You just know.'

'But I need a definitive answer.'

'Love doesn't work that way.'

I can feel myself getting worked up at Priya's ridiculous answers. For once, I have no interest in turning this into a debate and winning. I need her to argue her points and give me a definite signal for love. 'I can't work with grey-area emotions or guesses and hunches.'

'Look, all I can tell you is love is unique and you can't look for it, it finds its way to you and holds on.'

I think about this. 'Right...' I say, simmering down. 'Like how when we met he felt compelled to come back and see me. We were meant to be. He had no reason to come back and give me his number, did he?'

Priya looks pale, which is hard when you're Indian. And, is it me or is she squirming? 'Well,' she begins, 'maybe he had some reason.'

'What do you mean?'

She looks to the ground and speaks fast, 'Well he was fixing my laptop and we were making small talk and for some reason you came up...'

I wait for Priya to finish her sentence, 'And? What did you say about me?'

'Well, I just mentioned how you were intelligent and deserved romance. I told him that you weren't someone who went through tons of guys, but was classier than that and was waiting for the real deal…'

My mouth feels dry and I swallow but it doesn't help. 'You set us up?'

'Of course not!' says Priya trying to look indignant but coming across as flustered and guilty. 'Besides, it all turned out okay, didn't it? Love might have had a little helping hand, but it found its way. I'm still right about that.'

'For God sake, Priya!' I can't believe it! Then again, I should have known. Priya loves to be right, but I had no idea to what extent. I have a few choice words to say to her, but bite my tongue, because there are more pressing issues at hand.

After much grovelling, Priya leaves for work, and there's nothing else to do but wait. I sit in the kitchen, watching the door, with a cup of tea just to have something to hold.

There's a knock at the door. I get up and with heavy feet walk to open it. He sees me, and his face lights up. 'Morning babe,' he says, 'are you ready?'

Behind him, I see his car and that he's folded the back seats to accommodate my things. He stands clutching a spanner and some screwdrivers. It hurts to see how ready he is for me, when I'm not.

'No,' I say.

He frowns. 'Okay, well what do you have left to pack?'

'Shaun, come and sit.'

'What's the matter? Alexa?' He walks in and sits opposite me. I look at him; really look at him. I've always liked his hair and today is no exception. It's soft and clean and good to run your fingers through. He's handsome, albeit unconventionally so. His face is always soft and kind. He's never going to look at me like that again. I take a big drink of tea and wish it were something stronger.

'I can't move in with you,' I blurt out. Damn it. I had

rehearsed this so many times and was always much more eloquent and sensitive than that.

In that moment, his face changes. The big, puppy-dog eyes, that are always brushed with kindness or concern, start to narrow. 'What? Why? Are you getting cold feet?'

'It's not that...' I look down and focus on my hands because I can't look at him anymore. My cup is empty so I put it to one side. Now, there's nothing to hold on to. 'I should never have agreed to move in. It's not something I want. I'm sorry.'

'Are you serious?'

The anger and confusion in his voice echoes around the empty kitchen.

'What do you mean? You don't want to move in with me?'

His anger makes me want to retreat but he's right to be angry and deserves to know the truth. That said, my throat feels thick and when the words come they're quiet. 'No. I'm sorry.'

'Why?'

'It just doesn't feel right. I like living here.'

'Right...' he says, with that expression he always has when he's making mental calculations or figuring something out. 'Right. So you'll live here for a bit longer. It means it will take longer to save to buy for our own place but we'll make it work. We'll make it work, right?'

My heart sinks at his hopefulness. 'I mean, I don't know if that's something I want to consider just yet either.'

'I don't believe I'm hearing this.'

'Shaun, come on, we've not been together for very long. Can't we just stay as we are? Just dating?'

'I don't want to date, Alexa. I'm twenty-eight and I've been dating for ten years. I want to settle and I thought you wanted to settle with me.'

'In the future, maybe, but I'm only twenty-five and I have so much left to do. I want to build up my career, get a hobby, travel, live a little. I don't want to be an "us" before I even truly know who I am myself.'

'No,' he says with defiance, as though it's up for debate.

He drops his tools on the table with a clatter. 'We're perfect together. Alexa, you know we're perfect together.'

I shrug. So everyone keeps telling me. We're perfect and yet it haunts me every night that I don't feel as lucky as every single person tells me I am. I hang my head in shame. 'Maybe it's not enough.'

'What more do you need?'

'…I don't know.' I feel a lump in my throat and try to hold on to my emotions. 'I don't know! We're perfect on paper and everyone can see it and people won't stop telling me how lucky I am and I can see that, I can see that we're perfect, but I don't feel lucky. I just don't feel… "It".'

'It?'

'Yes. Whatever "it" is. The "it" that would have me running into your arms; it's not there. That knowing, that compelling feeling to be with you and share a life and a television and a bathroom with you, isn't there. Yes, things are "perfect" now but you'll stop sending flowers and taking me to Rome and then what? We'll spend our days sitting side by side whilst you watch football and I feel ignored and tell my friends I can't go out with them? I don't want to look back in ten years, full of regret because I was too scared to just say that actually, it's not what I want. I really am sorry.'

'Fine.' He springs from the chair and paces to the door. I want to run after him, say something that will make it all better, but I have to let him go. He leaves, and with one slam of the door I'm alone again.

Kylie

I'm on a train and that can only mean one thing: I'm going to see my parents. Or rather, I'm going over to see which of my childhood possession I want Mum to spare a trip to the skip. She rang me the other day and said, 'Kylie, I need you to come and decide which of your things you would like to take back to yours'. It completely threw me off because I moved out seven years ago and she put my things in the attic without a fuss. I guess I'll find the pressing storage space issue when I get there.

The train groans to my stop. I jump off and let my feet take me down familiar streets, back to the first home I ever had. There was never anywhere to hang out growing up, so my friends and I would roam these streets like nomads or skulk in the park and drink fizzy pop and then after a certain age (but not quite eighteen) cheap alcohol, if we could get our hands on it. It was such a waste of time, and yet filled with lots of happy memories. I still keep in touch with a few of those aforementioned street-dwelling friends.

When I get to my old home, Mum opens the door almost straight away. She looks at me; her lips pursed and eyes narrowed. 'Good evening, Kylie,' she says with forced politeness, 'come in.'

'What's the big rush to clear out the attic, Mum?' I ask, following her up the stairs.

'Nothing in particular, but it's taking up space and might as well be at yours.'

'I have no space.'

'Yes well, when one chooses to rent merely a room instead of a flat that tends to be an issue.'

Wow. So she's dragged me here and making me part with

my possessions just to have a dig at me? That's an insane level of pettiness.

Upstairs, the attic door sits open and boxes with my name on lie scattered all over the hallway. Dad's up in the attic, banging and crashing and moaning about said banging and crashing.

'Hi, Dad,' I shout up.

The noise stops and Dad pokes his head out of the attic, 'Hi, love.'

'Never mind chit-chat,' says Mum to Dad, 'get sorting them boxes.'

I peer into boxes and my past peers back at me. I spy my old jumper and striped tie, a sports day participation medal and an array of formal school photographs. There I am at seven with my two front teeth missing. Oh, and the less said about the ones of me hitting puberty the better. I don't want to take back any of this. But maybe my childhood bear, Rosie, and all my Jacqueline Wilson books. I thought I was too cool and grown up to take them to university. The truth is I wasn't cool enough to take them. 'This box, please, except the school stuff,' I say.

'Well put it over there and we'll call it the "yes" pile.'

I move the box and carry on looking. It takes a while to look through it all and decide what I want, but when I'm finished I have a box of CDs and music paraphernalia (minus a very primitive mp3 player), photograph albums and a bag of clothes, which I realise with horror will now be classed as 'retro'.

'But how am I going to get all of this back on the train?'

'You should have thought of that, Kylie,' Mum says with exasperation. 'You should be able to plan ahead.'

'I'll drop it off love one day this week,' says Dad.

'Thanks, Dad.'

'Not a problem. Is it about lunch time, Marie?'

'Yes, when Kylie gets off I'll make something.'

'Unless she wants to stay.' Dad turns from Mum and looks at me, 'you hungry, kid?'

I know Mum doesn't want me to stay. To be honest, that's

enough to make me say, 'Actually I'm starving.'

'Come on then.'

Downstairs, Mum dishes up a homemade quiche and salad. We sit to eat, Robbie included. He's eating with his head in his phone and Mum doesn't call him out on it. Typical.

'I love quiche,' I really do. 'No one makes it like you, Mum,' I say with honesty.

'Thank you, Kylie.'

'What have you been up to then?' I ask her.

'Oh, usual things...' she begins. 'Still working for the council. It's a humble job but it's good on top of Dad's income to ensure we have a nice quality of life. It might not be the most enjoyable job but some things have to take priority.'

And the digs keep coming.

'Well that's good.' I smile brightly, 'whatever makes you happy.'

But she isn't backing down. 'It's not about what makes me happy.'

'What does make you happy?' Neither am I.

'Dad, Robbie... you.' I'm in the same room as her and yet I'm still an afterthought. 'The house and our yearly trip to France. A nice glass of wine in the evening. This is a very odd conversation, Kylie.'

'It's not odd. I'm just taking an interest in what makes you happy. I respect what makes you happy.'

'Well what would make me happy now is you eating your lunch so you don't miss your train.'

She can't wait to get rid of me. I cut my quiche into tinier pieces and eat each bite with deliberation.

Mum ignores me and clears her throat, 'So Robbie has got himself a job.'

'Have you?' I ask Robbie, 'congrats, bro. What's it doing?'

'Just working in a restaurant. It's kind of lame,' Robbie says, shrugging without looking up from his phone.

'Nothing lame about it, son,' says Dad.

'No, that's really cool,' I tell him. 'I remember when I—'

'It'll be nice to earn yourself a little pocket money around going to college.'

'Absolutely,' I say.

'Besides, you won't be doing it forever,' Mum carries on, although no one has argued the contrary. 'You're too smart to be serving people for a living. You'll go to college and university and get yourself a proper job.'

'Marie...' begins Dad, or rather, begs Dad. He knows where this is going. So do I.

'What?'

Mum plays innocent.

'It's simply the truth.'

'Whatever career Robbie wants to do, we'll support it,' he says this meaningfully and I know it's aimed at me. He really is the best. I'll keep it together for his sake, and not take the bait Mum is dangling in front of my nose. Instead I look at my plate and focus on eating. Chew, swallow, chew, swallow, chew...

'Of course we will. Hopefully our supporting will count for something and he won't throw all of our hard work away.'

...Swallow. I take the bait. The giant, elephant-sized bait dangling in front of me that's putting me off my favourite dinner. Sorry, Dad.

'You know what, Mum? If you're so passionate about a career why didn't you get one?'

Suddenly, everything is silent. Robbie even looks up from his phone but Dad's gaze remains fixed on his plate, determinedly. Mum stares at me, not blinking, until she swallows what she was chewing. Then she says in the kind of calm voice that she reserves for when she's livid: 'Excuse me?'

Oh well, here goes nothing. 'I'm really sorry that you can't live vicariously through me now, and I'm sorry that I've disappointed you, but I have to live my life for me. I like working in a bar and you are going to have to accept that or see if my old job is taking vacancies and apply there yourself.'

She's staring right at me. Fork in mid air, quiche en route, hovering as she sits there rigid except the vein bulging in her neck that always gives away how mad she is. Shit.

'I really don't know what you're talking about, Kylie.'

'Sure you don't. You haven't been completely transparent about your feelings at all.'

Mum sighs and puts her fork on her plate. 'I just don't know why you quit your lovely job at that office. It was a step on the ladder, you were going somewhere, you were building a career.'

'I'd been on the bottom rung of that ladder for the last five years and I wasn't going anywhere. I was stuck in a rut, complacent and actually pretty miserable if I'm honest.'

'Darling, being miserable is no reason to quit a job. You persevere. You're an adult now and you have to be responsible and get your priorities straight.'

'I didn't quit, I was fired.'

Mum nearly chokes on thin air in sheer horror, 'You were fired? What did you do?'

'Nothing really. It just wasn't working out. Janine had it in for me.'

'I don't believe you. It's time to grow up, Kylie. It's time you took things seriously.'

'I am taking my life seriously and I don't know what your problem is. I have a job, I pay my way in life and I'm happy. Isn't that enough?'

'You're happy working a job that will never bring in decent money? You need to evaluate your life, Kylie, and where it's going. Do you at least have a boyfriend?'

'Nope.'

'Are you dating anyone nice?'

I sigh. Well, I might as well tell all now. In for a penny, in for a pound. 'I was dating a very well-off man who wore a suit to work and seemed pretty great but he was just using me for sex so that's off.'

Mum recoils at the word 'sex'. Dad becomes fascinated by his dinner, like it's a work of art. Robbie smirks, his phone abandoned on the table. Which is actually more significant than saying the word sex, if you ask me.

'Kylie, honestly, please. We're eating.'

'And I met a guy on a dating app but he's not really my type. We had sex anyway but we feel we're better off as friends.'

Dad has never studied a piece of quiche with this much devotion. Meanwhile, Robbie looks like he will explode with laughter at any second where as Mum looks like she's about to implode or spontaneously combust.

'Where has this new attitude come from? Getting fired and sleeping around. What does Alexa think about it all?'

Mention of Alexa nearly knocks the wind out of my sails. I take a deep breath and swallow, 'Well we're not talking right now,' I say trying to sound casual, not wanting to show weakness, 'so I have no idea what she thinks of it.'

'I feel like I don't even recognise you anymore.'

'Well, I'm Kylie. Nice to meet you. I work at a bar and I enjoy it. I have friends there and I wake up in the morning happy to go about my day. I'm single and for a while I was desperate to be with someone, anyone, no matter how little respect they had for me but now I'm cautious to date because I want to meet the right person and it's perfectly okay to be single even at twenty-five if not especially at twenty-five because I'm still young and I still have the whole world at my feet.' I feel like I should hold out my hand for Mum to shake for comedic effect, to take some of the tension away, but as it turns out I'm paralysed to the spot. Did I really just say all of that?

When I dare to look at Dad, I see he looks somewhat taken aback but there's pride on his face too. Robbie looks at me like he's looking at me for the first time.

'Nice to meet you, Kylie,' he says.

For a while, no one says a word. We eat, and Robbie picks up his phone again. Mum looks strained, but I think the battle is over, for now. 'You really do make the best quiche, Mum —'

'Who's ready for dessert?' asks Mum, to no one in

particular, and retreats to the fridge.
'What is it?' I ask.
'Apple crumble and custard,' says Dad, smiling.
'My favourite.'

Alexa

We broke up a month ago. Priya blames herself, although she shouldn't, and has been making me meals every night although I generally refuse to eat them. They're tainted somehow, everything is. Now I have a fridge full of leftovers and a stomach full of guilt. It weighs me down until I find myself lying in a fetal position on the sofa, which I'm doing right now.

It's been a long month with no one to turn to. Days have been spent working and spending my evenings alone. I know that I chose this and that I hurt Shaun, but I still grieved for our relationship and it was hard with no one to turn to and no one to be mad at but myself. It's given me fresh perspective that not every break up is black and white. I'm sure I'm evil to all who care about Shaun. I cared about him, I just wasn't willing to share a life with him and I never wanted to break his heart. He probably hates me, like his sister does. She stopped contact with me straight away. Things are awkward between Priya and me, and I'm never going to have a strong connection with my work colleagues. I'm utterly alone.

In my time of solitude and reflection I've come to realise that the reason Shaun and I were never going to work out is because I tried to make him fit into the Kylie-shaped-hole in my life and no one fits that mould but Kylie. I hate that we're not friends. It all started with Kylie's ridiculous insistence that we're on the 'wrong side of twenty-five' and her quarter-life crisis about how our lives aren't on track. At the time I thought she might be right, but not anymore. We didn't need anything before we thought we needed everything and now we have nothing. Well, now *I* have nothing, I should say, because Kylie's doing great from what I can see on social media. She's living her best life and I'm on the sofa alone on a Friday night, which was something I used to enjoy but now I'm just sulking and mourning for what once was. Look at me: I'm pathetic.

I sit up, and get out my phone. I'm not going to wallow in self-pity for a moment longer.

'Sam? It's Alexa.'

'Alexa!' she shouts down the phone, 'how's it going?'

'Great. Are you out tonight?' although I don't need an answer because I can hear music and people and a glass smashing in the background.

'I am indeed. I shall toast this drink to you, my dear.'

'Don't bother, I'm coming to meet you.'

'That's the spirit! But what about your serious relationship?'

'I'm in a serious relationship with myself and we want to celebrate it. Order me two drinks, I'm on my way.'

I arrive at my favourite club. For a moment, I never thought I'd be here again. I enter and somehow the hot lights, smell of spilled beer and hum of people, breathes new life into me. It's 2008 again and life has endless potential.

'Alexa!' says Sam, coming to meet me with two Cheeky Vimtos.

'I was kidding about the two drinks,' I say, laughing.

'You should never kid about alcohol, now get them down you and come dance.'

I join Sam and her new girlfriend on the dance floor, as well as some other familiar faces. Unfamiliar faces dance around us, in a blur, irrelevant to our fun. Because despite what Shaun thought, we don't come here to find men, or women. We don't come here to find anything. We come here to lose ourselves.

'Lex? Lex?' someone shouts. When I come out of my dance trance, I see that it's Sam.

'What?' I shout over the music.

'It's time to go.'

'Are you kidding? No way!' I can't leave now, I've just got started.

'We've been here for hours, come on, let's get some food.'

We grab a bite to eat from the nearest take-away and walk home. Sam and Izzy take the lead in front. I watch them side by side, laughing and joking, sharing a tray of chips. The scene is sobering and for a moment I feel emotional, but suppress it and shout, 'Get a room you two!'

Izzy looks back, 'Aww, Lex. Sorry, we're treating you like a third wheel, aren't we?'

'It doesn't matter,' I feel stupid for making a scene.

'Break-ups are hard,' sighs Sam with sympathy.

'What?' I ask, as they fall back and walk either side of me.

'You're upset about Shaun, right?'

'Oh yeah.' And now not only do I feel upset, but guilty that I'm not upset about Shaun.

Kylie

I'm rushed off my feet as Zara stands chatting with a customer, who she knows. She served them five minutes ago but they're still talking. Oliver's in the back room, sorting stock, too busy to help so I'm picking up the slack, as well as eavesdropping in on their conversation. I could join in, but I always make an idiot of myself when I do and besides, someone has to actually work. I give a customer their change and then wipe the bar near enough to listen.

'Oh that reminds me, you owe me ticket money,' they say to Zara.

'I'll pay you tomorrow,' she replies. 'I swear, my gig habit costs me more than rent.'

I myself haven't been to a gig since last year when I went with Alexa. We would go to a gig most weekends at the student union. Those were some great times, and ones we'll never have again. Sure I could go to more gigs, but they won't be the same without her. I swallow my sadness and keep busy.

'Are you broke?' they ask. 'Then I have bad news. Swallow Salvation is playing next week at Daze.'

'Oh, fuck, really? I love Frank Hadley too, the lead singer. He's so fit.'

'Hang on, you can't objectify men like that,' they say with mock-indignation.

Zara sighs, 'I don't like his artistic abilities better because of his looks, Sacha. I'm just saying he has bags of sex appeal. The things I'd do to him…'

'So, you want me to get you a ticket? I could get you in backstage if you're serious about snaring him.'

'Maybe,' she says. 'He's a total fuck-boy though from

what I've heard. Although I'm not looking for a marriage proposal so I don't know if that should bother me.'

'What's a fuck-boy?' I ask, forgetting I was eavesdropping. Shit. 'Like a male prostitute?'

They laugh, and then Zara explains, 'You'll know the type if not the title. Smooth and charming yet emotionally void and will dump you in an instant for the next girl.'

'Oh, I know the type.' I also now know a new name for Harry.

'Of course, the idea of monogamy is barbaric and unnatural. You just need to know where you stand. So, if you get with a fuck-boy, enjoy the moment and know it won't last. Spare yourself some heartache.'

'You don't agree with monogamy?' I ask.

Zara turns to me, 'I'm sure it's good for some people, but just think about it; do you want to be with one person for the rest of your life? People change and grow, what if your views stop matching theirs? Do you make it work anyway? It's all about compromise and sacrifice and the natural – but what with overpopulation no longer necessary – need to breed. I think a lot of people do it because it's expected of them.'

Am I just so used to Zara's elaborate thoughts or did that make sense? 'I never thought of it like that.'

'When you start thinking, really and truly thinking for yourself, and stop doing things just because it's what's expected of you, life gets a lot more fun.'

'I'll bare that in mind. I don't think I believe in monogamy, anyway. Or at least, it doesn't believe in me. I never bought into the whole love at first sight thing, either.'

'Monogamy is real, but a choice,' says Zara. 'Love at first sight is a misinterpretation of lust and endorphins.'

'And romance is a social construct,' says Sacha. 'We've been trained to accept the gifting of chocolate and flowers as a grand gesture of love. But showing grandeur isn't showing love.'

'Yeah. Giving someone flowers is no way to show love, which is supposed to be permanent,' I say. 'Flowers die. They're pretty but temporary.'

'What's your name?' asks Sacha.

'Me? Oh, it's Kylie.'

'Well, Kylie. Come on then, what do you think is a good replacement of flowers as a new and more sincere gesture of love?'

He's as weird as Zara is. 'I don't know,' I say as I consider the question, not wanting to say something moronic. 'Socks.' I blurt out. Socks? For God sake, Kylie.

'Socks?' asks Zara.

I'll have to run with it now. 'Yes. They give me warmth and comfort. Socks are reliable. What could be a bigger gesture of love than something comforting, reliable and long-lasting?'

Zara and Sacha look at each other. I wait for laughter and cringing, but instead Sacha nods in approval and raises his glass, 'I'll drink to that.'

'To socks!' says Zara, passing me a drink.

'To socks...' I drink and celebrate my small victory of feeling like, for once, I can carry a conversation with Zara and her friends. I can do this. I can engage in small-talk when needed without feeling like a complete idiot.

'So look, we're off out to Hinge after work. Want to come?'

I swallow with a gulp. Going to Hinge again might be biting off more than I can chew. But maybe Hinge will be different this time. Maybe I'll be different... 'Sure. That sounds good.'

I enter Hinge with Zara and Sacha with less anxiety than last time. Mostly because I know what awaits me, which is why whilst I'm not anxious, I'm not excited. Sacha waves at a group sat at a table and I follow him and Zara to it.

'Hey, Sacha, hey, Zara. Zara, I didn't know you were coming,' says some girl. She reaches over and hugs Zara as I stand behind wondering if I made a mistake coming.

'I bumped into her,' says Sacha as he sits down next to Zara. I stand, unsure what to do.

'Bumped into me... stalked me at my place of work...

same thing, right, Sach?' Zara smirks and Sacha elbows her gently.

'How is work?' asks the girl.

'Same old shit. Capitalism has me by the balls. Oh but Ollie's a great boss, right, Kylie?'

I'm a rabbit in the headlights as everyone at the table turns to look at me. Some look surprised, clearly not realising I was even here.

'He's erm,' I clear my throat and try to find my voice, 'he's great.'

'Kylie? I don't think we've met,' says the girl, 'I'm Shona.'

'Hi, Shona,' I say with a smile.

'Kylie works with me. Come and sit, Kylie.'

I sit next to Zara and hope the attention will be turned away from me soon.

'Kylie has this revolutionary idea about romance and love,' says Sacha, not helping.

'Really? Go on then, Kylie, what's your idea?'

Everyone waits, expecting something great. Help. 'Well, I, err…'

'That the socially accepted ways of showing love such as giving flowers are also temporary and short-lived, which isn't what love is supposed to be about. And we should give socks which represent warmth and stability. It's genius, right?'

Why oh why did I harp on about socks? I wish the ground would swallow me up as the group digests what Sacha has told them.

'It is,' says a guy who's sitting next to Shona. 'And it would certainly make courting cheaper!'

'You're a pig, Jack.'

'A broke pig,' corrects Jack, grinning. 'No, I'm only kidding.'

'He's right though, socks are cheap, and not aesthetically pleasing. Giving flowers as a display of affection is peacocking.'

'Well, we're all animals at the end of the day.'

'Right? But animals aren't monogamous nor do they mate

for life. So why should we?'

'Well that's not true, studies have shown that—'

'I'm just popping to the loo,' I interrupt. With a weak smile, I get up and leave the conversation about peacocks and God-knows-what-else. I head to the sink and make an art of washing my hands so I'm not just some toilet-loitering weirdo. I watch the water rinse away and then take a look at my reflection. I look like myself, but it's hard to feel like myself in this place. Why did I come here? And more importantly, how do I get out of here?

Alexa

The channels are dominated with festivity; the city centre is packed with last minute shoppers. It's Christmas Eve and there's nothing to do but sit and sulk at the fact that if Kylie and I hadn't fallen out we would be in the city right now, together, deciding where to go for dinner and having a great time. We had a Christmas Eve tradition of going last-minute shopping, more for Kylie's benefit than my own, having dinner, looking at the fairy lights and festive decorations before grabbing a hot chocolate and sitting on our favourite bench that has the best view.

'Are you sure you don't want to come with me?' asks Priya, as she gets ready to leave.

I smile, 'No, but thanks for the offer.' Priya's inviting me to her parents' house for Christmas. They're Hindu but consider Christmas a proud British tradition. 'Besides, I'll just be in the way.'

'I have six siblings, Lex. And three of those siblings have kids. We're all in the way of each other. That's what Christmas is about.'

'I appreciate the offer, but I'll be fine. I have a busy week planned.'

'Oh?'

'Yeah. I'm going to give the house a deep clean.'

Priya stops mid-mascara to look at me in exasperation. 'Seriously? That's your big plan?'

'Well, it needs doing.'

'Why don't you go see your mum?'

'She's still in Lanzarote. Honestly, I'm fine.'

She rolls her eyes and puts her mascara in her bag, 'Well you know the address if you change your mind.'

'Have a good Christmas.' I give her a hug.
'You too.'

I watch her leave and then head upstairs. After the day I broke the news to Shaun and he stormed out, I went back upstairs to unpack my stuff. It was back to normal within days, but my room still doesn't look right for some reason. I tried to brighten it up with Christmas decorations but it doesn't feel that festive. A small tree sits on a side table looking so pathetic I think I'm going to put it away.

I walk over to the Christmas tree and take off the ornaments. Each ornament was bought at different occasions and holds their own memories. One is from all the way back when I was young, one from my first trip to Disneyland, one bought in York when Kylie and I went to the Christmas Market. Usually I love looking at the tree and being reminded of good times. But that was before my life turned to shit. I pull off the fairy lights, scrunch the fake branches together and pick it up, taking it to the ottoman under my window.

When I open the ottoman, two shoes sit before me. One black and one white. I lift them out and put the tree inside, closing the ottoman, and hold the shoes in my hands. I should throw them away, but I can't let go. I don't want to let go. I'm suddenly really annoyed that they're odd, and both missing their other half. Some things are meant to be together. As I stand, looking at the shoes, something comes over me. I put on the shoes and head out.

Kylie

'So, to answer your question in a nutshell, I just don't agree with celebrating Christmas. It's not just because I'm atheist and believe that a secular society is a better society but I'm also against capitalism and materialism and Christmas ticks all of those boxes. It's a tedious, drawn-out celebration based on buying things people don't need as an enforced and therefore disingenuous way of showing affection, all in the name of a deity that the majority of the participants don't believe in. It's archaic, and wrong.'

I asked Zara if she was doing anything nice tomorrow seeing as it will be Christmas Day, and in return got a five-minute rant on how terrible Christmas is not just on a superficial level but on a moral level. I can usually handle her unique way of looking at things with good humour but not right now. All I can think of is how at this time every year, I'm usually with Alexa. We should be kicking off Christmas sat at our bench, bundled up in our best festive knitwear, soaking up the Christmas cheer. Instead, I'm with Zara whilst soaking up beer that's been spilled on the bar. I need to keep it together for the next ten minutes so I can go home and be miserable on my own. 'I don't know about all that,' I tell her, 'but I'm definitely not in the mood to celebrate anything.'

'Do you want to come to mine? I'm having a gathering. Don't worry, it'll be thoroughly secular.'

'No thanks... I'll be fine on my own.' Because I've already planned to watch Love Actually on repeat and eat my way through two packs of mince pies. I might be miserable, but it's still Christmas.

Just then, Oliver shouts from the stock room, 'Kylie, can I have a word?'

I put down my cloth and head over. He stands there, waiting, watching me as I enter the room. 'Everything okay?' I ask.

For a while he says nothing and it's unnerving. 'Yeah,' he finally says, 'everything's fine. You can finish up now.'

I look at the clock to check the time. 'But I don't finish until twelve, there's ten minutes to go.'

'I know. Go home and start your Christmas.'

'But I told you, I'm not doing anything special for Christmas this year.'

'Why? Do you find it to be a disingenuous way of showing affection?' He looks amused now. A hint of his signature wry smile shows on his face.

I smile and roll my eyes at the memory of Zara's rant. 'Something like that.'

'Well, I guess you don't want my Christmas present then...'

'You got me a present?'

Oliver puts a wrapped present in my hand, looking bashful.

'Can I open it now?' I feel excited but nervous. Why would he get me something? What could it be?

'Sure.'

Carefully and tentatively, I tear open the beautiful paper, and pull out... a pair of socks. Socks? But then I realise that Zara's rant can't be the only thing he's overheard recently. As I begin to process what this means, my heart starts to race, and my hands tremble as they clutch onto the socks. Finally, I look at Oliver and he's still standing where he was, but something's changed. The air between us isn't the same kind of air as it was a second ago. It contains a special kind of energy that's made every hair on my arms stand up. He looks back at me, but the wry smile has gone. 'I thought you could do with something reliable and long-lasting.'

I should reply, but I can't. My brain's too busy thinking of all the times he's made me feel foolish and immature and irritated. I've always thought he was cute, but figured he thought little of me, merely an employee that he took pity on.

But the way he's looking at me is how he looked at me when we had drinks in Zara's kitchen, before he left when he walked me to my doorstep, when he gave me the painting. And the way he's looking at me now is, oh shit, like he's going to kiss me. He moves in closer and life starts moving in slow motion, slow enough for me to realise that this is everything I've ever wanted. I have a job I love, and now a guy who loves me. I should kiss him and have a happy ever after. But, despite it all, I don't feel complete. This isn't how it's meant to be, and if I wait any longer I won't make it. I step back, 'Merry Christmas, Oliver.'

Keeping hold of the socks, I grab my coat and leave. I don't know if it's the cold air, excitement, or fear but I'm shivering. Never mind, I'll be warm soon, because I have to run.

I set off down the high street past a blur of fairy lights, ignoring the threat of a stitch in my side and keep going until I catch a glimpse of the bench... but she's not there.

I sit anyway, alone, ignoring the knot of disappointment gathering in my stomach as midnight strikes. But what did I expect? I messed up, big time. I was a total bitch to her when she was only trying to apologise. But we always start Christmas on this bench and a part of me thought she'd be here. Maybe if I messaged her... but what? What could I possibly say? I get out my phone anyway, and try to compose a message.

As I'm staring down at my phone, a pair of feet appear and I freeze. Someone is sitting next to me, on tonight of all nights. They're wearing odd converse shoes. One white and one black. And just when it hits me who it could be...

'Sorry.'

I dare to look up and for the first time in a long time I'm face to face with Alexa. I've thought about this moment for so long. I've acted out many theoretical arguments and thought about how upset or angry I would be. But seeing her after all this time, apologetic and with a sheepish smile on her face has melted any bad feelings. 'I'm sorry too.'

'This feels strange.'

'Can we go back to the way we were?'

Alexa smiles, 'That depends on what time period you had in mind.'

'Definitely post-Myspace but before the point in which we stopped talking.'

'So, somewhere on the right side of twenty-five?'

'Not necessarily. I'm fine with being on the wrong side of twenty-five, actually.'

'How come?'

'I possibly, maybe, over reacted. Everything else will fall into place in its own time, when I'm ready. What's the rush, anyway? I'm twenty-five, not thirty!'

'I agree.'

'It's a slippery slope to thirty but I've decided I won't panic much until then.'

'Good plan.'

'Thanks.'

For a while, we sit. Apart from the stars above, it's just us. I missed this.

Then she says, 'I should have told you.'

'It's not a big deal.'

'It is. I don't know why I didn't. I went about it all wrong. I'm an idiot.'

'You were. But I should have accepted your apology. Instead, I wanted to make you as hurt as I was.'

'Well I'm sorry that I hurt you in the first place.'

'I'm sorry too. I said things that I didn't mean. I'm sure Shaun is really nice.'

'He is… we broke up.'

'Oh. I'm sorry.'

'It's okay. Some things are meant to be… and some things aren't.'

'You'll be fine; you know that don't you?'

'I do. It's like that quote "behind every successful woman is herself".'

I roll my eyes, 'That's a terrible quote.'

'I knew you hated it,' says Alexa, sighing. But I see her smile in spite of herself.

'I hate it because it's wrong. It should say, "behind every successful woman is herself..., and *beside* every successful woman is her best friend, if she's lucky".'

'Well that's a bit long winded.' Her eyes meet mine and they're smiling. And then we both are.

With the running and the adrenaline, I hadn't realised just how cold it is. I rub my hands together. 'It's freezing.'

'Put on your gloves.'

'I don't have gloves with me.'

'What are those then?' she points to the socks next to me.

'Socks.'

'And... why exactly do you have a pair of socks with you?'

'It's a long story.'

'Come on, you can tell me at my place.'

And then like always, we get up and set off side by side to Alexa's. It's weird how so much has changed, but some things never will.

'Alexa...'

'Yeah?'

'Can we stop and get some cheesy chips?'

THE END

Fantastic Books
Great Authors

CROOKED CAT

Meet our authors and discover our exciting range:

- Gripping Thrillers
- Cosy Mysteries
- Romantic Chick-Lit
- Fascinating Historicals
- Exciting Fantasy
- Young Adult and Children's Adventures
- Non-Fiction

Visit us at:
www.crookedcatbooks.com

Join us on facebook:
www.facebook.com/crookedcatbooks

Printed in Great Britain
by Amazon